PRAIS
THE IMPOSS

OF L

"WONDERFUL. I read *The Impossible Truths of Love* by Hannah Beckerman in one gulp. The intrigue at this book's heart genuinely 'got' me."

—Marian Keyes

"Hannah Beckerman's writing is utterly superb: so finely crafted. I was gripped from the start and couldn't put it down. I LOVED this book and will be recommending it to everyone."

—Ruth Jones, author of *Never Greener* and writer / star of *Gavin and Stacey*

"This is an accomplished, moving, and deeply felt novel. I found myself thinking of it during the days and savouring it as I read it. It's affecting, elegiac, and highly relatable. Hannah Beckerman is the real deal."

—Alex Michaelides, author of *The Silent Patient*

"A page turner of a story, deeply felt, finely woven, and sharp as a tack about the unspoken conflict and isolation within families, as well as the lengths people can be driven by both love and loss. It made me think too about the nature of memory; about what exactly we own and what we assume or even imagine. It's an unflinching book and all the better for it."

—Rachel Joyce

"So beautifully written, involving and utterly heartbreaking."

—Rosamund Lupton

"Masterfully written and hugely powerful."

—Adam Kay

"This is a beautiful and heartbreaking novel about loss, family and grief."

—Kate Mosse

"Skilfully entwining the private lives of mother Annie and daughter Nell, *The Impossible Truths of Love* is not only a story of love, but also of duty, character, identity. You will turn the pages of this rich and moving novel with a full heart."

—Louise Candlish

"Powerful, beautiful and exquisitely written"

—Joanna Cannon

"A bold and moving story of tangled family lives, the awful things that parents do to compensate for grief and the way despite all efforts, the truth comes out. Poignant, dark and horrifyingly plausible."

—Amanda Craig

"A heartfelt story of secrets, past trauma, sorrow and love, *The Impossible Truths of Love* explores the true meaning of tangled family ties – impossibly tender."

—Lucy Atkins

"Utterly beautiful, desperately moving. This book is a finely crafted emotional powerhouse that will keep you up all night, desperate to discover what happens."

—Kate Hamer

"A gripping mystery about one ordinary family and a devastating secret. This story is compassionate, beautifully written, and had me hooked from the start."

—Louise Hare

"This is such a beautiful book. Moving, poignant, and compassionate, it forces the reader to consider how far they would go to protect the ones they love."

—Louise O"Neill

"Beautifully written, emotionally charged story of family and secrets that had me hooked to the end."

—Dreda Say Mitchell

"A fast-paced family story... I couldn't put it down."

—Cathy Rentzenbrink

THE
IMPOSSIBLE
TRUTHS
OF
LOVE

ALSO BY HANNAH BECKERMAN

The Dead Wife's Handbook
If Only I Could Tell You

THE
IMPOSSIBLE
TRUTHS
OF
LOVE

Hannah Beckerman

LAKE UNION
PUBLISHING

Text copyright © 2021 by Hannah Beckerman
All rights reserved.

Published by Lake Union Publishing, Seattle

www.apub.com

Amazon, the Amazon logo, and Lake Union Publishing are trademarks of Amazon.com, Inc., or its affiliates.

ISBN-13: 9781542029520
ISBN-10: 154202952X

Cover design by Emma Rogers

Cover illustration by Jelly London

Printed in the United States of America

For Adam and Aurelia,
who make life infinitely happier:

Oh, the places we'll go . . .

For, as I draw closer and closer to the end,
I travel in the circle, nearer and nearer to
the beginning.

Charles Dickens, *A Tale of Two Cities*

PROLOGUE

The baby in the cot beside her cries, shattering the silence.

The woman looks down into the crib, at the infant's crumpled face and scarlet cheeks, at its curled fingers and jerking limbs, and her heart tightens like a clenched fist.

There is a part of her that wishes she could disappear, take nothing with her. It is a weight of yearning so strong, as though something is pressing down hard on her lungs, squeezing the air out of them like the last gasps of a spent balloon. But she does not know where she could go, to whom she could turn. There is no one she can trust. She has learnt the consequences of telling people what she knows, how she feels. She dare not say more.

The baby howls and the noise is like a shard of glass piercing her thoughts. She lifts the baby out of the crib, jiggles it up and down, and although she knows this is what she must do, the action does not seem to belong to her. There is a sensation of having slipped outside her own body, of hovering on the periphery of the scene, watching herself perform this millenniaold act but feeling no connection to it.

The noise emerging from the baby is so shrill, so demanding, that it penetrates every pore of the woman's skin. She has to stop herself from fleeing the room, because she knows there is nowhere for her to go, nowhere to hide. There is no escape from the situation in which she finds herself. Instead, she puts the baby back in its crib, drapes a thin cotton sheet over its body. The baby looks up at her, eyes wide with disbelief that it has been returned to a place it has no wish to be, its cries filled with such need, such desire, the woman feels it may leach all the oxygen from the air and suffocate them both.

Love. She knows what this child needs is love. But whatever love she once may have possessed seems to have leaked out of her, like heat from a poorly insulated window, and she does not know how to capture it, bring it back.

The woman glances at the door, imagines herself walking towards it, through it, in search of a truth that is etched on her heart. But she knows it is impossible, that there is no one who will help her, no one who believes what she says. Instead, she sinks down on the bed, wraps the duvet tight around her and pulls a pillow over her head to muffle the sound.

In the crib beside her, the baby's cries accelerate.

Beneath the duvet, the events of the past three months spool through the woman's mind like a film in slow motion she has no desire to view but from which she cannot avert her eyes.

The moment of realisation. The disbelief on their faces. The impotent fury. The feeling that something is tearing apart in her chest that she fears may never be healed.

The baby wails and the woman's heart pounds.

Gripping the edge of the duvet, she tries to hold on to the hope that one day someone will believe her, and will help put right this unforgiveable wrong.

NOW

His breath smells tired, musty, like air that has been trapped in a room for too long.

Nell leans towards her father's sleeping face. 'Dad?'

She waits for an answer, to feel the whisper of his words on her ear. But there is nothing except a slow, laborious inhalation, followed by a thin wisp of air wheezing through his parched lips.

From the corridor outside she hears a nurse calling for a colleague, a telephone ringing, the squeaking wheels of a gurney being trundled across the grey vinyl floor. Nell glances along the row of identically furnished beds, the uniform white sheets, blue polyester curtains and brown melamine cupboards reminding patients not to get too comfortable, not to stay too long.

Under the stiff white hospital sheets, her dad's body is still, his eyes closed, his skin bleached of colour. Hollowedout cheeks sink into his face like the craters of volcanoes. Above his bed, his name is written in thick, blue, delible ink on a whiteboard she knows must have been wiped clean countless times before: 'William Hardy (Bill)'.

Panic crackles inside Nell's chest. She cannot understand how he can have deteriorated so quickly. Five days ago he had been sitting in the dark brown armchair overlooking the small front garden of Nell's childhood home, instructing her to stop fussing and get going, worrying she'd arrive home late when she had work in the morning. He had been thin, the cancer that had begun in his pancreas and spread to his liver and lymph nodes having denuded him of any appetite some weeks ago. But there had still been a brightness in his eyes, laughter in his voice. Nell had crouched down beside his chair as the early evening sun seeped through the window, squeezed his hand and returned his smile even as a pebble had lodged in her throat.

'Are you sure you don't want me to stay over? If I get up and leave early, I can miss all the rushhour traffic.'

'Honestly, love, there's no need. I don't want you getting up at the crack of dawn. I'll see you next weekend.'

Nell had nodded and kissed his cheek, told him she would visit again next Sunday.

As she had pushed open the kitchen door to say goodbye to her mum, Nell had found her leaning against the stainless steel sink, a saucepan in one hand, shaking her head, confusion pinching the bridge of her nose. *'I can't for the life of me think what I'm doing with this.'* Nell had taken the saucepan from her, put it away in the cupboard next to the oven, wrapped an arm around her mum's shoulder.

Four months since the diagnosis of dementia and still Nell is shocked, heartbroken, every time she witnesses the slippage in her mum's mind, every time she watches her stumble from the present to some unknown place in the past or future none of them are able to follow.

Now, sitting by her dad's hospital bed, Nell wishes she had stayed last Sunday night in spite of his protestations. They could have had the whole evening together. Nell does not know now whether there will be any more evenings at home with her father.

It has been only a couple of hours since Laura telephoned to say that their father had been admitted to hospital. Cancelling her students for the last seminar of the day, Nell had not dared imagine the worst. She had convinced herself that perhaps it was nothing more than a precautionary admission, that perhaps her mum had just needed a break. It is only now, sitting by his bedside, watching a saline drip feed into the back of his hand, another delivering morphine into a vein at the crook of his elbow, that she acknowledges the falsity of hope.

Her dad's eyelids flicker and Nell tightens her fingers around his skeletal hand, which was once solid and strong. His eyes open slowly, cautiously, as if he is peeking out from behind closed curtains, unsure of what he might find. They slide from right to left, and when they land on Nell his desiccated lips inch towards a smile.

'Hello, love.' The words are hoarse, scratching their way free from his throat.

'Hey, Dad. How are you feeling?' She knows it is a rhetorical question. She can see the answer for herself, but everything she wants to say is trapped beneath the rubble of her anxiety and she cannot find the words to set it free.

'Oh, you know . . .' Deep, hacking coughs interrupt him and he turns his head to one side, tries to clear whatever is in his lungs, but does not appear to have the strength to lift himself from the mattress.

Nell slides a hand under his back, is shocked to feel the angularity of his shoulder blades jutting out like stunted angel wings beneath the blue cotton of his pyjamas. As she helps him onto his side, she feels the vibrations in his chest, disease rattling through him in an unforgiving hurry, and it seems perverse to her that here is a man who was once renowned for hitting the bell on the High Striker at every school fete, winning her the biggest teddy each year, and yet now it is she who is lifting his body from the mattress of a hospital bed.

The coughing subsides and Nell lays him back down, his clavicles rising like desert ridges from the dry parchment of his skin. She notices the change in the colour of his flesh, now tinged with yellow, like oncewhite bed linen that has not been replaced for years.

'Work okay? How long are you going to keep me waiting for that Nobel Prize?' His lips twitch in a poor imitation of the smile that had once, not so long ago, illuminated his face.

Nell tucks the sheet back round him, pushing the loose edges under the mattress. It has been a running joke between them ever since she undertook her degree in Physiological Sciences at Oxford University. Seventeen years later, as an Associate Professor in stem cell therapies at UCL, the joke is still going strong. For the first time, Nell wonders whether it is not meant entirely in jest, whether her dad – who has worked all his life with his hands, crafting furniture from wood, and who has never been ashamed to confess that Nell's career is like another language to him – actually believes that one day it may happen. And the thought that he might have such faith in her, that he may believe her capable of such greatness, causes a chasm to open up in her chest. 'I'm working on it. You'd have to buy a new suit for the ceremony though.' She can hear her attempt at levity but her voice seems to have been flattened by the truth.

He closes his eyes and drifts off to sleep. Nell watches him, strokes the back of his hand, waits to see if he will wake. A nurse stops at the end of the bed, offers Nell a sympathetic smile. Nell watches as the nurse studies the clipboard hanging on the end of the bed frame, as she walks towards the drip stand, looks at the bag of morphine hanging from it and checks the medical notes before tapping some numbers into the small electronic monitor. She smiles at Nell once more before heading to the next cubicle.

Nell sits in silence next to her father's sleeping body, watching the rise and fall of his shrunken chest. Time seems to lose all sense of itself, as though the world's clocks have been suspended and all Nell can do now is wait. Around her, the ambient noise of the hospital hums: beeping monitors; the murmur of voices; deep, guttural coughs from elsewhere on the ward.

'He's sleeping again then?'

Nell turns, sees her sister, Laura, standing behind her, still in her work uniform – navy blue trousers and matching tunic – which could easily have her mistaken as a member of hospital staff. 'The nurse just came and fiddled with his morphine. I don't know if she increased it a bit?'

'Possibly. It's all just about keeping him comfortable at this stage.'

At this stage. Nell knows that Laura will have witnessed this scene hundreds of times in the residential home where she works as a care assistant, but it is a new situation for Nell and she does not trust herself to speak without her voice fracturing.

'Look, I don't want to rush you but Mum wants a bit of time with Dad by herself before visiting hours finish.'

'Of course. Where is she?'

'In the coffee shop with Clare. Clare's getting a bit . . .' Laura thinks for a moment, as if searching for a word that is both truthful and tactful to describe their older sister. '. . . impatient.'

Nell glances down at her watch and then back at Laura. 'Just a couple of minutes more?' She sees a glimmer of something – sympathy or apprehension, she is not sure which – flicker behind her sister's eyes.

'I don't know. Clare was quite insistent.'

Nell hesitates. She has faced Clare's insistence enough times not to want to make Laura the gobetween. 'I promise I won't be long. Then I'll come and get Mum. There's still nearly an hour until visiting time's over.'

Laura takes a deep breath, her wide shoulders inching up and then down again. Laura's tall, sturdy frame is so similar to their mum's – so different from Nell's petite build – that her mum and her sisters might have been cast from the same mould. 'Okay. We're in Costa, on the ground floor.'

Nell nods and watches her walk out of the ward. She wonders how it is possible that seven months ago both her parents seemed to be in good health, and yet now her father is lying in a hospital bed while her mother struggles to remember events from one day to the next.

She turns back to her dad, studies his pale features, his face diminished as though all the buoyancy has been sucked from his cheeks.

His fingers tighten around her hand and his eyes open. 'Nell? What are you doing here? Shouldn't you be at work?'

Nell swallows against the narrowing of her throat. She shakes her head, reminds herself that it is the morphine making him confused. 'It's Friday evening. I've finished work for the week.'

He drifts off again, the skin around his knuckles puckered beneath her fingers, veins rising from the back of his hand like a sequence of river deltas. When he finally opens his eyes, he looks at her with an expression she has never seen before: something at once both troubled and urgent.

'Nell?'

He pauses and it is as if everything else in the hospital has fallen silent, as though a sound engineer has reduced the volume so that all she can hear are her dad's laboured breaths. She watches him swallow slowly, suck in a long, steady stream of air and let it out again, an almost imperceptible twitch at the outer edges of his eyes betraying the effort of it. And then he turns back to her, fixes his eyes on hers, and there is a faint popping sound as his lips peel apart. 'I want you to know that I've always loved you. I never stopped, even for a second. You have to believe that. You need to know that I've always loved you even though you were never really mine to love.' His grip loosens on her fingers, his eyelids slowly drooping towards sleep.

A cold draft inches down Nell's spine. 'What do you mean?'

He looks at her through halfclosed eyes, as though he cannot pull her into focus, does not answer.

Nell places her hand on top of her dad's arm, feels the loose skin and protruding bone where once there had been flesh and muscle. 'What do you mean I was never really yours to love?' Her voice is low, quiet, but she can feel the urgency creeping around the corners of her consonants. 'Dad, can you hear me?' Her heart begins to thud gently and she strokes the back of his hand, silently implores him to come back to her, even if just for a few moments.

Her dad's eyes close fully as a single tear trickles across his temple and pools inside the well of his ear.

'Come on, you've had ages already.'

The interruption is brusque, sudden, and Nell turns to see Clare standing behind her, hands on hips, like a bouncer at the door of a nightclub. Her hair, Nell notices, has been cut since the last time she saw her, a bob mirroring the line of her jaw, the severity of which seems to emphasise the irritability in her expression. 'Mum wants some time with Dad by herself now.'

'Just one more minute?' Panic leaks from Nell's voice and she does not know how to contain it.

'No, Mum wants to come in *now*. She's just popped to the bathroom and then she's going to sit with Dad, by herself.' Clare's tone is resolute and this is the moment Nell would usually acquiesce, walk away. But today she cannot. Her dad's elliptical words hum in her ears and she knows she has to try to speak to him before she leaves, to find out what he meant.

'Please, Clare. Just a couple of minutes more.'

9

Clare's eyes flit to the entrance of the ward and Nell follows her gaze towards the empty doorway. Turning back to Nell, her sister shakes her head. 'For God's sake, you're not the only one who wants to spend time with him. Stop being so selfish.' Impatience skews Clare's words into sharp, unforgiving syllables.

There is a moment's stalemate between them, but then Nell spies her mum walking through the door into the ward, Laura guiding her arm. Her mum is still tall, broad, and yet she seems shrunken, somehow, as though the dementia is stealing not just her memories but a part of her body too, rendering her diluted, diminished. As their mum walks towards them, Nell feels a rush of love for her so great she has to empty her lungs to make room for it. She steals another look at her dad, silently willing him to wake up before she has to go, but his face is passive and unreadable behind his closed eyes.

'The nurses will phone us, won't they, if anything . . . changes?' She cannot bring herself to say it aloud, bland euphemisms filling the space where her worst fears lie.

Clare nods. 'Course they will.' Clare's voice softens fractionally, like an outoftune note on a piano being brought up to pitch.

'And someone will phone me? If anything . . . I want to be here. Whatever time it is, even if it's the middle of the night.'

'Laura's already said she will.'

Their mum and Laura reach the bed, and Nell takes hold of her mum's hand, rises out of the seat she has been occupying, helps her mum into it. 'Are you okay? Can I get you anything?'

There is a shift in her mum's expression as though a curtain has been drawn over her thoughts. She shakes her head. 'No, I'm fine, love. You get back off to Oxford. I don't like you travelling all that way in the dark.'

Nell does not correct her, does not point out that she has not lived in Oxford for fourteen years, that she now lives an hour's drive north of her parent's house, on the other side of the Thames. She does not remind her mum that it is early evening in June and the night will not be drawing in for a couple of hours yet. It has been a process of rapid adjustment, learning to interact with her mum in a world in which she can exist in multiple time frames at any given moment. Glancing now between her parents, she is aware that she is losing them both simultaneously, albeit in different ways, a realisation that drums inside her chest and makes her crouch down, cloak an arm around her mum's shoulder.

'I'll drive carefully, I promise. But I won't leave until you do. I'll be in the coffee shop with Clare and Laura. We'll come back and get you at the end of visiting hours.'

Her mum raises Nell's hand to her lips, brushes her mouth lightly against Nell's knuckles. Nell leans forward, kisses her dad's forehead, whispers her love for him into his ear and walks away before her mum sees her tears.

From outside the ward, she watches through the glass, sees her mum take hold of her dad's hand, sees her press it against her cheek. Her mum and dad. Annie and Bill. Married for fiftytwo years. Nell cannot imagine them ever having to be parted.

A wave of confusion and sorrow washes over her as her dad's words circulate in her head like a playground taunt that will not be silenced. *You need to know that I've always loved you even though you were never really mine to love.*

Stealing a final glance at her parents, she heads towards the nurse's station to ask what time she can return in the morning; tomorrow, she thinks, she will arrive as early as she can and try to find out what her dad meant.

THEN

Annie holds on tight to Bill's hand, anticipation fluttering beneath her ribs.

Opposite them, the midwife reads from some notes on her desk, nudging the glasses up onto the bridge of her nose where they keep slipping down. October sunshine streams through the window, making patterns on the floor through the vertical louvre blinds, and Annie feels like a child awaiting the verdict on her school report.

'Everything's looking fine, Mrs Hardy. The baby's head's engaged and everything's in order. As far as I can see, you're on track for a perfectly healthy delivery.'

The midwife smiles and Annie turns to Bill, sees the pride and relief in his eyes. She had told him she was happy to come alone today, that it was just another routine checkup. He has been to so many appointments with her already, she didn't want him taking more time off work. But Bill wouldn't hear of it. *'Don't be daft. You're not going on your own. Course I'm coming with you.'*

'If I had to hazard a guess, I'd say that if Baby decides to be born in the next twentyfour hours, it'll be around the eightpound mark, but don't hold me to that. So what are you hoping for – a boy or a girl?'

Annie is still considering her answer when Bill replies. 'We don't mind either way. As long as it's healthy that's all we care about.' He squeezes Annie's hand and she feels the strength of his reassurance. It is one of the things Bill is good at, one of the reasons she loves him. His ability to give her something – love, encouragement, laughter, comfort – without her ever needing to ask. It is one of the many reasons she chose to marry him fifteen years ago.

They have talked about it so much since they found out. This surprise fork in their lives, this new, unexpected adventure when they thought the path in front of them was predictable, welltrodden.

When she had begun to tell people she was pregnant again, she could see it in their faces: the surprise, the embarrassment, the silent assumptions. *No*, she had wanted to say, *it wasn't planned. But that doesn't mean we're not thrilled now it's happened.* But she'd said nothing because she hadn't wanted to seem defensive, and the question had never actually been asked.

She is thirtyeight. Their daughters are eleven and seven. She does not need anyone to tell her that this turn of events is unconventional, that the new baby might upset the equilibrium of their family. She does not need to be warned of the financial burden a third child will place on them: there have already been plenty of sleepless nights wondering how on earth they will cope. What she would like, most of all, is just to look forward to this baby's arrival, to be able to celebrate its imminent appearance without other people electing to worry on her behalf.

'As I always say to parents, the best baby is a healthy baby. Nothing else really matters at the end of the day.' The midwife smiles approvingly at them. 'And how are your daughters feeling about the impending arrival? Excited about being big sisters?'

Annie thinks back six months, to when she and Bill told Clare and Laura they would have a baby brother or sister by the end of the year. Annie had been worried they might feel anxious, jealous, rejected even. Laura, especially, had been a cause for concern: for seven years she has been the baby of the family and Annie had feared she would not want the role taken away from her. But both girls seemed genuinely excited. The only bone of contention was Clare's resistance to sharing a bedroom with Laura, given the baby will need a room of its own. But since moving to a bigger house is not an option, it is just something they will all have to manage, and she feels certain Clare will adapt, in time. 'Yes, they've been helping me get the baby's room ready. And they've got some strong opinions on names.'

Bill laughs. 'Very strong. Clare's gunning for Fallon if it's a girl – she's a *Dynasty* fan, in case you couldn't guess. But I think we'll probably go a bit more traditional.'

'Well, I'm sure whatever you choose, it'll be lovely. You're clearly very wellprepared.' The midwife stands up, and Annie and Bill follow suit. 'I'll pop you in for an appointment at the beginning of next week, but we may not need it if Baby decides to make an appearance before then.'

Annie smiles and nods. Alongside the excitement and joy, she is aware of the ambient hum of concern. It is not the thought of starting all over again with nappies and nightfeeds, prams and playgroups, although plenty of her friends have said they don't envy her having to revisit all that. She is, in truth, looking forward to those aspects of motherhood. Now that Clare and Laura are both growing up and at school all day, it will be lovely to have a new baby in the house when everyone else is out. The fear is, instead, the inexplicable anxiety that somehow she will have forgotten how to do it. That perhaps her first two outings as a mother have been a fluke, and this time she won't be so lucky. She knows it is an irrational fear but a part of her wishes they could fast forward to the day of the baby's arrival so they could meet the newest member of their family and begin life as a quintet.

'Any problems in the meantime, just give me a call. But I don't expect you'll need to.'

She opens the door, and Annie and Bill thank her before walking into a waiting room full of women at various stages of pregnancy. Most of them, Annie notices, look at least a decade younger than her.

'Well, that went well.' Bill places his hands on either side of Annie's swollen stomach, leans his head towards her bump. *'Now we just need you to make an appearance, little one, whenever you're good and ready.'*

Annie laughs, heat flushing her cheeks, aware that the other women in the waiting room are watching. 'Don't be daft. It can't hear you.'

'How do you know? It might be able to. *Hurry up and come out – we want to meet you.'*

Annie nudges Bill, slips an arm through his. As they step out of the hospital's double doors into the crisp autumnal air, towards their Talbot Sunbeam parked at the far end of the car park, she holds close her excitement, shuts her ears to her concerns. She knows she is older than most pregnant women, knows all her friends finished with babies years ago, but perhaps that is a good thing. Perhaps she will be able to offer this baby things she couldn't when she was younger: more patience, more experience, more deepset gratitude for this unexpected chapter in their lives.

As the two of them head for home, discussing baby names they still can't decide upon, she knows that she and Bill can do this. They have done it twice before. They can do it again.

NOW

Nell opens her eyes and squints against the early morning sunshine. Two years since moving into her flat, having scraped together a deposit during her first frugal years as an academic, she still hasn't found the time to change the thin cream curtains that came with the purchase.

Peeling a curled lock of hair from her cheek, she is aware of a difference in the air, a change in the weight of the mattress. Shuffling onto her side, she remembers: Josh lies beside her, facing the wall, his naked back to her, deep breaths indicative of sleep. Six months since they began dating and still there is an element of happy surprise on the mornings she wakes to find him in her bed.

As she had driven home from the hospital late the previous evening, she had resigned herself to a quiet couple of hours with a book and a glass of wine before heading to bed. But then she had called Josh to update him on her dad, and she had not realised until she heard his voice how much she wanted to see him. He had been out with friends – drinks in the pub to celebrate the official end of the working week, although Josh often worked weekends too – but by the time she arrived home he had been waiting on her doorstep, a bottle of red wine in one hand, a bar of her favourite chocolate in the other. Sitting on the sofa, he had pressed her for details of her father's symptoms, and she had described her dad's somnolence, his discombobulation. She had questioned Josh on the likely effects of the morphine – how confused it might make him, how disorientated – relying on Josh's expertise as a senior registrar in A&E to fill the gaps in her knowledge. She had known, from the way Josh's voice had softened, from the way his fingers had tightened around her hand, that it was unlikely her father would recover sufficiently to be able to return home. But she had found herself unable to confide in Josh about her dad's strange pronouncement, her father's words still murmuring in her ears like white noise that would not be silenced.

Josh had wrapped an arm around her shoulders, pulled her close and they had drunk wine and watched half of a subtitled Korean movie until exhaustion had propelled Nell towards bed. Josh had joined her and she had been relieved not to have been alone with only her thoughts for company. But soon after he had enfolded her in his arms, Josh had fallen asleep while she had remained restless until the early hours, the conversation with her dad rotating in her head like a record someone had forgotten to take off the turntable.

Wiping the encrusted sleep from the corner of her eye, she recalls again the events of the previous evening. *You need to know that I've always loved you even though you were never really mine to love.* Whichever way she turns her father's words over, however hard she tries to mould them into something comprehensible, she cannot fashion them into a shape she recognises.

The clock beside the bed tells her it is just gone six fifteen. There is almost an hour and a half before she can leave for the hospital. When she asked at the nurses' station the previous evening about visiting times, she was told at first to come between three and eight. But then the nurse asked who she was visiting and, when Nell told her, the woman's expression shifted and she said Nell

17

could come any time from nine. Nell had not known whether to feel grateful or terrified.

The tannins from last night's wine coat her teeth and she craves a cup of coffee. Her eyes scan the nightstand for her phone but it is not there, and she remembers leaving it on the arm of the sofa when she went to bed. There is a moment's panic, the fear that she may have missed a call in the night, but then she remembers having left the ringer on its loudest setting, knows that she would have heard it had anyone phoned.

Lifting the corner of the duvet, she shifts her weight to the edge of the bed, trying not to cause too great a fluctuation in the mattress. She has just pressed her feet into the soft pile of the rug when she senses Josh stir behind her, holds herself still to see if he will settle.

His hand finds the small of her back. 'What time is it?'

She turns around, rests her palm on the warm skin of his arm. 'Early. Six fifteen. Go back to sleep.'

Josh rubs his eyes. 'Why are you awake already?'

Nell exhales a long stream of air, aware of the acridity of her breath. 'Just couldn't sleep.' She shifts her body, moves to stand up. There is a restlessness in her blood this morning and she needs to be up and about. Catching sight of herself in the mirror, she sees the smudges of mascara beneath her eyes, cannot tell where the dark rings of sleeplessness end and the makeup begins. On top of the chest of drawers is a bottle of cleanser and some cotton wool, and she picks them up, begins to wipe the ointment across her eyes.

'My mum texted yesterday, to check your dietary preferences again. I think lunch next weekend might be a bit . . . full on. Are you sure you're up for it?'

Nell smiles at his reflection in the mirror, wipes at clumps of mascara that are refusing to be detached from her eyelashes. 'Are you trying to put me off?'

He slides across the bed towards her, wraps his arms around her waist, burrows his head against her hips. 'Course not. My parents are going to love you. How could they not?' He lifts the back of her tshirt, kisses the base of her spine, his overnight stubble brushing against her skin.

She turns around, leans down, kisses him on the mouth. 'I hope so.'

Next Sunday's lunch will be Nell's first meeting with Josh's parents, her first visit to his childhood home in Wiltshire, a home about which she already feels an intimate knowledge given all she has heard about it, all the photos she has seen. She has met Josh's brother and sisterinlaw, often spends Saturday night or Sunday brunch with them, but meeting his parents is different. Significant. There have been boyfriends in the past whose parents she has met, and those encounters she has taken in her stride, has not found herself worrying over whether or not she will be liked. She has always thought it slightly hysterical – oldfashioned – when her friends have, on her behalf, imbued those encounters with such import. It is only now, feeling the flutter of anxiety at the thought of meeting Josh's parents next weekend, that she understands why: somewhere, deep down, she must have known that those previous relationships – with Tom, with Will, with Alex – would not go the distance, that her investment in those parental meetings was not crucial to her future happiness. With Josh it is different. She is keen – more than keen – for Josh's parents to like her. To approve of her. To welcome her into their fold. It is still relatively early days in their relationship and yet frequently, at unexpected moments – when she is leading a seminar of undergraduates, when she is examining data in the lab, when she is lunching with a colleague – she will find scenes of an imagined future slipping into her head. Prosaic, domestic scenes of cohabiting life: cooking dinner, reading in bed, entertaining friends. She has not shared any of these fantasies with Josh – does not want to risk scaring him off – but sometimes she thinks she can sense it in him too: a tone, a timbre, a rhythm to their relationship that marks it out as different from those they've each experienced before.

'They will love you, I promise.' Josh places his hands either side of her face and returns her kiss, the morning tartness of their breaths mingling in the air between them. Lying back down on the bed, he rests his head on his arm, watches her return to the mirror.

Nell attacks her other eye with cleanser and a cotton pad, the mascara stubborn and unyielding, reminding herself that this is why she is usually so disciplined about removing her makeup before going to sleep.

Glancing at Josh in the mirror, she experiences a pang of regret that he did not get to meet her parents before her father was diagnosed with cancer, before her mother's dementia took hold. In the time she and Josh have been dating, Nell's fortnightly visits home for Sunday lunch have been dominated by talk of hospital appointments, care plans and new medications, and while she knows Josh would take such conversations in his stride – that his input would be helpful, even – she has not felt it was the right time. A voice in her head has repeatedly reassured her that such a meeting can be postponed to a future when her parents are stronger, fitter, better. When they are more like their old selves. Only now does she realise that such a time may never arrive.

She thinks about how much her dad would like Josh: how, in spite of their superficial differences – their education, their profession, their class – he would approve of Josh's solid work ethic, his sense of duty, his compassion for others. He would like Josh's sense of humour: wry, subtle, clever, so that sometimes it takes a few seconds for the sophistication of his jokes to land. Whenever she has spoken about Josh to her parents, she has caught their surreptitious glances across the elm wood dining table, the shared expression of parental knowingness that Nell's tone of voice is different talking about Josh than about other boyfriends in the past.

She has a sudden, childlike urge to speak to her mum, to find out how her dad has been overnight. Heading into the sitting room, she picks up her phone from the arm of the sofa and sees it immediately: the blank screen. Her pulse taps at her wrists and she hurries into the kitchen, plugs the phone into the charger next to the fridge, waits a few interminable seconds before the power returns, before she is able to switch it on. The phone yawns into action, one app at a time blinking into life. And then there they are, the sight of them narrowing the wall of Nell's throat: notifications telling her she has a stream of missed calls. Opening them, her eyes scroll down the list: fifteen, twenty missed calls from Laura over the course of the past few hours while Nell's phone battery was dead and she was sleeping.

She does not listen to any of the eight voicemails that are waiting. Instead she calls Laura's number, her hand shaking, has to wait only a single ring before it is answered.

'Where have you been?' Laura is crying on the other end of the phone. 'I've been trying to reach you for ages.'

'I'm sorry. My battery ran out.'

There is a heartbeat of silence and Nell knows what is coming before Laura begins to speak.

'It's Dad. He's gone.'

THEN

The baby snuffles and Annie feels the warmth of his cheek against her shoulder. With one hand she runs her fingers gently across the top of his head, his fair hair so fine it is like stroking air, the soft down on his cheek almost translucent in the artificial light. His top lip sticks out slightly and it is all she can do not to bend forward and kiss it repeatedly. The smell of him is something she does not have words to describe but she breathes him in, inhales him into her lungs.

'God, he's adorable. Can I hold him?' Pam sits down on the sofa next to Annie, arms outstretched. Annie does not blame her oldest friend for wanting to hold him: babies, she knows, have an almost magical power over adults, like catnip over kittens. And her baby, she is sure, is even more beautiful than most.

'Course you can. He's out like a light. I don't think anything'll wake him until it's time for his next feed.' Prising her fivedayold son from her chest, she feels a sense of sudden, abrupt loss as she places him in Pam's arms, as though she is losing a part of herself, like a fifth limb. She read somewhere recently that the first three months of a baby's life are like a fourth trimester, that it is natural to want to keep your baby close. She had thought it sounded like hippyish nonsense – she was sure she'd settled Clare and Laura into a routine almost immediately – but now it feels true to her in a way she couldn't have imagined a week ago.

'Don't you be getting any ideas, Pam. Three under six is enough for me.' Pam's husband, Alan, stands next to Bill, rolling back and forth on his heels.

'My hands are more than full, thank you very much. But that doesn't mean I can't think this one's a cutey, does it?' Pam leans her face towards the baby, makes a cooing noise as she strokes his cheek, and Annie feels a pang of something in her chest, a need to scoop her child back into her arms. She tells herself to stop being silly: the baby is fine, she will have him back soon.

'So, have you decided on a name yet?'

Annie glances at Bill and he nods. 'We have actually. We decided last night and told the girls this morning.' She shifts her bottom to the back of the sofa, conscious of the way her stomach still tests the waistband of her maternity trousers. When the community midwife had visited yesterday, she'd said breezily that as long as Annie kept active and ate healthily, she'd lose the extra weight in no time. Never having been a small woman, Annie remains unconvinced. It is not that she is fat, so much as tall, big boned: a teacher at school once told her she 'cut an imposing figure' and Annie hadn't known if it was supposed to be a compliment or a criticism. Even outside of pregnancy it is rare that she can find a bracelet to accommodate her wrist, has not been able to squeeze into anything less than a size sixteen since her early twenties. Until she met Bill, she'd worried she might never find a husband who didn't make her feel like a giant.

'Don't keep us in suspense. What are you going to call him?' Alan lingers by the gas fire as though he does not dare fully enter this female space of postnatal baby chat.

'You tell them, Annie. It was your idea.'

Annie rests a hand on the baby's head, as if drawn to touch him by some invisible, magnetic force even when he is not in her arms. 'We're calling him Danny. Daniel William Hardy. William after Bill, obviously, and Danny because . . . well, we just like it and we think it suits him.' Tears fill her eyes and she is aware all too late that she is about to cry.

'Oh, love, is it a touch of the baby blues?' Pam smiles sympathetically. 'I had them after Melissa was born. They'll pass in a few days, once your hormones settle down.'

Pam places Danny back in Annie's arms and she feels a flood of relief to have his head against her shoulder once again. She does not contradict Pam, but these are not the baby blues. The midwife gave her a leaflet about those a few weeks ago, and Annie has read the whole thing from beginning to end. It is not the blues affecting her. She is not sad or anxious or depressed. She is crying for no other reason than she is happy. All those weeks of worrying that she might have forgotten how to be a mother and now – five days after Danny's birth – she already cannot imagine life without him.

'Mum, we're thirsty. Can we have something to drink?' Laura runs into the lounge, puffing and ruddycheeked from where she has been playing in the back garden with Pam's two boys. She is wearing her favourite pink rahrah skirt over navy blue tights and red wellington boots. An orange scarf – a handmedown from Clare – is wound around her neck, on top of the purple woollen jumper Annie knitted for her last year, which thankfully still fits. 'Can we have some Coke? Please? There's some in the fridge.'

'Go on then, but make sure you share it out equally between you. And see if Clare wants some too.' Glancing over Laura's shoulder into the garden, Annie sees Clare playing swingball by herself, wearing nothing more than a denim jacket over her jumper and jeans, no protection at all against the bitter November chill that snapped into the air during the night. She looks younger, somehow, than her eleven years, and Annie wonders if she is okay: whether she is happy playing by herself, pleased to be absolved of the responsibility of entertaining Pam's young sons, or whether there is another reason she has chosen to be alone.

'Thanks, Mum. We will!' Laura skips out of the lounge, Pam's boys trotting behind her like faithful puppies. Darren, at six, is only a year younger than Laura, but a head shorter and half a shoulderwidth slighter. Gary, Pam's middle child, has only just turned four but Laura is kind and patient with him in a way that gives Annie little cause for concern about how she will interact with her new baby brother over the years to come. Melissa, Pam's eighteen-monthhold, is asleep in her pushchair in the hall.

The doorbell rings and Bill leaves to answer it. Annie hears a familiar voice and then Denise enters the lounge wearing a black-andwhite polka dot blouse over a tight red pencil skirt, her hair blowdried PrincessDiana style.

'I hope you don't mind me popping in. I didn't realise you'd be here, Pam. I won't stay long. I just wanted to bring you this.' She holds out a present wrapped in pale blue paper but Annie's hands are already full with the baby, and it is Bill who reaches out to take it.

'Don't be silly – sit down. That's really kind of you.'

Denise perches on the edge of the armchair, her eyes fixed on the baby.

'Would you like to hold him?' The words slip out of Annie's mouth and she regrets them as soon as they're gone.

Denise shakes her head. 'God, no, I don't know anything about babies. I'd be scared I'd drop him. He's beautiful though. He's going to be a real heartbreaker when he grows up.'

Annie feels a rush of affection for her, for not taking Danny from her arms when she doubts very much that Denise – who spent her

25

teenage years babysitting half the children in the neighbourhood – has any real concerns about dropping him.

'Mum, I'm bored.' Clare slouches into the room, remnants of salt around her lips from the packet of crisps she's holding.

'It'll be time to eat soon. I expect you're hungry.'

'I'm not. I'm bored. There's nothing for me to do.' Clare frowns and Annie would embrace her if she were not already holding Danny. She knows it is not much fun for Clare, spending Saturday morning at home with only her little sister and two young boys for company.

'Why don't you see if Ali wants to stay over tonight?'

'Really?'

'Go on, give her a ring. Make sure she checks it's okay with Debbie though.'

Clare is already in the hallway, closing the door behind her when she replies. 'I will! Thanks, Mum.'

The arm supporting Danny's back is beginning to numb and Annie shifts position. He is a large baby, relatively speaking – eight pounds twelve ounces, so the midwife had not been far off – but to her he seems tiny. She had forgotten how small babies are, how vulnerable, how their limbs do not yet seem fully attached to their bodies. How gently she has to change his nappy, slip a vest over his head, ease his toes into the feet of a fresh babygrow. Next to him, Clare and Laura look enormous when less than a week ago she still thought of them as little girls.

'So you've shut up shop today, Bill? That can't be good for business.'

There is joviality in Alan's voice, but Annie and Bill exchange a surreptitious glance. They had this conversation only this morning, Annie telling Bill he should go to work, that it was silly for him to stay at home when she'd have Pam and Alan for company; they couldn't afford the lost revenue. The past few years have been tough enough, their belts already tight with two children to look after, but now with an extra mouth to feed, she knows Bill is going to be under pressure to keep the furniture commissions coming in. Closing the shop on a Saturday is problematic for the week's income: it is when most people go shopping for the kind of furniture Bill makes. They can't depend on the repair jobs he does – the wobbly tables, broken chairs, family heirlooms in need of a French polish – for a reliable income. But he insists he's found a solution, and although Annie is yet to be convinced it's the silver bullet they need, she doesn't want to pour cold water on the idea when he's so enthusiastic about it.

'It's only one Saturday. And it's not every week you bring home your son from the hospital.' Bill leans forward, kisses the top of Danny's head. 'Anyway, it's not going to be an issue any more. I'm taking someone on in the workshop. She starts a week on Monday.'

'*She?* You're taking on a woman? Bloody hell, that's brave of you.' Alan laughs a little too loudly, and Pam waves a shushing hand in the air at him.

'Say what you like, but I interviewed half a dozen young people and she was head and shoulders above the rest. She's got a real eye, and is obviously a hard worker. And she's got some great ideas for winning more business. We'll see how it goes.'

Annie says nothing, rests her lips on the baby's head. She can feel them all watching her, waiting for her response, but she has no desire to share her thoughts. She is not worried, not in that way. Bill is not that kind of man: she would never have married him if he was. But he has always been such a solitary craftsman – has always said that he cannot be productive in the workshop if there are other people around – so it has come as a surprise to discover that he intends to have someone with him all day, every day. And hiring a woman is not what Annie had expected. She cannot pretend not to have felt a twinge of jealousy when Bill told her. But it is only

27

on a trial basis. Three months, that's all: if it doesn't work out, that will be the end of it.

'So what's her name? When does she start?' It is Pam asking the questions and Annie can hear the ellipses at the end of them: the inquisition she is saving up for when the two of them are alone.

'Elsa. She starts next Monday. She's only just moved down from Glasgow. Big transition for a twentyoneyearold. But soon enough for me to get a bit of time with these two.'

Bill lowers himself onto the edge of the sofa, places one hand on the baby's back, the other around Annie's shoulder. She feels a rush of love for her husband, like the giddy feeling she had when they first met. Whatever her reservations about Elsa, she is happy to be having more time with Bill at home so they can share these first few precious weeks of their son's life together.

NOW

It is raining on the morning of the funeral. Not heavy rain, but a misty drizzle that had clung to Nell's hair, her clothes, her skin as she had run the short distance from the car to the crematorium.

Now, standing in the doorway, in a line that comprises her mum, Clare and Laura, Nell glances over her shoulder to where the room is filling up behind her. She cannot bring herself to look all the way to the end, to where her dad's coffin is lying on the high wooden catafalque, the altar's rim scuffed around the edges from the weight of previous incumbents. She does not want to see the metal rollers underneath, which will, within the next hour, slide her dad's coffin through the ruby velvet curtains to the furnace beyond. Only by focussing on the arrival of mourners can she stop herself from imagining her dad's body, stiff and inert, his face waxy and frozen, nothing more now than a shell of the father he had once been.

There had been a moment, this morning, when she had thought she was not going to be able to endure the day ahead. Standing in front of her bathroom mirror, dabbing concealer under her eyes to mask the dark rings beneath, a tidal wave of grief had forced her to the floor where she had sat with her back to the bath, knees hugged to her chest, her shoulders convulsing with sorrow. It had been so overwhelming, so powerful, that she had not been able to stem the momentum of it until she was already ten minutes late in leaving. Her makeup had been applied in the car and, even then, the blotched skin around her eyes was still visible.

It is not that she has failed to grieve over the past ten days. There have been tears, insomnia, headaches, anger. There have been mornings of waking to a temporary amnesia before she has remembered this new reality and the shock has hit her again and afresh, as though she is learning it for the first time. There has been the chasm deep in the pit of her stomach, as though her body is not yet ready to acknowledge her loss. There have been those rare moments she has been so busy with funeral arrangements that she has, perversely, forgotten that it is her father who has died. And then she has remembered and the guilt that she had forgotten, even momentarily, is almost as acute as her grief. But this morning, sitting on her bathroom floor, it was as though none of that grieving had taken place, as though it was only now, on the day of his funeral, that she understood the enormity of her loss.

Glancing towards her mum, she notices how much older she looks, how much weaker, and the awareness twists in Nell's stomach. Her face has altered, so that where once her cheeks were full, her eyes bright, her complexion smooth, now there are deep grooves across her forehead and her expression has dulled as though someone has dimmed the lights. Perhaps, Nell thinks, her mum has been ageing imperceptibly for years now, the change so gradual Nell has not noticed. Or perhaps grief has rounded the curve of her shoulders, hooded the lids over her eyes, deepened the crevices across her skin. Nell is overcome by a deep urge to protect her, to restore the malfunctioning neurons in her mother's brain, to shield her from the horror of grief. She reaches out, wraps an arm around her shoulders, wonders whether this is, eventually, the inevitable order of things: the reversing of roles between parents and their children, the shifting of responsibilities, the transferal of concern.

'Are you cold?' Nell holds onto her mum, aware of the slight trembling beneath.

Her mum grasps Nell's hand, shakes her head, her other hand fiddling with the brass clasp on her black patent handbag, snapping it open and shut: click, snap, click, snap. The music being piped from the speakers inside the crematorium slips into 'Abide With Me' and Nell recalls all those FA Cup Finals she watched with her dad over the years, even though his beloved Bromley FC never got within touching distance of the trophy.

Turning back towards the car park, Nell sees Elsa walking towards them and relief washes over her. She has spoken to her father's former business partner almost daily since his death, but it is reassuring to see her in the flesh, petite and elegant in a tapered black trouser suit, her sandy blonde hair tied into a loose chignon, looking a decade younger than her fiftyeight years.

Elsa reaches the portico where the four of them are lined up and stands in front of Nell's mum, her hand outstretched. 'I'm so sorry, Annie. You must all be devastated.'

There is a momentary silence, anticipation humming in Nell's ears. She feels her mum's fingers curl into tight balls, her arms stiffen by her side. 'He was my Bill, not yours.'

The words are clipped, abrupt, and Nell cannot tell if this is one of those moments when her mum's grasp on reality has slipped or whether, in fact, she knows exactly what she is saying. Nell squeezes her mum's hand before she lets go, steps forward, takes hold of Elsa's elbow and guides her towards the chapel door. It is only when they are out of sight that Nell embraces her. 'I'm sorry about Mum. She doesn't know what she's saying half the time. She didn't mean to be rude.' It is possibly only half a truth but Elsa smiles, places the palm of her hand on Nell's cheek.

'Nothing to apologise for. It's a dreadful time, for all of you. How are you today?'

Nell turns Elsa's question over in her mind, unsure how to answer truthfully without opening the Pandora's box she fears will lead to a repeat of this morning's breakdown. There are so many aspects of her father's death she is mourning beyond the finality of his passing. There is the guilt that she does not, like Clare and Laura, live within walking distance of her parents' house, that she had not seen as much of her dad since his diagnosis as they had. There is the fury with herself for not having charged her mobile phone overnight and having missed her chance to be with him as he had taken his last breath. There is the torment that her dad might have known she was not by his side at the end, might not have forgiven her absence. 'I'm not sure I know, to be honest. It still feels surreal, like a bad dream I can't wake up from.' It is less than a fortnight since his death and already these platitudes feel familiar on her tongue, as though she has swallowed a guidebook to grief and can now regurgitate it at will.

'It'll take time. I know how close you two were.'

For a few seconds Nell cannot speak, does not know how to navigate the ocean of her grief. She is aware of it eddying inside her, knows she must throw down an anchor to steady herself. She breathes, slowly and deeply, swallows against the constriction in her throat. 'It's hard for you too. I'm sorry Mum was a bit . . .' There is no way to finish the sentence without being disloyal.

'Don't worry. But you know I'm here for you, whatever you need.' Elsa tucks a stray strand of hair behind Nell's ear, and for a few moments Nell feels as though she is eight years old again, sitting on the bench in her dad's workshop, watching Elsa carve a piece of wood while Nell chatters about her day at school.

Glancing over her shoulder, Nell catches her mum frowning at her and is aware of a familiar guilt curdling in her stomach.

'Why do you have to encourage Nell to spend so much time with her?'

'It's not right, how much interest that woman takes in our daughter.'

'You can't possibly keep an eye on her when you're working, and what does Elsa know about looking after children?'

The memories throb in Nell's head and she turns back to Elsa, guides her to an empty seat at the end of a pew. 'I'd better get back to Mum. I'll see you afterwards.'

She hugs Elsa and hurries back to the entrance where her mum is greeting her oldest friends, Pam and Alan. The two women share inaudible murmurs, their heads bent close, their hands entwined, and Nell is reminded of all those afternoons when they would sit together on the sofa, Nell playing quietly on the rug in front of them, trying to decode their grownup conversations, the meanings of which always seemed just fractionally out of reach.

'You bearing up okay?' Alan rests a hand on Nell's shoulder. Capillaries spread in a fertile delta across his nose, his cheeks ruddy and flushed.

'I think so. I suspect I'll feel better once today's over.' Nell forces her lips into a smile, baulking at these strange funereal customs: the stoical reassurances, the innocuous small talk, the brave face while inside she is howling.

'Let's make sure we give him the sendoff he deserves.' Alan pats her arm and Nell nods in silent reply.

As Pam and Alan make their way inside, Nell's phone vibrates in her jacket pocket and she scrabbles to retrieve it, fingers fumbling to open the app.

Hey sweetheart. Just to say I'm thinking of you. I hope it goes as well as it possibly can. Let me know if you want to meet up later. I love you. J xx

Reading the message, she wonders whether she has made a mistake, refusing Josh's offer to accompany her today. But then she looks at her mum, at her lost expression as if she is floating out to sea and Nell is the buoy destined to keep her afloat, and she reassures herself it was the right decision. It is not that she wouldn't have appreciated Josh's presence today, but her focus must be on supporting her mum, helping her through, providing whatever comfort she needs. It would not have been the right time – the right occasion – for Josh to meet her family.

'For God's sake, put your phone away. Jesus Christ.' Clare's voice is sharp and heat floods Nell's cheeks as she turns off her phone, thrusts it back into her pocket, but not before she registers the time: 10:43. Fifteen minutes to go. Silently she implores time to slow its steady march forward. For ten days people have been telling her that the funeral will be cathartic, that it is an important step in the grieving process. But there is a finality to it that feels premature, an ending for which she is unprepared.

A different tune begins to pipe through the speakers. 'Tell Out My Soul', one of her dad's favourites: *Tell out my soul, the greatness of the Lord, to children's children and forever more.* She can hear her dad's voice now, as clearly as if he were standing next to her: *'I've never been a religious man, but the church does know a thing or two about a good tune.'*

Denise Silva arrives – another old friend of her mum's – and the two women clutch each other's elbows as if unsure which of them is holding the other up. More people file in, offering their condolences as they pass, faces Nell recognises but is unable to place, like being handed an old school photograph full of grainy portraits that spark a flicker of recognition but nothing more.

The officiant tells them it is almost time to begin, and Nell takes her mum's arm on one side, Clare the other, Laura behind, and they walk along the aisle of the packed chapel, dozens of eyes boring into the skin on the back of Nell's neck. Her mum grabs hold of Nell's hand and clasps it so tightly it almost hurts, but it is better than the other pain, the one pressing down on Nell's chest, shortening her breaths, squeezing the air from her lungs.

Her mum lowers herself onto the front pew, sandwiched between Nell and Clare. Nell sits with a straightened back, her free hand curled into a fist in her lap, fingernails pressed into her palm. She recalls the feel of her hand enclosed inside her father's, the rough skin on the pads of his fingers, but the memory is too painful to handle, like loose pins, and she buries it in a corner of her mind to be examined later, when she is alone. For now, she fixes her gaze firmly forward, holds her body close to her mother's, and tries to convey silently to her mum that she is not alone, that she is loved, that they will get through this together.

'Well, that was a beautiful service. Your dad would have loved it.'

The words are fuzzy in Nell's ears but she smiles and nods at Pam. Her eyes scan the 1970s church hall with its faded walls that had once been white but are now a nameless shade of cream. Its narrow wooden floorboards have been scuffed by decades of footfall, its fraying blue curtains held open by yellow tiebacks from which stray strands hang limply towards the floor. It had been the venue for so many childhood jumble sales, Christmas fairs and amateur pantomimes that stepping into it now is like opening the door on a wardrobe that leads into a past Nell had all but forgotten.

On trestle tables along the far wall, a sequence of thin paper tablecloths are held down by plates of ham sandwiches, sausage rolls, stainless steel urns of tea and coffee. Nell watches as guests load up paper plates with quartered pork pies and slivers of quiche they are eating with their fingers because neither Nell nor her sisters remembered to buy plastic cutlery.

The room is packed. Nell had assumed that in walking the fifteen minutes from the crematorium to the village hall, they would lose half the congregation. But there must be fifty people there, possibly more.

Across the room, Nell sees Laura carrying Tupperware boxes full of sandwiches towards the table where some of the foil serving plates are already halfempty. Her sister's hair is scraped into a short ponytail, from which strands of fine hair are already coming loose. She is wearing a cream chiffon blouse with silver buttons, black flared trousers, and Nell realises that she cannot remember the last time she saw her sister in anything other than jeans or her work uniform. She excuses herself from Pam and makes her way through the tightly packed mourners, finds a box of sausage rolls, begins to lay them out.

'Thanks, Nell. What is it about funerals? It's almost as if people need to eat to prove they're still alive.'

Nell takes a pile of dirty paper plates from Laura. 'Let me tidy that up. You've done more than enough already.' She finds a bin bag under the table, shoves the plates inside. When she stands up, Clare is standing by Laura's side, eyes pinched with suspicion. At seven inches taller than Nell, both Clare and Laura tower over her, and standing opposite them she feels like a dwarf in a fairy tale. Clare picks at the skin around her thumbnail – a tic she has had for as long as Nell can remember – the cuticle red and angry beneath. Her face is free of makeup, her nose pinker than the rest of her skin, the crevices around her eyes suggestive of insufficient sleep.

'Have you told her?'

Laura shoots Clare a look and they engage in a pantomime exchange of silent communication.

'Told me what?'

Laura shakes her head. 'Nothing.' She turns to Clare, eyebrows raised in mute warning.

'I just assumed—'

'Well, I haven't.'

Nell stands opposite them, observing the interchange like a spectator following a tennis match. 'What are you talking about? What's going on?'

There is a moment's silence before Clare speaks. 'We've accepted an offer on the house.'

Laura exhales loudly, will not meet Nell's quizzical gaze, and it takes a few seconds for the information to compute inside Nell's head. 'On Mum and Dad's house? Since when?'

Laura hesitates, glances at Clare, waiting for her to fill in the blanks, turns back to Nell when it is clear their sister has no intention of completing the explanation. 'It only happened yesterday. We were going to tell you today. It's just been so full on with getting everything ready . . .' Laura's voice trails off and she does not make an effort to chase it back.

'You could have phoned me, or texted. We've got joint power of attorney. You can't just make unilateral decisions without me.'

'We're telling you now.' Clare folds her arms across her chest. 'It's a decent offer, we'd have been mad to turn it down, and they wanted an answer straight away. What should we have done? Lost the buyer just so you could be consulted on something we were all going to agree on anyway?' Clare's voice is like jagged rocks and Nell almost retreats, in search of a place of safety. But then she remembers the day, five months ago, that their parents signed over joint power of attorney, making them promise that if they ever needed to use it, they would take decisions between them.

'What about Mum? Where's she going if the house is sold?' Nell takes a step back as a woman she doesn't recognise reaches in front of her for an egg and cress sandwich.

There is another wordless communication between her sisters: Clare's frown; the almost imperceptible shaking of Laura's head.

37

'She's got a place at Birchwood.' Laura's voice is apologetic and she looks away, fiddling with the buttons on the cuff of her blouse.

Nell is aware of her pulse accelerating, is not sure whether it is shock or indignation causing it to race. 'When did that happen?'

'My manager's done me a favour – bumped Mum up the waiting list. If we hadn't taken it, it could've been a year before another room came free. And we did all agree that if we could get Mum into Birchwood it would be the best place for her. You know she can't stay living at home now . . .' The end of Laura's sentences keep eluding her, as though she misplaces them halfway through and does not know where to find them.

Nell tries to marshal her thoughts into a straight line but they are like unruly children at the end of playtime. It is true that she and her sisters have agreed, since her mum's diagnosis, that when the time comes for her to need fulltime care, the ideal solution would be for her to move into the residential home where Laura works as a care assistant, just ten minutes from their childhood house. Money for this eventuality has been put aside by their parents, from the sale of Bill's carpentry business to Elsa eight years ago, an act of prudence that now seems almost prescient. It is also true that her parents' house has been on the market for nearly six months and that there has not been a single offer in that time. Nell knows that Laura is right, that it is not feasible – not practical – for their mum to live alone now that their dad is not there to keep an eye on her. There have been so many close calls over the past few months. The front door left wide open for hours on end. The reading glasses found in the vegetable drawer of the fridge. The missed hospital appointments, letters for which their mum claims never to have seen. And her mum's condition seems to have deteriorated further since their father's death: the day after he died she had tripped over the leg of a diningroom chair and banged her cheek on the skirting board, a purple bruise flowering on her flesh, the yellow residue still visible on her skin.

They are all legitimate reasons to move their mum into a care home. And yet still Nell cannot shake the feeling that she is a small child again, listening at the closed door of her sisters' bedroom to conversations they do not want her to hear.

'It all happened so quickly. You know how overwhelming the last ten days have been. I'm sorry we didn't call you yesterday, but we really didn't think you'd mind.' Laura's voice is softer than Clare's, but both her sisters' accents are still so different to Nell's. Over the years, Nell has learnt to mould her vowels and consonants to replicate those of her Oxford peers and Bloomsbury colleagues, until there is no hint left of her south London childhood. Her accent now is anonymous, placeless: a voice of no traceable origin.

'I'm just worried she'll hate it.' Nell glances from Clare to Laura. 'And should we be making such a drastic move for her right now? Isn't the advice not to make big changes soon after a bereavement?'

Laura opens her mouth to reply but Clare barks out the first response. 'What's the alternative? Are you going to give up your job to come and look after her?'

'No, but—'

'Exactly. It's all very well for you to play the concerned daughter but you're not the one dealing with her every day. You just rock up once a fortnight and have the red carpet rolled out for you, while Laura and I are the ones dealing with it day in, day out.'

'That's not fair—'

'Isn't it? What do you do except turn up for lunch twice a month and get treated like the prodigal daughter?'

'I organise their supermarket shopping every week—'

'Oh, big deal—'

'And you know how much research I did into Dad's condition, how many people I spoke to about whether there were any treatments he could try, any trials he could get on.' Nell feels her voice beginning to crack, sucks in a deep breath to ward against it, but Clare interrupts before she has a chance to continue.

'And you really think that compares to the amount Laura and I do?' Clare rolls her eyes as if tolerating the complaints of a small child. 'You're not rushing round there every day because she's lost the remote control or can't remember how to use the kettle or she's in floods of tears and doesn't know why. You're not rebooking her doctor's appointments because she threw the letter away without opening it, or cooking her meals or making sure she's had a shower each day. You're not having to deal with all of that while working every shift you can get at Tesco's and cleaning people's houses in between. You just sit in your poncy flat doing a job you think makes you better than the rest of us, while it's me and Laura doing all the hard graft, for all the thanks we get—'

'Clare—'

'What?' Clare whips her head around to scowl at Laura. 'I'm only telling it how it is. Why should we always be pussyfooting around her?'

None of them speaks. Clare's face tightens like a fist, and Nell turns away, not wanting either of her sisters to see the tears stinging her eyes.

There is no easy response to Clare's accusations. It is true that Clare and Laura have borne the lion's share of responsibility for their parents, true that it is they who are called upon first for any immediate needs, of which there have been many during the past six months. But that is not because Nell doesn't care. It simply does not make sense for Nell to be called first in an emergency when the trek across London can sometimes take two hours if the traffic is bad. It is not practical for her to visit her parents during the week given she is often in the lab until nine or ten at night, by which time her parents are already in bed. She knows, in theory, that visiting her parents for lunch every fortnight does not make her a negligent daughter, knows that she sees them more frequently than most of her friends and colleagues see their families. And yet, even as she hears the wellrehearsed arguments in her head, she knows she has to take responsibility for decisions she has made. It has been her choice to move away, to have separated her life from theirs with fourteen miles of road and a millenniaold river.

You just sit in your poncy flat doing a job you think makes you better than the rest of us. The barb stings, not because it is true but because it is so unjust. Nell is careful never to talk about her work in front of Clare and Laura, rarely mentions it to her mum except in the sketchiest of detail, knows that it makes her family uncomfortable that she spends her life doing something they do not really understand. It was only ever her dad who took a genuine interest in her work, who read the articles she sent him, who tried to understand the way she read genetic code like other people might read a book, searching for ways to manipulate faults, find cures, develop regenerative tissue from the body's own stem cells.

Thinking about her father now – about the way he had listened so attentively to whatever she was trying to explain, the way she had almost been able to hear the processing of his brain as he absorbed the information she was giving him – causes the back of her throat to burn with loss and she turns her head, looks around the room.

Across the sea of people she sees Clare's son, Liam, drinking from a can of lager, his arm around a woman Nell does not recognise but assumes is his girlfriend. At almost thirty, he is only five years younger than Nell, nearer to her in age than either of her sisters, but she has never been close to him. Clare had been eighteen when she had fallen pregnant with Liam, nineteen when she had given birth, a single parent by the time Liam was six months old. Nell can remember all the whispered conversations between her parents and Clare at the time, conversations she had not understood then, did not understand until years later: her parents' efforts to persuade Clare to move back home when her relationship fell apart, to bring the baby with her, to let them help her raise him. But Clare had been resolute, had moved into a council flat and secured a sufficient roster of cleaning jobs in the affluent houses of Dulwich to support herself, parking Liam's pram in wide hallways as she'd vacuumed carpets and scrubbed bathrooms. Somehow, she had managed to scrape by financially, though Nell has always assumed her parents helped too. Looking at Liam now, Nell recalls all those Saturday mornings when Clare would drop him off before breakfast, en route to those houses she cleaned that didn't sanction having a young baby in tow, and how Nell had watched her mother playing with Liam, had witnessed the care she had given him, trying and failing to suppress the pang of envy that her mother's attention was being bestowed on another child.

Her eyes wander further across the room. Leaning against a window, Laura's husband, Sean, is laughing with their two children, Dylan and Keira. Dylan has shot up since Nell saw him last – at fourteen, a young man, suddenly, rather than a boy, and Nell realises with a stab of guilt that she hasn't seen her niece and nephew since Christmas, almost six months ago. Neither Laura nor Clare tend to pop by on Nell's fortnightly trips to their parents' house for Sunday lunch. She knows that Laura takes her children to visit Annie and Bill every week, knows that Annie dotes on her grandchildren, the boys in particular, as though having had three daughters of her own, the novelty of girls has perhaps worn off. Over the years, Nell has been aware of how much both Clare and Laura have relied on their mum for advice and reassurance about aspects of their parenting, wonders if they now feel fully equipped to be mothers independent of her guidance or whether they are already mourning the loss of her counsel.

On the other side of the room, sitting on a pair of blue plastic chairs, scuffed with years of stacking and unstacking, she sees her mum and Denise, heads bent, deep in conversation.

Turning back to Clare and Laura, Nell tries to keep her voice neutral. 'So when's the room in the nursing home coming free?'

Clare shoots Laura a warning look and it is as though time has reversed, as though Nell is five years old again and has walked into a room where Clare and Laura are talking, their voices falling silent as she enters. So many times as a child, Nell experienced a feeling of being on the outside looking in, like a little girl at a sweet shop, face pressed to the glass, watching Clare and Laura inside selecting treats from oversized jars, knowing she was not permitted to go in and join them but wondering – hoping – whether there would one day come a time that she was.

'Let's not do this now. We can talk about it later, once everyone's gone.' Laura's voice is quiet, placating, and it reminds Nell of all the times during their childhood when Laura adopted the role of peacemaker, smoothing over tensions with Clare that Nell could sense but not fully comprehend.

'Don't be ridiculous. We've started now, so we might as well finish.' Clare drains the last of her wine glass. 'She's moving on Monday.'

Nell turns to Laura, seeking confirmation, and finds the answer in her sister's flushed cheeks. 'On Monday? As in, six days' time? And you're only telling me now?'

'For God's sake, it only happened yesterday and we're telling you today. Jesus, I thought you'd be pleased we've sorted it all out without you having to lift a finger.' Clare shakes her head, expels a long, heavy breath.

'So what's happening to everything in the house? To Mum and Dad's things?' Nell's voice sounds strange in her ears, as though it has been retuned at a slightly higher pitch.

'Clare and I will get going on it this week. We'll do the bulk of it at the weekend. The estate agent said there's no mad rush but we might as well get it done before Mum moves.'

Nell thinks about the scuffed rosewood wardrobe filled with her dad's shirts, trousers, jumpers, shoes. All those ties, in a multitude of colours and patterns, that he insisted on wearing every day to the workshop in case a customer came in. She thinks about his collection of records, all those decadesold LPs of Frank Sinatra, Dean Martin, Sammy Davies Jr, Ella Fitzgerald, that he would listen to in the chair overlooking the garden on a Sunday evening as Nell did her homework at the dining table. She thinks of the framed photograph of her and her parents on the day she was awarded her degree, her dad's arm around her shoulder, his broad smile illuminating the picture, a photograph that has sat on his bedside table since the day Nell graduated. 'I'll come and help. At the weekend. I've got nothing on I can't cancel.' She thinks of lunch with Josh's parents, knows he will understand, can only hope that they will too.

'There's no need.' Clare's words snap at the air.

'I want to.'

'Laura and I have got it all in hand, haven't we?'

'Well, actually—'

'We'll be fine. We can manage without you. Right, I'm going to the car to get more wine. Can you see if there are any more sandwiches?'

Clare walks away without waiting for a response. Inside Nell, something seems to crumple, like a paper bag being scrunched into a ball. Laura lays a hand on her arm.

'Don't take any notice of her. If you've got time to come and help at the weekend, that would be great. Now I'd better go and find out why Sean thinks it's a good idea to feed the kids nothing but crisps all lunchtime.' Laura smiles before heading through the crowd, and Nell watches as Sean wraps his arm around her sister's shoulder, kisses the top of her head, offers her his glass of wine.

Across the far side of the room, Nell spies her mum sitting alone. She makes her way over, sits down next to her, the seat still warm from where Denise has only recently vacated it. 'Are you okay?'

Her mum looks at her, a thin film over her eyes, and reaches for Nell's hand. 'You're such a good girl, to be here today. It would have made Bill so happy to know you'd come.'

Nell strokes her mum's liverspotted skin. 'Of course I'm here. Where else would I be?'

Her mum does not answer, does not seem to have heard, her eyes roaming the room, and Nell wonders whether it is a collection of familiar faces she is seeing or whether her memory has rendered them all anonymous. Her mum turns to Nell, fingers tightening. 'You're a good girl. Whatever anyone says, we brought you up well, Bill and me. No one can ever take that away.'

Her mum looks around vaguely and the words thrum in Nell's ears. 'What do you mean? Of course you and Dad brought me up well. Why would anyone ever say differently?'

She waits for her mum to answer but there is a distant look on her face, as though a door has been closed that she does not know how to reopen. Nell thinks about asking the question again but suspects it will not reap an answer. Her mum's words niggle at her like an itch she cannot reach to scratch. She tries to tell herself that it is just the dementia talking, but the memory of her dad's final words to her in the hospital whisper quietly inside her head, and she cannot shake the feeling that there is something more, something she cannot grasp. For the next twenty minutes she sits holding her mum's hand, stroking her thumb along veins rising from skin like a pale blue mountain range, hoping there is some reassurance for her mum in her presence. As the two of them watch the wake unfold before them, Nell replays her parents' words over and over in her mind, trying and failing to find the source of her unease.

THEN

Annie leans over the handlebar of the pram, tucks the blankets tighter around Danny's shoulders. The November wind whips across her face and she halfwishes that she had not promised to take the girls swimming this afternoon, but she knows it isn't fair to keep them cooped up at home on a Saturday. It is hard enough for them to discover they are no longer the recipients of all her attention without changing their weekend routine too.

Danny's lips stretch open into a wide, gummy yawn, and Annie is aware of holding her breath so as not to make a sound even as a lorry rumbles past on the main road beside her. He has been asleep for only twenty minutes – just long enough for her to get the girls' swimming things together and corral them out of the front door – and if he wakes now it will make for a miserable bus ride to the pool. But as she watches, rocking the pram gently back and forth, he sucks his lips together, rests his head to one side and drifts back to sleep. Love floods Annie's veins. He has been in their lives for only thirteen days and yet already she cannot remember their family without him. Sometimes the feelings are so overwhelming that she does not know where her love for him ends and her protection begins. She had assumed, having been a mother twice before, that the experience the third time around would feel familiar, straightforward even. But whether it is because there have been seven years between Laura and Danny, or whether it is because this third child was so unexpected, it sometimes feels to Annie as though she is experiencing all the joys and anxieties of a new baby for the first time. Perhaps, she thinks to herself, wrapping her scarf tighter around her neck, it does not matter how many children you have: perhaps each one feels like a tiny miracle. Perhaps each one remakes you as a mother.

'Come *on*, Mum. If we don't get there soon, we won't get any time in the pool.' Clare doesn't wait for a response as she turns and strides ahead, the duffle coat Annie and Bill bought for her last birthday straining across her shoulders. Sometimes Annie thinks her girls must grow exponentially during the night while they're sleeping: their shoulders wider, their calves thicker, a few millimetres added to their height. There are days when it seems only moments since they were Danny's size and she cannot understand where the last eleven years have gone.

'Can I push?' Laura places one hand on the bar of the pram and Annie steps aside. Laura has been so sweet with Danny – both girls have – and now Annie wonders why she spent so much of the pregnancy worrying about how her daughters would adjust to their new sibling.

They reach the door to the shop and Clare heads in first. Annie pauses in front of the wide glass window displaying a pair of newly polished dining chairs and an antique trunk Bill has just finished restoring. She glances surreptitiously through the window, trying to catch a glimpse of the woman she has come to meet, but the winter sun is shining against the glass and all she can see is the reflection of cars trundling past on the main road behind her. Before she has a chance to hone her vision, Bill steps into the open doorway, beaming, ushering them inside.

'How are my three favourite ladies doing?' He kisses Annie on the lips, his hand on the small of her back, and leans his head into the pram. 'And how's my little man this afternoon? Has he been okay?'

Annie nods. 'Absolutely fine. The girls watched him while I had a bath. I'm taking them to the pool but we thought we'd pop in and say hello.' She has tried to keep her voice casual, but Bill knows her too well for her to disguise what she has really come for.

'Come and meet Elsa.'

They follow Bill through the scuffed wooden door to the Tardislike workshop behind. Annie remembers the first time Bill brought her here, almost a decade ago, when he was contemplating signing the lease and starting his own furniture restoration and cabinetmaking business. At the time, he had been employed by the man he'd worked for since leaving school at fifteen, the man who'd taught him everything he knew but was now retiring, bequeathing his clients to Bill. Annie had been wary at first, feeling it was too great a risk. With a small baby to care for, she had wanted him to find employment with an established firm, where he would have a regular income and no financial risk. People like them, she thought, did not run their own businesses: people like them spent their lives grafting for others. But as Bill had taken her through the shop front – previously a haberdasher's – and walked into the expansive space beyond, talking nineteen to the dozen about where he'd put the workbench, in which corner he'd store his tools, how he'd keep the space nearest the back door for the finishing area, she hadn't been able to resist his enthusiasm. And he'd made a decent fist of it. Money was tight but he kept things ticking over. People liked him and trusted him, and they came back when they needed something fixing. Some of his more affluent clients from Dulwich or Sidcup returned multiple times with fresh commissions: a toy chest for a grandchild, a coffee table for a sitting room, a bookcase for a new study. Business wasn't exactly booming but they got by. And now, apparently, his new employee was going to help invigorate the shop's fortunes.

Annie steers the pram through the doorway, wheels crunching over the wood shavings on the floor.

Standing at a workbench, planing a piece of wood, is a young woman so contrary to Annie's expectations that it takes a moment for her to adjust her preconceptions.

The woman is not the solid, muscular Elsa of her imaginings. This woman is slender, elegant, dainty, the kind of woman on whom clothes hang effortlessly, as if on a perfectly proportioned coat hanger. Her blonde hair is bunched into a haphazard ponytail that manages to look both careless and stylish at the same time. She is dressed in denim dungarees over a tight white tshirt, a checked redandwhite scarf tied around her head. If Annie had opened one of the fashion magazines she occasionally looks at in the doctor's surgery, she would not have been surprised to find Elsa within its pages. Her face is wiser, somehow, than her twentyone years, and it contains a knowingness that Annie finds strangely unnerving, as though there are thoughts inside this young woman's mind that Annie wants to know but suspects she will never be told.

'Annie, meet Elsa. Elsa, this is Annie, and Clare and Laura.'

Elsa picks up a cloth from the workbench, wipes her palms before extending her arm towards Annie, her handshake confident, her skin softer than Annie is expecting.

'It's nice to meet you, Elsa.'

'You too. I feel like I already know you, Bill's told me so much about you.'

There is only the lightest hint of a Scottish burr in her voice and it takes Annie by surprise. She has expected Elsa to sound more . . . Scottish. Instead she sounds posh – almost London posh – but with an undertone of Gaelic so subtle you might miss it if you weren't listening out for it, like an offwhite paint in which you see the extra pigment only if the light is right.

'I've heard a lot about you too.' It is not strictly true. Bill has said very little about Elsa since she started working with him five days ago, and Annie cannot help wondering what Bill has told Elsa about her during all the hours they have so far spent together.

Elsa says hello to the girls, shakes their hands, and Annie watches her daughters' awkwardness: they are not a handshaking family. Clare and Laura begin telling Bill about the Search for a Superstar contestant on *Saturday Superstore*, and Annie envies her daughters' apparent indifference to their father's new employee. As the five of them stand in a circle in Bill's workshop, Annie cannot help feeling that she and the girls are taking up too much space: their limbs too heavy, their bodies too cumbersome next to Bill's elfin assistant.

'This must be Danny. Congratulations. Can I take a peek?'

Annie feels her fingers grip the handlebar. 'Of course. He's sleeping at the moment though, so I won't get him out.'

Elsa waves a hand in the air. 'God, no. Only a crazy person would wake a sleeping baby.' She peers over the hood of Danny's pram, turns back to Annie with a smile Annie thinks is genuine but cannot be sure. 'He's beautiful. No wonder Bill's besotted. Must be exhausting though, having a newborn baby.'

Annie rubs her eyes in Pavlovian response. 'He's a pretty good sleeper. We're very lucky.' She hears the defensiveness in her voice, does not know where it is coming from. 'How are you settling in?'

'Great, thanks. I'm renting a flat just near the Horniman Museum. And Bill's been brilliant – filling me in on the best shops and cafes to go to. I still feel like a tourist, but I guess I will for a while yet.' Elsa laughs and there is something so unselfconscious in it that Annie wishes she could bottle it and save it for future use.

'I keep telling him that I'd have been lost without his advice this past week.'

Both Elsa and Bill laugh, and Annie tries not to disclose her surprise at the ease with which they share a moment of good humour after less than a week in each other's company.

'I was about to make a cup of tea. Would you like one?' Elsa reties the scarf around her hair with a nimble flick of her fingers.

Annie shakes her head. 'No, thanks, we need to get going.'

'How about you, Bill? Do you want your usual?'

Your usual. The words prickle Annie's skin. She tells herself she is being ridiculous. She and Bill have been married for fifteen years. Their third baby is asleep in the pram by her side. And yet the sight of this beautiful, selfassured young woman walking over to the sink to fill the kettle and make Annie's husband 'his usual' provokes an urge both to flee and never to leave at the same time.

'So you're off swimming? Well, I hope this little one behaves himself watching his big sisters. And you two be good for Mum, okay?' Bill wraps an arm around each daughter, kisses the tops of their heads, one then the other.

'Which pool are you going to? I want to find an outdoor pool, or a pond like the ones up in Hampstead. Is there anything like that round here?'

Annie waits for Bill to answer but he is listening to something Laura is saying.

'There's Brockwell Lido. But it'll be deathly cold at this time of year.'

'I don't mind. I loved swimming in lochs and rivers back home. I hate having a roof over my head when I swim – makes me feel so claustrophobic.'

Annie nods, trying to banish the image that's popped into her head of Elsa in a bathing suit, legs lean, stomach flat, not a dimple of cellulite on her thighs. Annie does not swim with the girls when they visit the local pool: she has never been a fan of it, hates the sight of her body in a swimming costume. Even when she was younger – before the thread veins appeared on her thighs like indelible lines of ink, before the extra weight she gained in her first pregnancy refused ever to leave – Annie had felt uncomfortable in her own skin. She cannot shake the feeling that her body – with its wide hips, thick ankles and chunky calves – has mistakenly been cast three sizes too big. It is a curse she has passed onto her daughters but Clare and Laura do not, so far, seem to be besieged by the same selfconsciousness, and for that Annie is grateful.

'So what made you leave Glasgow for Bromley?'

There is a fractional hesitation, an almost imperceptible twitch of the eyebrows; Elsa blinks and it is gone.

'*Mum*, can we go now? The pool's practically going to be closing by the time we get there.' Clare heads for the door, leans on the doorframe.

A thin channel of sweat trickles along Annie's spine, her thick winter coat too much in the electricfanheated workshop. 'Okay, fine.' She turns back towards Bill and Elsa. 'I'd better get these two to the pool. I'll see you at home later. It's nice to meet you, Elsa.'

'You too. See you again soon, I hope.' Elsa turns back to her workbench, her arm gliding the plane smoothly along the grain of the wood, a clear line demarcating the contour of muscles in her upper arm.

Bill kisses Annie on the cheek: just a light grazing of his lips against her skin. As Annie follows the girls out of the shop and into the November chill, she rechecks the blankets around Danny, still sleeping soundly in the pram, and tries to ignore her unease that in visiting Bill and Elsa at work, she has intruded on a space in which she was never meant to be.

NOW

Nell parks her car outside her parents' house, looks at the pale beige pebbledashed walls and small square windows: two at the top, one at the bottom through which, if the light is right as you're walking past, you can see straight through to the back garden.

Switching off the engine, she finds herself hesitating before opening the car door. It is such a customary feeling, yet no less unnerving for its familiarity. The sense that before she enters her parents' house, she must shed a version of herself – the adult, professional Nell – in order to inhabit the filial space she occupies here. Sometimes she feels like a chameleon, adapting herself to suit whatever environment she is in. Other times, it is as though she brings out different incarnations of herself, like outfits in a wardrobe, befitting the occasion. There are times when she wishes there was a way to fuse the various aspects of her life so that she no longer felt comprised of jigsaw pieces that don't quite fit together. But then she wonders whether perhaps she likes it better this way: that perhaps this compartmentalising suits her, given that this is the way she has chosen to organise her life.

Walking along the short path towards the white PVC front door, she wonders how many times she has stepped onto the dove grey paving slabs, how many times she has heard the creak of the metal gate behind her, its paint peeling, tangerine rust collecting at its hinges. She can count on one hand the times her parents have visited her in

London, remembers with a blend of guilt and disappointment how uncomfortable they had been, first in her houseshare in Highbury, more recently at her flat in Stoke Newington, like creatures taken out of their natural habitat and placed somewhere foreign, illfitting. Nell's interactions with her parents have invariably taken place here, at her childhood home, and much as she loves her mum and dad, she cannot shake the feeling, as she heads towards the front door, that she is shrinking herself to childhood size in order to fit through, like Alice, potion in hand, at the bottom of the rabbit hole.

In the small front garden she notices the dry earth and crinkled leaves in the flowerbeds. Unopened fuchsia buds litter the paving stones like discarded confetti. Sweet pea stems cling limply to trellis slats, their petals curled and fading. The colour has drained from her mum's roses, their heads drooping towards the ground as though spent of the energy to look up towards the sun.

It is thirteen days since her father's death and time seems to have taken on a new dimension. Days seem longer somehow, heavier. Normal life – her research in the lab, her lectures to students, the supervision of PhD candidates – marches on, but now she is accompanied at every turn by a new companion, and there are moments when she is unable to bear the weight of it by her side, moments she has to disappear to the toilet, lock the door and surrender to her grief.

Reaching the end of the path, she presses a finger to the bell. Laura opens the door, ushers her into the hall. 'Were the trains okay?'

Nell shakes her head. 'I drove.'

'God, that was brave of you on a Friday night. Why didn't you just get public transport?'

Nell does not know how to answer her sister truthfully. She does not want to say that she always drives to Bromley as a means of maintaining some independence, of reminding herself that she is an adult, even as she feels herself regress. 'I thought having the car might be useful – you know, if there are trips to the dump or the charity shop that need doing.'

'There definitely will be. So how's work?'

'Fine, thanks. How about you?'

'Yep, all good.'

It is such a wellrehearsed interchange, as if they are both reading from a script, and Nell wonders whether it is simply a habit they have got into – this perfunctory engagement with each other's lives – or whether there is something more to it: some inability to share their true feelings with any degree of honesty, of openness.

Following Laura into the sitting room she finds it almost unrecognisable. Boxes occupy the available floor space, piled high with ornaments and nicknacks their mum has collected over the years. The walls bear the imprint of recently removed pictures, the discolouration of the paintwork like scars the house never intended anyone to see. The mantelpiece is bare where once it had been cluttered with framed family photographs, leaving behind an outline of dust like a photographic negative. The boxes represent the accumulation of a life's possessions, packed and crated, awaiting trips to the dump. It is not, Nell knows, just the dismantling of a home, but the disassembling of a family and of the lives that have been lived inside its four walls.

In the corner of the room, in the armchair that had, not so long ago, been her dad's favourite, sits her mum, staring out onto the street. A navy blue cardigan is wrapped around her shoulders, her arms free of its sleeves, her hands kneading each other with a steady, almost hypnotic rhythm. She has lost weight since Bill's funeral, and there is no longer the sense that here is a woman who can fix any problem, right any wrong. It is disorienting, this new version of her mum, and Nell cannot imagine that she will ever acclimatise to it, wishes she did not even have to try.

'Look who's here, Mum. Nell's come to stay with you for the weekend. She's going to help sort out the house.'

Annie turns, looks at Nell, and there is a moment's blankness, her expression like that of a waxwork dummy, features fixed in another time and place. 'Have you been out in the park with your dad? Make sure he wipes his boots properly. I've only just hoovered and I don't want muddy footprints all over the carpet.'

Nell crouches down, places a hand on her mum's arm. 'Don't worry. No one's going to put muddy footprints anywhere.' Her mum does not respond and Nell is not sure whether she has heard. She would give anything to be able to flick a switch, have one more day before the dementia took hold. Just one more day without her mum forgetting where she is or what year they are living in. Just one more day of listening to her mum recount stories about friends and neighbours, their conversations always revolving around the personal, the domestic, never politics or current affairs, a fact which had, at times, frustrated Nell in the past but for which now she would be inordinately grateful. Even though it has been only a matter of months since the diagnosis, already Nell fears that her own memories of her mum – of the lowered, conspiratorial voice she would adopt when sharing details about her friends' lives, of the way she would pause before a story's punchline – are being slowly eroded by this dwindling shadow of the woman her mum once was.

Behind her, Laura clambers over an obstacle course of boxes, reaches for her denim jacket. 'Now that you're here, I'd better get going. I gave the kids their tea earlier, and Sean's at home, but I should get back.' She hesitates for a moment. 'Dylan had a bad asthma attack yesterday. We ended up in hospital half the night. He's still a bit shaken up.' She delves into her handbag, roots around, retrieves her car keys.

'God, that's horrible. Is he okay now?'

'He'll be fine. Just a bit of a shock. Reminded me of some of the horrible attacks I had when I was little. I want to keep a close eye on him for the next couple of days, much as he'd rather I didn't.'

She laughs, slings her handbag over her shoulder. 'Right, I'll be off. Mum's had her tea so she won't need anything else to eat, and don't let her drink anything after eight o'clock or she'll be up half the night going to the toilet. I've left you some shepherd's pie in the fridge. I'll be back on Sunday afternoon – I couldn't get off work tomorrow. But Clare will be over at some point.' Their eyes catch and there is a fleeting moment of complicity. 'Call me if there are any problems.'

Laura kisses their mum goodbye and heads into the hall. Nell hears the click of the frontdoor latch and a stillness descends on the house, a preternatural silence that Nell feels the need to break.

'Can I get you anything, Mum?'

Her mum turns around and there is a moment when the fog lifts from behind her eyes and she reaches out, takes hold of Nell's hand, clasps it tightly beneath fingers that are still surprisingly strong. 'When did you get here?' Her mum is smiling, no trace of the consternation that had beset her just moments before.

'A few minutes ago.'

'Can you stay long? I know how busy you always are. Makes me tired just watching you.'

Guilt pools in the back of Nell's throat. It is a refrain her mum has used so often over the years, Nell fears that perhaps she has inadvertently given her parents the impression that her fortnightly visits home are an inconvenient interruption to her busy life. 'I'm staying the whole weekend. I don't have to go back until Sunday night, Monday morning, even.' She thinks of the lunch she is missing on Sunday with Josh's parents, of the kindness and understanding in his mum's reply when he had texted to cancel. There is a residue of disappointment that it cannot take place this weekend, though even without the house clearance Nell is not sure she would have been able to immerse herself in the heart of someone else's family when hers has just suffered such a loss. There will, she is sure, be other opportunities to meet Josh's parents. Other chances, she hopes, to make a good impression.

Her mum's smile broadens, the sight of it so rare these days that it tugs at the muscles binding Nell's ribs. 'That's lovely. What a treat. If only you lived close by, like Clare and Laura, I'd be able to see you every day.'

There is nothing pointed in the way her mum says it, no sharp edge of accusation, but Nell feels it nonetheless, does not know what to say in response.

'You know I always love it when you're home.' Her mum brings Nell's hand to her lips, kisses the back of it, the gesture so familiar it is like reversing time, spinning through the years, recalling all the countless times her mum has performed such acts in the past.

'Yes, it's just the two of us this weekend.' As soon as Nell has spoken, she sees it: the shadow cast over her mum's expression, as clearly as if a dark cloud has rolled off the sea. Silently, Nell chastises herself for her stupidity, for making any reference – however oblique – to her dad's absence, but it is too late, and she watches as her mum disappears somewhere Nell cannot follow.

'Can I get you anything, Mum? A drink, or something to eat?'

Her mum turns to her and frowns, as if hunting through a chest of drawers in her mind, unsure what she is looking for. 'Put the . . . the hot water jug on, there's a good girl. I'll have . . . what I always have.'

Nell does not allow her expression to betray her. 'I'll make us some tea.'

Heading into the kitchen, she fills the kettle, flicks the switch. Looking out onto the back garden, once her mum's pride and joy, she sees it is now a tangled web of shrubs and weeds after months of neglect. At the edge of the narrow patio stands the intricately carved wooden bird feeder her dad had made, empty of food yet still beautiful even in its weathered state.

She closes her eyes, memories slipping into her head. She thinks of the Sundays she and her dad would take a train from Bromley to Croydon, then a second train to Lewes, stepping out into the clean country air, walking through the town before heading up Chapel Hill, past rows of picturesque period cottages on their left, the River Ouse on their right, towards the green hills beyond. How the two of them would tramp across the South Downs, her dad identifying the calls of skylarks, lapwings, yellowhammers, greenfinches – Nell trying to guess them too, keen to impress him but invariably failing. The two of them climbing to the top of Mount Caburn from where a distant view of the sea would, on a clear day, be visible on the horizon. How they would sit on the bench at the top of that ancient, Iron Age fort, surrounded by birdsong and wild flowers, eating clingfilmwrapped ham sandwiches, and how Nell would always want the day never to end.

The kettle boils and Nell hears voices from the television in the next room. The clock on the cooker flicks to 7.32 p.m. and she carries the cup of tea into the sitting room, places it down on the side table next to the sofa, her mum's eyes fixed on the TV screen.

Looking around the room, she notices the halfempty sideboard, realises Laura must have been midway through clearing it when she left. Kneeling down, she begins to pull out items that appear not to have been touched for years: a box of white taper candles – brittle with age and covered in dust – that Nell imagines must be as old as her parents' residency. She cannot recall them ever lighting candles, does not know if they even own candlesticks. A faux leather case containing the canteen of stainless steel cutlery her parents received as a wedding gift, saved over the years for special occasions, which Nell has only ever seen used on Christmas Day. Beneath the cutlery there is a stack of photo albums, their padded plastic covers scuffed at the corners.

Picking one up, she looks inside, is greeted by a photograph of an elaborate wall of flowers, Nell sandwiched between her mum and dad standing in front of it, their faces radiating happiness. The date underneath tells her it was taken two years ago, and as Nell studies the picture, her heart contracts at the thought of how much can change, how quickly. It had been taken at the Chelsea Flower Show, the second year running Nell had treated her parents to tickets: booked them, organised the day, taken them for dinner afterwards at an Italian restaurant that was special enough to make an occasion of it, but without ostentation so that her parents wouldn't feel intimidated by the surroundings. For three consecutive years, it had been an annual event – just the three of them – her mum thrilled to be witnessing so much horticultural splendour, her dad happy just to be out with the two of them. There had been tickets bought for this year, too, tickets Nell had held on to even as her father's condition had deteriorated, even as her mother's memory had declined. She still has the tickets, in her bedside drawer at home, a month after the flower show has closed. She hadn't felt able to give them away. It would have seemed like an admission of defeat, an acknowledgement of changes she is still not ready to accept.

Lifting the next album from the pile, time rewinds as she is greeted by a photo of herself, aged six, crouching in the back garden, trowel in hand. Behind her, kneeling on the burnt orange cushion that was once her mum's gardening mat – that will probably still be in the shed when Nell clears it out – is her mum, smiling beatifically. Flicking through the photographs, Nell is greeted by a host of similar images, her childhood self growing taller with each turn of the thick cardboard pages: she and her mum planting seeds from thin paper packets, dropping them into predug holes; the two of them side by side, tilting watering cans towards the earth as the sun sets behind them; Nell holding up muddy hands towards the camera, her mum laughing behind her; standing proudly beside a sunflower towering over them both. Nell's eyes devour the pictures, trying to locate in her mind the memory accompanying each one, unsure whether she is recalling each moment for real or whether it is little more than a screen memory. She thinks about all the hours she and her mum have spent in the garden over the years – planting, watering, pruning, deadheading – all through childhood and into adulthood. So many of her Sunday visits home over the past decade have followed the same, comforting rhythm: a cup of tea with her parents in the front room; her mum putting the Sunday roast in the oven; the two of them heading into the back garden, fetching trowels and forks, gloves and cushions from the shed, an hour or two passing in peaceful collaboration, pulling weeds from the soil, cutting back overeager shrubs, tidying disorderly borders. Her parents' garden is not large but somehow she and her mum have always found things to do before returning through the back door, into the kitchen, where her mum would baste the roast potatoes and Nell would set the table for lunch. She had always found it calming, meditative almost: not just the act of gardening, but the quiet intimacy with her mum, sometimes working together in silence, other times the mindfulness of their work accompanied by easy, companionable conversation. They haven't gardened together for months now, and as Nell looks at the last of the photos and shuts the album, she closes the lid on thoughts she is unready to accept.

Pulling another album onto her lap, its ringbound spine creaks as she opens the cover. Inside, trapped beneath a transparent layer of thin, protective plastic, is a selection of rectangular, yellowing photographs, their colour bleached as though left out too long in the sun.

Nell's eyes roam across the quartet of pictures on the first page. A baby swaddled in blankets. The same infant held against her father's chest. Two photographs of her mum in a hospital bed holding the baby close, her dad perched on the edge, one foot flat on the floor to steady himself, one arm curled protectively around her mum's shoulder.

She looks at the date written in her mum's handwriting on the inside cover: the year of Clare's birth. Nell turns the pages, leafing through fragments of a family life that predates her. Photographs of Clare in a plastic baby bath tub, of her lying naked on a towel, of her sitting in a square red paddling pool. Photos of Clare reaching for a tower of plastic blocks, of her perched in a high chair, of her laughing into the camera, face smeared with food. Nell leafs through the collection until the final page, where Clare beams behind a cake adorned with a single candle.

She puts the album aside, finds a similar photographic story in the next one documenting Laura's first year of life. The two babies look almost identical: fine, fair hair that appears as though it may fly away in a gust of wind; hazel eyes; a top lip that extends beyond the bottom, giving them an impish smile. Nell would have thought they were the same child were it not for the date written in biro specifying the year, and for the photograph of Clare, aged four, standing next to a plastic hospital crib, peering at her new sibling inside. In another photograph, Annie lies in bed with Laura in her arms, Bill and Clare either side of her as though keeping guard. There is a symmetry to the photo that Nell finds unnerving: the kind of photograph an advertiser might use to portray a perfectly proportioned family.

So many times over the years it has occurred to Nell that the story of her family is a play in two distinct acts. Four performers in the first half. And then, after a lengthy intermission, the second act in which Nell arrives and the cast are transformed into a quintet. Sometimes she wishes she could go back in time and find out what her family was like in those years between Laura's birth and her own. Discover whether her parents and sisters were changed by her arrival, and in what way. Meet the people they had been before.

Opening the next album, she is greeted by her own reflection, thirtyfour years earlier. On the first page, she grins into the camera lens, a bright pink balloon in the shape of a number one behind her head. In another she stands holding on to the handle of a red wooden truck, her bare thighs chubby beneath a disposable nappy.

There are photographs of her laughing, playing, splashing in a puddle in yellow wellington boots. On each page, she watches herself age incrementally until, on the final page, she is sitting on the floor, a wooden jigsaw puzzle by her side, a cake with two candles perched on the coffee table in front of her.

Delving into the sideboard, she hunts for an album containing the first year of her life, but finds only photographs of later years: school plays, sports days, family camping trips to Devon. As she searches, it dawns on her that she does not remember seeing a similar album of her first twelve months. She cannot recall ever seeing a newborn photograph of herself.

Holding the albums on her lap, she experiences a strange sense of dislocation, like a key that will not turn in a lock. She does not know where the feeling comes from, or why it has swollen inside her like a balloon she cannot deflate. Only that, in looking at these photographs, she has a sense of peering through a window at a past she was never supposed to witness, of spying on a version of her family she was never meant to see. It is a feeling she has had many times in her life before: a sense that, in being so much younger than her sisters, she had arrived late to a party that was already in full swing.

Putting the rest of the albums into a box destined for the care home, she takes the one of her toddler years and tucks it into her overnight bag.

From the other side of the room, her mum tuts beneath her breath. Nell turns, finds her staring at the television, muttering and shaking her head. On the TV screen, a middleaged man and woman are arguing in the middle of an otherwise empty street.

'That's just what he said when I told him.' Her mum's voice is flat as though her words have been ironed before leaving her lips. 'He didn't believe me . . . I knew as soon as I saw . . .' The fragments of speech are disjointed, like a chain in which some of the links are broken.

Nell rises from the floor, sits on the edge of the sofa next to her mum. 'What's that?' She is aware of having softened her voice, as though speaking to a small child who has lost her bearings in a department store.

'They made me stay . . . I didn't want to . . .' Her mum stares ahead, face blank.

'Who did?'

She ignores Nell's question, does not appear to have heard. 'He was white as a sheet . . . I told him . . . They should've listened.'

An inflection of panic has seeped into her mum's voice, her thoughts like a silver sphere in a pinball machine, careering in too many directions for Nell to follow. 'Who should've listened?' She studies her mum's face, searching for a flicker of a clue that might indicate what she is talking about, where her memories have taken her. But her face is impassive, wiped free of expression like the screen of a child's EtchASketch.

'It wasn't my fault . . . I tried . . . And then he cried . . .' She shakes her head, hands fidgeting in her lap.

Nell places her own hand on top to try to steady her. 'Who are you talking about?'

Her mum's eyes narrow, twitching at the edges, as though she does not want to see whatever is behind them. 'I'd only ever seen him cry once.'

Nell tries to order the fragments into a story, like tiles in a slide puzzle, but cannot slot them into a meaningful picture. 'Who cried?'

Her mum reaches into the sleeve of her cardigan, pulls out a crumpled tissue, lets it sit in the palm of her hand for a few moments before looking down at it, wrinkling her nose as though someone else must have placed it there, and dropping it onto the carpet.

There is a silence during which Nell senses that the scattered breadcrumbs of memory are about to disappear. But then her mum sucks in a long, deep breath. 'He wanted to tell them . . . I couldn't let him . . . Stupid risks he took . . .'

Her mum's thoughts trail off and Nell is conscious of instructing her voice to remain neutral. 'Tell what?'

There is no flicker of acknowledgement that her mum has heard as she turns back to the television. Lights flash on the screen as characters dance out of time with the music. From one of the cardboard boxes on the floor comes the muted ticking of a discarded carriage clock.

'It was too late . . . I couldn't bear it . . .' The urgency has disappeared from her mum's voice, replaced by a quiet melancholy.

Nell edges closer until their knees are touching. 'What was too late?'

There is no response and somewhere in her mum's face, a curtain is pulled shut. Nell watches the nostalgia evaporate from her eyes, her focus fixed back on the television screen. She squeezes her mum's hand, trying to resuscitate her memories, but her mum reaches for the lukewarm cup of tea, says nothing more.

Nell replays the words in her head, trying to work out what the missing links might be, but it is like attempting a piece of analysis in the lab when half the data is missing.

She is aware of a compression in her chest, grief that it is no longer possible for the two of them to have a normal conversation. The deterioration of her mum's memory has been so rapid, with so little time to prepare, leaving Nell with a paradoxical feeling of having lost her mum even while she is still alive.

Holding hands, the two of them sit in silence while on the TV screen a collection of makebelieve characters live out their fictional lives. And all the while, Nell repeats the shards of broken sentences silently in her head, trying to unravel her mum's tangled weave of memories.

THEN

Annie peels open her eyes, pulls into focus the illuminated digits of the alarm clock beside the bed.

6.58 a.m.

It takes a few seconds for her brain to catch up. It is nearly seven o'clock, the latest she has woken for almost five weeks. There is a moment's disquiet that she should have slept so long before she reminds herself what the community midwife keeps telling her: take every bit of rest you can because a wellrested mum is a patient mum. Straining her ears, she listens for any sign of movement in the house but the only noise is Bill's deep breathing beside her. Her head feels leaden and she lets it sink deeper into the pillow.

Since they brought Danny home from the hospital five weeks ago, he has been like a human alarm clock, awake for a feed at midnight, at three, and again at six thirty. Every day, Annie has risen at half past six, fetched Danny from his cot in the bedroom next door, and taken him downstairs so as not to wake Bill or the girls. She has prepared his bottle with one hand, while holding him against her shoulder with the other. They have sat together on the sofa, watching Selina Scott and Frank Bough deliver the morning's news on *Breakfast Time*, Annie grateful for the company of early morning TV, a luxury that didn't exist when Clare and Laura were little. Danny drinks his milk while Annie finds out the weather forecast, watches the Green Goddess in her bright leotard, listens to her horoscope even though she knows it's nonsense. When Danny has finished his feed and she has winded him, she lays him on the sofa, fetches some of his toys – his shiny rattle, the flashing lightup rabbit, the bunch of pastel plastic keys – and the two of them play until the seventhirty news, when she carries him upstairs and into her bedroom to wake Bill. It has become their early morning ritual, and there is something magical about this time with Danny: she loves the calm, the quiet, the sense that the world is still sleeping while she and her son begin their day.

Next to her, Bill emits a single snore before turning onto his side. He will be pleased Danny has slept a little later this morning. Over the past week, he's told Annie she's looking tired, has asked her to wake him for the early morning feed so that she can have a lie-in. But Annie doesn't want Bill doing that, not when he's got a whole day of work ahead. She can always have a nap in the afternoon when Danny is sleeping – not that she ever does, there is always so much to do – but Bill doesn't even have that option.

Lifting the duvet, Annie feels a draft of cold air rush to greet her bare legs. The heating does not come on for another hour – the pipes clank and have a habit of waking Laura – so she slides her feet into the slippers beside the bed, reaches for her dressing gown hanging on the back of the door, heads into the hallway.

Pushing open the door of Danny's room, she halfexpects to hear a gurgle of greeting but the room is silent. Feeling her way in the darkness, she walks along the wall and towards the cot: she does not want to wake Danny with the harsh beam of a lightbulb. It was Pam who had advised them to install a blackout blind and it's been perfect for Danny's afternoon naps, will be even more useful come spring when the sun rises earlier.

Her eyes adjust to the darkness, and she sees the outline of the wooden cot Bill made before Clare was born, and which has since been used by all three of their children. Reaching inside, she rests a hand gently on the small silhouette lying on the mattress. There is no immediate sensation of the rise and fall of his chest, and her heart seems to skip a beat as she adjusts the weight of her hand so that she can feel not just the cotton of his babygrow, but the flat bone of his sternum. Closing her eyes, she trains all of her senses on the feel of his body beneath the palm of her hand. She tells herself it is just the darkness playing tricks on her, that there is nothing to worry about, that he is just sleeping, and yet she runs to turn on the light, flicking the switch, rushing back to the crib. Scooping Danny out from under the blankets she feels it straight away, the looseness of his limbs, and she knows that something is not right, that there is a floppiness to him that is just not right. Cradling him in her arms, she brings his face close to hers, holds her own breath while she listens for his, but she cannot hear anything, cannot feel anything, there is no tiny exhalation on her cheek and she cannot detect the milky smell she has inhaled every morning for the past five weeks. There is a voice in her head telling her that she is wrong, that she just needs to quieten the pounding of her own heart long enough to hear him breathe, but she hooks her hands under his arms, holds him up in front of her, and that is when she sees it: the faint blue tinge around the edges of his lips.

She is not aware of shouting out into the silence until Bill is beside her, asking her what is wrong, fear flooding his voice, his hand tight on her shoulder.

'What is it? What's happened?'

Bill's questions are woolly in her ears and she opens her mouth to respond but nothing comes out.

'*Annie*. What's wrong?'

She turns to Bill, sees the panic in his eyes, and it shocks the words out of her. 'He's not breathing. I can't feel him breathe.' She is clasping Danny to her chest as tightly as she dares, because surely that will give him whatever he needs. Surely if he can feel her heartbeat he will respond with his own, if he can sense her breathing, he will follow suit. Surely if she cradles her baby boy, her love will make him breathe again.

But then Bill is taking Danny from her arms and she sees it in his face immediately – the fear, the urgency, the dread – and it is the most terrifying thing she has ever witnessed.

'Clare! Dial 999 and ask for an ambulance *now*. Tell them there's a fiveweekold baby and he's not breathing.' Annie whips her head around, sees Clare and Laura standing in the doorway, faces drained of colour, terror in their eyes, and she knows she should go to them, put her arms around them, but she cannot because her feet are glued to the floor, her arms wrapped across her chest as though if she does not hold on tight to herself, she may fall apart.

'*Now*, Clare! Do it *now!*'

Clare runs to the bedroom next door and Annie hears her daughter's voice speaking into the telephone but the words are muffled in her ears.

'What's happening, Bill? What's wrong with him?' Desperation claws at Annie's throat as her mind splices in two: one half reassuring her that it is going to be fine, that Bill will make it all better; the other half shrouded in dread descending like a dark cloud from which there is no escape.

Bill does not answer, leaning over their baby, breathing into his mouth, and Annie tells herself over and over that Bill will cure whatever is wrong, Bill will make Danny okay.

'Dad! They want to speak to you.' Clare shouts through the wall, and Annie hears the tears in her daughter's voice. She watches Bill carry Danny out of the room, follows close behind, into their bedroom, where Bill takes the phone from Clare, Danny still cradled in his arms. She listens, blood pulsing at her temples, as Bill answers questions that seem to take forever, and she wants to grab the phone, scream into it, tell them to stop talking and just get here, just please send somebody to make her baby better. And then Bill is placing Danny on the floor, kneeling down beside him, the phone cradled between his ear and his shoulder, and she watches him tilt back Danny's head, one finger under his chin, puff five times into Danny's mouth, and then he is pressing two fingers onto Danny's chest, up and down, again and again, so many times that Annie wants to shout at him to stop, that he's hurting him, that her baby's body is too small, too vulnerable, for anyone to do that to him so many times. But the muscles in her throat will not move, and Bill continues the compressions, and then he is puffing again into her baby's mouth, and Annie stands over them, watching them, a voice in her head telling her that it is going to be fine, Danny is going to be fine, Bill is going to make him better.

She hears a noise behind her and she jerks her head around, and there are Clare and Laura, tears streaming down their cheeks, and Annie reaches for them, takes one girl under each wing, cleaves them to her body as they watch Bill deliver air from his own lungs into Danny's.

She does not know how long they stand there, waiting for some sign of movement, but all the while Annie pleads silently in her head, makes a string of promises about what she will do, the life she will lead, the person she will become if Danny is okay. And then the doorbell rings, and it is Clare who runs to answer it. And then there are two paramedics in bottlegreen uniforms, asking Bill to stand back, crouching over her baby, holding his wrist, leaning their ear against his mouth, and she wants to shout at them to stop checking him, to start doing something, that they haven't got time to waste. And then they are performing the same CPR that Bill had been doing, and she hears herself begging them to save him, begging them to do whatever they can to make him breathe again. And then one of the paramedics is lifting her baby and carrying him down the stairs, and Bill is asking them what's happening, where are they taking him, and the other paramedic is answering in a voice that is trying to stay calm but is filled with urgency that they are taking Danny to the hospital, that one family member can travel in the ambulance with them. And then Bill is telling Annie she must go, that he will follow on in the car, and Annie runs after the two paramedics, down the front path and into the back of the ambulance, and it is only once the doors have closed and they have pulled away that she realises she is still in her dressing gown and slippers.

The paramedic lays Danny down on a stretcher and places a mask over his face, pumping a ball at his side, and Danny is so small, so fragile, that a part of her is desperate to scoop him into her arms, have him close, hold on to his tiny, delicate body, but she does not move, knows she should not, watches impotently as the paramedic attends to her son.

The siren begins to howl and through the window she can see the flash of blue light in the winter darkness. They are travelling at speed but there is no speed great enough for Annie. She wants to be at the hospital now, wants her baby to be in the care of doctors who can do whatever it is that needs to be done. Sitting on a seat beside the paramedic, she watches oxygen being pumped into her baby's lungs, her stomach churning with a feeling she dares not give a name to, and she prays for the first time in her life, making the same silent promise over and over again through closed lips to whomever might be listening. *Please make him okay. I'll do anything – anything – as long as you make him okay.*

From somewhere behind them, a baby screams, and Annie jolts. Further along the hospital corridor a young woman stands under the harsh strip lighting, a baby no older than Danny pressed to her chest, bouncing him gently up and down, murmuring softly. Annie looks away, studies her thumbnail, bitten to the quick. She does not remember doing it, has not chewed her nails since she was a child.

Bill squeezes her free hand and even though she can feel the heat of his gaze on her cheek, she does not turn to look at him, cannot face the possibility of seeing her own terror reflected back at her.

The clock on the wall tells her it is eleven minutes to eight but she thinks it cannot be right, surely it must be later. It seems to be an eternity, the time she and Bill have been sitting there, waiting for news, waiting for someone to tell them what is going on. It is as though time has warped, as though the seconds are forgetting to tick, as though the minutes are being stretched like dough in a baker's kitchen until they have lost all sense of shape.

In a room somewhere along the corridor lies her baby, surrounded by doctors doing things to him she cannot bear to imagine, and it is taking every ounce of her selfrestraint not to scour the hospital until she finds the room he is in, demand to know what is going on. But she does not move because her muscles have become fluid, her limbs no longer under her control.

She looks at the clock again. Five to eight. It is almost half an hour since she arrived in the ambulance with Danny, over fifteen minutes since Bill appeared, telling her he'd dropped the girls at Pam and Alan's. Since then they have not spoken. Unable to find any words to fit around her panic, Annie has instead slipped her hand inside Bill's and not let go.

There is the swoosh of the double doors along the corridor and they both look up, Annie's heart knocking against the cage of her ribs. But a woman in blue scrubs walks past without a second glance and Annie tells herself that this is good, feels a flutter of relief like the beat of a hummingbird's wing.

The double doors swish again and a man approaches them wearing navy trousers with a tight pleat along the leg and a pale grey shirt. He introduces himself as Dr Laverty, asks them to follow him, gesturing with his arm back down the corridor. Somehow Annie manages to rise to her feet even though her legs are shaking, even though her heart is pounding so fiercely she fears it is going to pummel all the breath out of her. She keeps hold of Bill's hand as they follow the doctor through the double doors and along the corridor, towards a room in which Annie expects to see her son, to be told what is wrong with him, to be reassured that everything is okay. But when they walk inside there is no bed, no cot, no bank of nurses. There are no beeping machines, no saline drips, no polyester curtains separating one bay from the next. Instead there are four padded armchairs arranged around a low wooden coffee table, and Annie has to stop herself from reaching out, grabbing hold of the doctor's cotton shirt sleeve, telling him he has made a mistake, he has brought them to the wrong place, that she wants to be taken to the other room, the room her baby is in. She just wants to see her son.

The doctor gestures for them to sit down and even though Annie does not want to be there, both she and Bill comply, and then the doctor lowers himself onto a chair, leans forward, elbows resting on his knees, hands clasped beneath his chin as if in prayer, and he sucks in a deep breath, looks at them both, Bill and then Annie, and a gap of time seems to open up into which Annie senses she may tumble and never find her way back. And then the doctor begins to speak but he is not telling them where Danny is, what is wrong with him, when they can go and see him. He is apologising, in a quiet, calm voice, and he begins to say words so horrific, so abominable, that Annie knows they cannot be true, that there is no world cruel enough in which his words could possibly be true. But he carries on saying them, his voice low, as though he knows the world is not yet ready to hear them, and Annie shakes her head from side to side, so vigorously that pain jabs at her temples, and she is telling him that he has got it wrong, that he has made a mistake, that he has to let her see her baby. But the doctor just keeps apologising and Annie wants to scream at him to stop saying sorry, to realise he has got it wrong, that it is not Danny he is talking about. But he will not stop saying it, will not stop apologising, and Bill is squeezing her hand so tightly that it hurts, but she does not want the doctor's apologies, she does not want Bill's hand, she just wants her baby back.

And then Bill is crouching down beside her, wrapping his arms around her, the weight of his anguish against her body, and she cannot bear it, cannot bear the ferocity of his grief, and she hears a sound reverberating in her ears, a sound so primitive, so desperate, filling the room, and it is only when she feels the rawness in her throat and the heat in her chest that she realises the sound belongs to her.

NOW

She has left her mum in the sitting room, watching a hospital drama series that has been running since Nell was a child but which she hasn't seen since leaving home.

Above her head is a darkened square, the loft hatch already open. A ladder extends in front of her, waiting for her to climb it. Nell tucks her phone into the back pocket of her jeans, treads carefully, the metal steps creaking beneath her feet.

Her hand instinctively fumbles in the darkness to find the light switch just beyond the entrance and she is relieved to see the bulb illuminate above her head. As she climbs the last few steps and pulls herself into the loft, the enormity of the task ahead hits her. The plywood flooring her dad laid decades earlier is covered with a jumble of tattered cardboard boxes and longdiscarded furniture. The air is stale and Nell imagines thousands of invisible dust motes being sucked through her lips and drawn down into her lungs.

Pulling open the lid of the nearest cardboard box she finds the tangled thread of Christmas lights that have been decorating the family's artificial tree for as long as Nell can remember. Dragging the box to one side, she leaves it by the hatch ready to carry downstairs and add to the collection awaiting a trip to the dump. The next few boxes meet the same fate, filled with old bits of crockery wrapped in newspaper, ancient light bulbs, audio cassettes devoid of any means to play them.

On top of an old bedside cabinet is a box inscribed in fluorescent orange pen with the cursive script of Nell's childhood, as though her handwriting were playing at being grown up long before she was an adult. 'Nell's Private Things. Keep Out!' Inside, she is surprised by how neatly packed the box is, a cornucopia of items individually wrapped in sheets of yellowing kitchen paper. She lifts one out, unwraps it, finds a snow globe housing a family of penguins. Tipping it upside down, she places it on her palm, watches a flurry of silver glitter rain down on the birds. She cannot remember when she got it, or from whom, imagines it may have been a present from Father Christmas long before she had begun to doubt his existence. Next she uncovers her old recorder, fingers slotting instinctively over the tone holes. She brings the mouthpiece to her lips, but it smells murky, rancid, and she slips it back inside the box. Beneath an old notebook is a framed photograph of Nell sandwiched between her parents, holding up a birthday cake in the shape of a space rocket, six candles waiting to be lit. She is aware of a memory on the periphery of her vision, closes her eyes and it is there, waiting for her. She has just blown out the candles when she looks up and sees that her mum is crying. Tears are spilling down her cheeks and Nell wonders what she has done wrong, the panic of a perfect birthday being tipped on its head, spun one hundred and eighty degrees from joy to sadness. She asks her mum what the matter is and her mum pulls her face into a tight smile, wipes her tears with a sweep of her fingers, and gives Nell an excuse she does not believe but does not want to question because all she wants is for this feeling to go away and for her birthday to be happy again.

Nell opens her eyes, the memory lingering like the flash of a camera bulb long after the shutter has clicked open and closed. Pulling out a stack of papers bound by a desiccated elastic band, she finds birthday cards featuring teddy bears, butterflies, birds and balloons. There are Christmas cards depicting fat red Santas and smiling snowmen, a Valentine's card she does not remember receiving, signed inside with a single, oversized question mark written in patchy blue biro. Nearly every card is written in her mum's spidery handwriting, each word slanting to the right like the Leaning Tower of Pisa.

Flicking through them, she pulls one out that is different from all the others: a reproduction of Van Gogh's 'Sunflowers'. Opening it, her breath catches in her throat as she sees her dad's handwriting, small and neat in black ballpoint pen, such incongruous writing to emerge from such a large, sturdy man.

She is aware of her throat constricting as her eyes glide from one line to the next, absorbing this little slice of her father from beyond the grave.

To our clever Nell

Well done on passing the 11+! We are so proud of you. We know you will be every bit as clever as the other girls at the grammar school and are sure you're going to really enjoy it.

With all our love
Dad and Mum
xxx

Her eyes sting and she runs a finger across letters where the ink has longsince dried. She imagines her father's pen pressing down on the thin white card, imagines his wide fingers wrapped around it, imagines – as she traces his words – that she can feel his presence in the soft indentations.

It is as she reaches the final line that she notices it: how her mum has not signed her own name, her dad signing for both of them. She stares at it for a moment, unsure why it feels like a riddle in need of solving. She remembers how her mum had always been so conscientious when Nell was little about everyone signing their own name at the end of every card: birthday cards, anniversary cards, piles of Christmas cards they would pass along the table like items on a conveyor belt in a factory production line. '*If I sign them from all of us, it's like no one else in the family really cares. Come on, it won't take long.*'

She stares at her mum's name written in her dad's hand on the card, and it is as if she is back there, sitting halfway up the stairs on a Sunday morning twentyfive years ago, listening to a conversation she knows she is not meant to hear.

'*I don't want her to go. It's too far away.*'

'*But we can't stop her. You know we can't.*'

'*Why not? You know how I feel about it. Why can't you just back me up?*'

Nell hugs her knees to her chest. She is not used to hearing her parents argue, can recall only a handful of times she has ever heard them raise their voices. Now that she thinks about it, their arguments have always been about her: about parties she is invited to, school trips she is due to attend, friends she is having over to play.

'*Because it's a fantastic opportunity. This could change her life. You know how bright she is. Her teachers have been telling us for years. You can't seriously be suggesting we don't let her go?*'

'*Why does she need to go to a school miles away when there's one five minutes down the road? It was good enough for Clare and Laura. Why shouldn't Nell go there too?* Nell hears something creep into her mum's voice that she doesn't recognise: panic, fear, anger and despair all mixed up together.*

'Because the grammar school's better. You know that as well as I do. She'll have opportunities there she'll never get at the comp.'

'It's too far. I can't have her travelling all that way on her own every day. I can't— Anything could happen.'

Neither of them speaks for a moment and Nell feels something shrivel inside her, like a decaying piece of fruit on a timelapse video. Ever since they got the letter two days ago, Nell has been able to think of nothing else. She does not have the words to describe the feeling she had, almost nine months ago, when her dad had taken a Saturday morning off work and driven her to the open day at the nearest grammar school, at the suggestion of Nell's headteacher. She had listened to a speech about the kind of girls who thrive at the school and had felt a yearning deeper than anything she had ever known that this was the place she wanted to spend the next seven years of her life. And when one of the sixth formers had given them a tour of the school – of the enormous science labs and expansive playing fields – she had dared to imagine herself there, in the bottlegreen uniform, surrounded by people who didn't call her a nerd or a swot because she liked learning. For the next six months she had worked feverishly at every practice paper her teacher had given her, had spent hours at Elsa's house, being guided in subjects her parents would not have known how to teach her, trying to fit six years of a different kind of education into the space of a few months. As Nell had sat in the examination hall working through question after question, first in maths, then in English, she had known that coming here was what she wanted more than anything else in the world. And when the letter had arrived, when her dad had hugged her and told her how proud he was, she had felt like a butterfly emerging from its chrysalis, pumping water into its wings and preparing to fly.

In the kitchen, a cupboard door closes with a bang.

'It's not fair of us to stop her.'

There is a heartbeat of silence and when her mum replies, Nell has to strain her ears to hear, her mum's voice low and rigid as though

79

every word has a steel rod running through it. 'And it's not fair of you to ask me to let her go.'

Neither of them speaks and then Nell hears the click of the kitchen door and she scrambles to her feet, up to her bedroom, onto her bed. She picks up her book, the words swirling in front of her, heart thumping with the fear that she has got so close to taking up that place – in her mind, she is already there, heating chemicals over Bunsen burners, playing hockey on the sports field – and yet now her mum might, inexplicably, snatch it all away.

Nell snaps open her eyes, adjusts them to the light. She remembers how, for the whole of that summer term and the school holidays beyond, she had lived with the ambient anxiety that her mum and dad were going to tell her they'd changed their minds, that she was going to the local comprehensive instead. How she had been on her best behaviour, fearing that if she wasn't, they might think her unworthy of the opportunity. How she had felt that the future she wanted for herself was held so tenuously in her grasp, that it could disappear at any moment like a puff of smoke in a magic trick.

She doesn't know what other conversations took place between her parents that summer, what discussions, arguments or persuasions may have occurred without her eavesdropping. All she knows is that when it came to the first day of the new academic year, she had got dressed not in the navyblue skirt and jumper of the local comprehensive but in the bottlegreen uniform of the grammar school.

Nell breathes deeply, flooded by memories she has not thought about for years. The geography field trip to the Outer Hebrides that her mum had refused to sanction on the basis that it was too far to go when Nell was not yet fourteen. The skiing trip her mum had said they couldn't afford, even though her dad had already told her that they would find the money if she really wanted to go. The Duke of Edinburgh expedition her mum had fretted about for weeks, while all her friends' parents had been busy buying rucksacks, thick socks, water bottles and supplies of chocolate. The sleepovers, parties, invitations for weekends away with the families of more affluent friends: the catalogue of excuses her mum had conjured up as to why they weren't convenient, why Nell couldn't go. It had been a childhood lived to a soundtrack of caution, as though the world was filled with dangers, and Nell was safe only if she stayed close to home. And, on those rare occasions when she had ventured out of the family orbit on sleepovers or school trips, there was always that invisible tug of her mum's apron strings reeling her back home.

Standing alone in her parents' loft, she experiences the feeling as viscerally as if she were a child again: the fear that if she strays too far from her mum's care, she leaves herself open to a world of unimaginable harm. And now, in place of that juvenescent fear, there is a different awareness: the knowledge that her attendance at the grammar school – and the place at university that followed, the career in academia – have set her apart from her family. However much she loves her parents, those decisions have – just as her dad predicted – set her on a different path, one which has taken her away from them, not just physically but in other, intangible ways too: in the way her family do not truly understand the work she does, the career she is passionate about, the adult she has become. Sometimes, returning home, Nell is overcome by a sense of loneliness: an intense feeling of dislocation that she is at once returning to the heart of her family, to the place she is most loved, and yet also to a place she is not entirely understood.

Nell closes the lid on the box of her childhood possessions, resolves to take it back home and look through it properly when she has more time.

Moving through the avenue of boxes, she peers inside at shoes that cannot have been worn for decades, motheaten crocheted blankets, paintbrushes stiff with age.

In the far corner of the loft, beneath a black bin liner containing two mildewy pillows, she finds a box bound with brown parcel tape. The parched tape comes away easily, and as she opens the lid, what greets her is not a sight but a smell: the musty scent of old paper, as if she has buried her head in the pages of a wellthumbed paperback or stepped through the doors of a secondhand bookshop. But when she looks inside, what she sees is not a collection of cherished novels but a jumble of notebooks, envelopes, postcards and letters.

Reaching forward, she picks up the postcard lying on top. It is from Pam, sent thirteen years ago, from a holiday on the Kent coast where, apparently, it had been raining every day for a week and the B&B breakfasts were inedible. Rifling through, she discovers that many of the letters are brown envelopes with a clear plastic panel, stamped with the name of a GP surgery, a hospital, the local council. She puts them to one side, continues digging.

Right at the bottom is a pale green cardboard folder, tattered at the edges. Nell pulls it free, upending other pieces of paper, leaving them in a vertical stack. Perching on an old chest of drawers, she lays the folder in her lap, opens the flap. As she pulls out a handful of its contents, she sees they are all newspaper clippings, their sides jagged as if cut in haste from larger pages. Picking up one and then the next, she sees that each clipping contains a photograph of a baby: babies winning local beauty competitions, babies surviving illnesses, babies in features about sleeping, eating, weaning. Babies in advertisements for nappies, formula, clothing chains. As Nell pulls out more and more handfuls of cuttings she notices they are not all from the local newspaper, the only paper she has ever known her parents to buy. Some are from publications as far afield as Glasgow, Cardiff, Bristol, Brighton. There are national newspapers as well as local, and Nell cannot imagine where someone in her family got all these cuttings from or why they might have collected them.

In some clippings, the print has begun to fade. The paper on others has turned from cream to yellow, from soft to brittle like fallen autumn leaves. As Nell leafs through them the effect is vertiginous. She cannot understand what would have possessed someone to accumulate such a curious collection.

It is then that she notices the date on one of the cuttings, where the article has been printed at the top of the page. She assumes it is an anomaly. Thumbing through the clippings, she finds a second, and then a third, and before long she has a dozen pieces of paper in her hand, each containing the date they were printed.

She is aware of her breath accelerating as she puts the folder on the floor beside her, keeps the dated extracts on her lap. She spreads them out, eyes darting from one to the next, trying to draw a meaningful narrative from something that makes no sense.

Because every one of the cuttings is dated during the first six months of Nell's life. And whichever way Nell tries to shape that fact in her head – however she tries to craft it into something comprehensible – there is no explanation she can think of as to why anyone in her family would have spent the first halfyear of her life collecting pictures of other people's babies.

THEN

Annie lies curled in a ball, duvet pulled up to her chin. She does not open her eyes. To open her eyes would be to confront a reality she cannot face. She lies still, as if by minimising her movements – keeping her eyes closed, causing no disturbance to the air around her – the world might forget her existence. She breathes slowly, steadily, and yet inside, beyond her control, something pulls deep in the pit of her stomach – pulls and tugs, pulls and tugs – as though she is being turned inside out like the fingers of a glove.

Her head is heavy on the pillow, her mind shrouded in a dense winter fog. She does not sleep at night, cannot rouse herself during the day. Instead, she exists in a state of perpetual limbo in which she is neither asleep nor awake, neither a part of the world nor physically absent from it. There is a weight upon her chest that she cannot lift, does not know whether it bears down on her from above or whether it is inside her and cannot be excised without wrenching apart her own ribs.

An image slips into her head, an image she sees so often she thinks it may be etched onto her retina: standing in a darkened room, the flat of her palm against the soft cotton of a babygrow, holding her breath, waiting to feel the gentle undulations of air travelling in and out of infant lungs. That moment of knowing and yet willing herself to be wrong. Sensing the fear tiptoeing across her skin, leaving a trail of goosebumps in its wake, shivering in spite of the dressing gown tied tightly around her waist. The split second before she turned on the light, a moment suspended in time, full of equal parts fear and hope, panic and disbelief. And then, with the light, despair. Being led into a sterile hospital room, seeing the truth pinched into the skin across the doctor's forehead even before he begins to speak, aware that she is standing on the precipice of a different future, one she does not want to inhabit and yet knowing that it is not within her gift to step back from the edge, to avoid the inevitable fall. And then feeling herself tumble – down and down, round and round – waiting to hit the bottom which cannot be seen in the darkness. Eleven days later and still she is tumbling, cannot imagine that she will ever stop. She is not sure that she wants to stop, because if she does, what then?

She pictures the stillness of the hospital room after the doctor left, her body enfolded in Bill's arms, their twin grief tangible in the vibrations of their flesh as shock reverberated between them.

She recalls the soft Welsh lilt of the policewoman asking questions that would not form intelligible sentences in Annie's head, hearing Bill's voice replying, his words viscous in her ears. The policewoman asking for permission to access their house, Bill telling her that their nextdoor neighbour had a key, and Annie not wondering until later what it was the police were looking for.

She pictures her and Bill being led into a room where her baby was lying on a bed much too big for him – so big, far too big for his tiny body – and a nurse stepping back as they approached. And there had been her little boy, her baby boy, under an unforgiving white hospital sheet, and she had lifted him into her arms, had felt the slackness of his limbs, the stillness of his chest, and yet still she had believed that she could breathe life back into him, that there was no medical science in the world greater than a mother's love. She had held him close, one hand behind the balding patch on the back of his head, rough where thirtysix nights of sleep had rubbed his hair away, the other hand beneath his bottom, whispering to him, over and over, that she loved him, that she would never stop loving him, that he would always be her precious baby boy. She had stood in that sterile room, with Bill's arms wrapped around them both, and had cleaved her son to her body as if protecting Danny from a biting wind, willing him to turn his head, to puff up his chest, to suck in a deep gulley of air. *Breathe, Danny, please breathe, I know you can do it, I know you can, please, Danny, breathe for me.*

She remembers Bill telling her that it was time to leave the hospital, that they should get back home, see the girls, tell them what had happened, and Annie had not been able to understand what he was saying, had not been able to comprehend that they were to leave Danny there, at the hospital, alone. It did not make any sense to her, that they should leave him behind, that she was to go home without her baby. It was like saying she should go home without one of her limbs, or her lungs, or her heart. And yet, eventually, she had lain Danny back down on the bed, had leant forward to kiss him, had watched as her tears had dropped onto his cheek, his forehead, his lips, and still she had thought that perhaps her grief might bring him back to life. But Danny had lain on that toobig bed, unmoving, and somehow she had allowed Bill to lead her out of the room, through the hospital doors, towards their car. And as they had left, it was as if her chest had opened up, was spilling its contents through the corridors, down the stairwell, across the car park, like a trail of breadcrumbs in a fairy tale so that Danny could find his way back to her.

She pictures the girls sitting on the sofa in the moments before Bill told them, but the memory is blistering, like flesh against a flame, and she presses the heels of her hands against her eyes, pushes as hard as she can until it hurts and all she can see are flashes of light against the darkness.

In the days since, as her heart has torn apart in her chest, as the tears have fallen, she has known that she will never forgive herself for having slept in that morning, for not having known instinctively that something was wrong. She will never absolve herself of responsibility for not being with Danny the moment his final breath had passed through his lips.

From somewhere downstairs she hears voices, indistinct and yet familiar. The clattering of cutlery against crockery, the persistent beep of the microwave, the gentle thud of a cupboard door closing. The sound of daily life. Annie buries her head further beneath the duvet, presses her head deeper into the pillow. She cannot bear them, these sounds of normality. They are an affront to her, to her grief, to her belief that the world stopped spinning eleven days ago. It is as though each of these sounds – every word, every rattle, every vibration – widens the gap between her and Danny, stretches the space between them, takes him further away from her. To Annie, it feels as though life were put on pause the moment she walked into Danny's room and could not feel him breathe, the moment she switched on the light and saw his pale blue lips. She does not wish it to be any other way. She is closer to Danny this way. If she can pause time, he is not so very far away from her.

Her breath is hot and damp under the duvet and she lifts her face from beneath it, feels the December chill on her cheeks, shivers even though the rest of her is clammy. She does not know what to do with this feeling: this sense of panic, restlessness, agitation colliding with such overwhelming inertia. She does not have the strength, the will, the desire to move, and yet the need to escape pulsates beneath her ribs. She wishes there were a switch she could flick to turn off every thought, every feeling, every memory, that she could be emptied of it all: a blank, a vacuum, a void.

She does not understand where he has gone, how he is no longer asleep in the room next door. It does not make any sense. It is like a conundrum she cannot solve, one she does not want to solve. How can it be possible that she put him to bed one night, held him in her arms as he drank from a bottle of milk, laid him down in his cot, kissed him goodnight, watched him drift off to sleep, and when she woke up the next day he no longer existed? How is it possible that his life could just disappear, that he could suddenly be gone? There is an incomprehensibility to it, a madness, with which her brain cannot grapple. Sometimes she thinks it is some dreadful magic trick, and that surely – surely – someone will pull back a curtain and reveal where they have been hiding him all along.

It cannot be possible that she will never see him again.

Her heart twists beneath her ribs as she pictures the tiny coffin being lowered into the ground yesterday morning. It is monstrous to her that her baby should be sealed in a box, that he should be buried beneath the earth, that he should lie there all alone. The whole time she had stood by that deep hole in the ground listening to the vicar reciting prayers, a single thought had revolved inside her head: *What if he wakes up?* It is such a hellish thought she wishes she could stop thinking it, but now, every time she closes her eyes, it is there: the image of her baby, sealed in a mahogany box, buried six feet underground, wailing for her, his cheeks damp, his eyes red, his terrified fingers curled into fists, and nobody hearing him. It had taken Bill holding on to her elbow, his other arm wrapped around her shoulder, for her not to have climbed into Danny's grave with him, not to have lain down on his coffin and wrapped her arms around that unfeasibly small wooden box. Now, lying under her duvet, she does not understand how she can possibly have allowed herself to be led away, how she could possibly have left him there all by himself. What kind of a mother buries her child and leaves him all alone in the darkness? What kind of a mother sleeps beyond her baby's usual waking time, does not intuitively know that there is something wrong, something horrifically wrong? What kind of a mother does not reach her child in time to save him?

A car drives past on the street outside her bedroom window. The front door to a neighbouring house slams and voices carry from the pavement to Annie's ears: people on their way to work, school, buses, trains. She does not understand how those things can be happening, how other people can continue with their lives oblivious to her grief, how the world does not acknowledge her loss.

She cannot believe that she will never see him again. Cannot believe that she will never watch him take his first steps, hear him utter his first words, hold his hand on his first day to school. She cannot believe that she will never watch his school plays, stand on the sidelines of his football matches, meet his first girlfriend. She will never wish him luck for his first job, never sit as a passenger in his car, never watch him fall in love, get married, have children of his own. She cannot believe that she will never get to watch him grow up, that he is frozen in time at thirtysix days old, that he will only ever lead an adult life in her imagination. They are thoughts she cannot stop thinking, thoughts that cause her chest to collapse in on itself, like a sinkhole opening up and swallowing everything in its path.

There are footsteps on the stairs and Annie holds her breath, listens, waits. It is Bill's heavy tread and she can almost hear the weight of grief in his footfall. She hears him pause outside their bedroom door before there is the scrape of wood against carpet, before he is walking towards her side of the bed. She keeps her eyes closed, regulates her breathing to mimic sleep, senses him hover over her. She hears something being placed on the bedside table beside her, does not move. She feels him watching her, wonders whether he knows she is feigning sleep. Eventually she hears him turn and walk away, pulling the door gently shut behind him.

Guilt presses down on her chest, heavy and unforgiving. She knows that Bill is suffering too, knows that something has ruptured inside of him just as it has in her, but she dare not get too close to his grief. It is too much already to bear her own. She fears that the ferocity of their collective mourning would ignite such heat within her – such rage and despair, such melancholy and heartache – that it would burn right through her: through her organs, her flesh, her muscle, her skin. Other people's grief is a flame she dare not approach. She does not want to hear their memories, their stories, their condolences. She does not want to hear the sorrow leaking from their voices, as it had, again and again, at the funeral. He is her baby, her child, her loss to grieve. With every mourner's expression of sympathy, every recollection of his thirtysix days of life, she feels they steal a little part of Danny away from her.

There are more footsteps on the stairs, and then there is Laura's voice asking Bill if she can go into the bedroom, say goodbye before school. Annie senses the hesitation before Bill's reply, hears the apology in his whispered voice. 'Mum's still sleeping. Let's leave her to rest. You'll see her after school, okay?'

'But I want to show her the decoration I've made for the class Christmas tree and she won't get to see it if I don't show her now. You said last night I could show her in the morning.'

Something compresses in Annie's chest. She knows she should call out, confess she is awake, let Laura come in. But when she opens her mouth to speak, nothing emerges.

'I know, love. But how about I ask Mrs Raynor if you can bring it home at the end of term, and we can hang it on our tree and Mum can see it then?'

Annie tries to lift herself onto her elbows but it is as if she has been bound to the mattress with metal chains.

'Okay.' Laura's voice is small, hesitant.

'Come on, let's get your teeth brushed. You don't want to miss assembly.'

Annie listens to the footsteps heading towards the bathroom, to the sound of running water, to Bill's voice filling the space where Annie's presence should be, asking Laura about the school Christmas play, about the present for her teacher, about remembering her hat and gloves. She hears them head back down the stairs and then Bill is calling Clare, telling her to get her coat on, and there is rustling in the hallway. And then the front door opens and closes and they are gone. The house is empty.

A wave of grief billows and swells in the silence where the sound of her baby should be. She should be singing to him, rocking him in her arms, rolling his toy car along the floor. The day should be stretching out before them, seven hours with just the two of them before the girls finish school. There should be time for a walk to the park, a visit to the local motherandbaby group, a cup of tea with Pam. Instead, there is nothing.

Tears spill from her eyes in steady streams as though a tap has been left on. She has never felt grief like this before. Her mother, her father, each of her four grandparents: she has grieved them all but nothing like this. She has never before felt this great cavern open up inside her like a wound threatening never to heal. Whatever she does, wherever she goes, this grief will be there, like a daemon shadowing her for the rest of her life. And she does not want it to mend, does not want it to fade. She needs it there beside her, a part of her. Her grief is all she has left of her son.

Crawling out of bed, the change in air stipples her skin. She unhooks her dressing gown from the back of the bedroom door, creeps onto the landing, listens to check that the house is empty. Walking towards Danny's bedroom, she pushes open the door and for a splinter of time it is there, as it is every day: the momentary hope that it has all been a bad dream, that when light pours into the room he will be there, lying in his cot, waiting for her, ready for the day to begin.

In the halflight, she walks towards the empty cot, curls up on the floor beside it. She stretches a hand through the wooden slats and rests her palm flat on the indentation of the mattress where her baby once lay. There are folds in the sheet, loosened by her son's movements, and if she closes her eyes she is sure that the bed is still warm, that the heat of his body still permeates the soft cotton.

Closing her eyes, she listens for the sound of her son's breathing. If she concentrates hard enough, she can hear it: tiny snuffles in and then out again. The faint sucker of his lips. The muted snore. With her eyes closed, she can feel his soft skin beneath her fingers, can sense the fluctuations of his chest as he breathes, can smell the milkiness of his breath.

Lying on the floor next to Danny's cot, eyes closed, she listens to him sleep. His tiny body is safe beneath her hand, his flesh warm beneath her fingers, and the same three words repeat over and over in her head, somewhere between an oath and a lamentation: *I love you. I love you. I love you.*

NOW

Nell opens her eyes and reaches for a glass of water. Glancing at the time on the clock by the bed, she hears herself groan: three minutes past five. The house is silent and she wonders whether it is the strangeness of being in her childhood bed that has woken her so early, or whether dreams she has now forgotten have stirred her from sleep.

Switching on her phone, she sees a message from Josh, sent just before midnight.

> *Hey you. Just got home from a monster shift. Remind me why I do this job again?! Anyway, I'm definitely off tomorrow night, so I thought I could pop down to Bromley & take you out for dinner. Or we could meet in Dulwich if you'd rather not do the whole meetthefamily thing. Wdyt? J x*

She reads the message once, then again, trying to understand why her pulse is racing. It is not just the prospect of introducing Josh to her family at this moment in time, when there is already so much going on: with her mum, with Clare, with the house. There is something more, though she cannot pinpoint exactly what it is. All she knows is that her head feels full, and she does not think there is space for anything – anyone – else right now.

Leaning up on her elbows, she types a response.

> *Hey. Sorry you had such a late one. That sounds really tough. You do the job because you love it (even if it might not always feel like that at midnight on a Friday night!) and because you're brilliant at it. That's a nice thought about tonight, but I ought to stay in with Mum. She can't be left on her own and I can't really ask Clare or Laura to sit with her when they've been with her every other night.*

She taps out *Speak later?* and then deletes it, though she is not sure why. Only that the events of the past twelve hours seem to be pressing down on her temples and she does not know how she would recount them, would rather not have to explain herself – her feelings, her thoughts – to Josh, to anyone.

Instead, she closes the message with three kisses, watches her finger hesitate over the screen before pressing down on the 'Send' button.

Lying in bed, she is aware of a yearning weighing heavily in her chest. It is, she knows, grief for her father. But it is more than that too. She thinks of her mum in the bedroom next door, realises that tonight will be her penultimate night in a house she has lived in for almost fifty years, cannot help fearing that her mum is unprepared for the move.

Flicking back the duvet, she swings her legs out from underneath, a sudden desire to get moving, get some air. Tiptoeing out of the bedroom, she heads towards the closed door of her parents' room, behind which she can hear the deep breaths of her mum sleeping. Laura has told her that their mum rarely wakes before eight o'clock, which gives Nell more than enough time for a

94

decent run. Heading back into her temporary bedroom, she pulls on leggings and a tshirt, slips her feet into socks and trainers, ties a hoody around her waist in case she is greeted by a morning breeze. Grabbing her mobile and headphones, she creeps down the stairs, remembering to avoid the fourth step, which creaks however lightly you tread on it. She retrieves the spare keys from the hall cupboard, lets herself out of the house, pulling the front door gently towards her, the Yale lock clicking quietly into its latch.

There is a light breeze and the sun is not yet high enough above the horizon to warm the sky, but she leaves the hoody tied around her waist, zips the house keys into the pocket. Plugging the buds into her ears, she selects a Haydn cello concerto on her phone, opens her running app, slips the phone holder around her upper arm.

She heads left, towards the main road, alongside rows of terraced houses she must have passed thousands of times before; en route to primary school, to catch the bus, to the grammar school, to the shops, to the park. There is something unnerving about running here, as though she is racing through the avenues of her past.

She makes her way along the main road, quiet save for the odd car and occasional bus, cuts up through residential streets her memory still knows how to navigate, as though a map of her childhood has been filed away in her brain all this time. She passes the Forest Hill Pools, unrecognisable since she used to go swimming there with her mum, then an old Victorian building that had once housed separate pools for upper- and working-class swimmers, now a modern cube clad in wood with a long metal tail resembling a spaceship or a whale. With the loose cuff of her hoody she wipes a line of sweat from her brow, glances at the app on her phone, sees she has been running for almost half an hour already. There is still time to run further before she will need to get home for her mum, and her feet pound faster against the concrete as she heads onto

Lordship Lane, past the Horniman Museum, skirts around the edge of Dulwich Park, the gates still locked for another ninety minutes.

It is only when she is standing outside the shop that she realises where her legs have carried her. She looks up at the sign above the window in its Farrow & Ball duck-egg blue and something tightens in her throat at the sight of the name. Pressing her face to the glass and cupping her hands around her eyes, she peers inside, sees a light on in the workshop at the back. She checks her watch again: just gone 6 a.m. She ought to feel surprised but isn't, cannot help wondering whether, as soon as she woke this morning, she had known unconsciously that this was where she needed to come, and that the person she wanted to see would already be here.

Her knuckles wrap on the glass door and the sound rattles through the empty street. Inside, the door to the workshop opens and Elsa walks out in blue dungarees and yellow espadrilles, surprise and then pleasure spreading across her face.

The bell above the door jangles as Elsa opens it. 'What a lovely surprise. What are you doing here so early?'

Nell steps inside, the door clicking closed behind her. 'I woke at five and needed some air. I wasn't sure you'd be here until I saw the lights on.'

'You know me – always up with the larks. And Saturday's the busiest day in the shop, so I like to get a head start. I was just about to make some peppermint tea. Would you like one?'

Nell shakes her head. 'Just some water would be great, thanks. I've still got to run back.' Following Elsa through to the workshop behind, the smell that greets her fills her nostrils with nostalgia and grief: freshly sawn wood, varnish, glue. It is the smell of a thousand afternoons visiting the workshop after school and countless days in the holidays when she would accompany her dad to the shop. All those occasions she would sit on a stool in the corner, hands cupped around a mug of hot chocolate or a glass of orange squash, watching her dad work at one bench, Elsa at the other. All those Saturdays she would slip her hand inside her father's, drive with him to work and potter around the workshop while her dad and Elsa bevelled edges, fixed mouldings to cabinet doors, dovetailed joints with meticulous precision. To Nell it had always been a place of unbridled freedom. In her dad's workshop, she had been allowed to wrap her fiveyearold hand around a hammer, her dad helping her to hold it steady, bashing nails into a piece of wood. Here, aged nine, she had been handed a chisel by Elsa and challenged to carve her initials into an offcut of oak. Aged eleven, she had made her first wooden box, complete with hinged lid and crimson felt lining, which still sits on her bedside table at home. It was here that Nell had confided in Elsa so many of her ambitions for the future.

It wasn't until years later that Nell understood why she had loved spending time at the workshop. Because in spite of the sawdust that got up her nose and the table saw that shrieked in her ears, it was a place Nell felt she could breathe. In the workshop, there were no interrogations about the status of her friendships, about whether strangers had tried to speak to her on the bus, about which teachers were taking a particular interest in her. With her dad and Elsa she could confide whatever she chose without ever feeling she was disappointing them for not disclosing more.

Her mum had never liked her going to the workshop. Nell had heard enough whispered conversations between her parents during her childhood to know.

'It's not a safe environment for a child, all that sawdust getting into her lungs.'

'How can you possibly be sure she won't get hurt on any of the tools?'

'Why on earth would I want Elsa, of all people, looking out for her?'

But her dad had prevailed and by the time she was at grammar school, she would head there once or twice a week to do her homework at the little table in the corner where Elsa would help with her Latin declensions or English essays, and where nobody grilled her about the specifics of her day.

Nell lets her eyes roam around the workshop. It has changed little since all those childhood visits. There is still Elsa's workbench on the righthand side, on which sits a narrow walnut drawer awaiting a handle. There is still, on the opposite wall, her dad's bench, empty now for seven years since his retirement, when he sold his share of the business to Elsa for less than it was worth. *'It was you who made the business what it is, Elsa. It wouldn't be fair – it wouldn't be right – for me to take any more.'* There is still the table saw in the middle of the room, still the hooks nailed to the wall on which a selection of tools hang. There is still, Nell notices, her father's slate-grey apron hanging on its peg by his workbench, the sight of which causes Nell to bite down hard on her bottom lip.

'You're welcome to have it if you like. It's been there since he retired. I could never bring myself to give it back to him.'

Nell turns to Elsa, shakes her head. 'I wouldn't dream of it. It belongs here, with you. I just wasn't expecting to see it, that's all.' She takes the glass of water, drinks from it thirstily. 'So how are things? Looks like you're busy?'

Dotted around the workshop, at various stages of progress, are a small oak cabinet with eleven identical slender drawers complete with distressed brass handles, the top of a coffee table made from a single plank of walnut and a toybox on which the recipient's name is in the process of being carved.

It had been Elsa's idea to move the shop from Bromley to Dulwich, where the clientele had more disposable income and where customers from further afield would be more inclined to visit. It was soon after the move that Bill had made Elsa a partner in the business. While Bill had continued with his traditional work, Elsa had developed her own style, built her own list of clients. On paper, the partnership shouldn't have worked but somehow it did and they had, over the years, managed to build a viable business.

'Yes, all good. More work than I can handle, to be honest, but you know I never like turning anything down. I should take on an apprentice really, but . . . well, I just can't imagine anyone else working at your dad's bench.' Elsa brushes some loose wood shavings from the table to the floor. 'How's your mum? It can't be easy for her, leaving the house after all this time.'

Nell thinks for a moment, realises that she hasn't spoken to her mum directly about the move, wonders whether she has fully grasped what is happening. 'To be honest, she's pretty confused most of the time now. She's gone downhill so much since Dad died.' Nell feels her throat constrict and she gulps another mouthful of water even as she knows it will slosh in her stomach on the run back.

Elsa touches her lightly on the arm. 'If there's anything I can do to help, you know you only have to ask.' Their eyes catch and there is a fleeting moment of recognition, both of them knowing that, however authentic the offer, it will not be acted upon. Nell has never understood the friction between her mum and Elsa, knows only that her mum has always bristled at Elsa's presence in their lives. And yet Elsa has always been there for Nell, at every major junction. It was sitting exactly where she is now, perched on the tall wooden stool from which her feet still don't reach the ground, that Elsa had taken hold of Nell's hand and reassured her that grammar school was going to change her life. It was leaning against the butler sink while Bill served a customer that Nell had told Elsa she was being awarded the Year 11 Science Prize, had decided to study the subject at university. It was on one of Elsa's regular visits to Oxford, during Nell's second year as an undergraduate, that Nell had confided – before telling anyone else – that she was planning to do a PhD, to aim for a career in stem cell research. She'd asked Elsa that day whether it was too ambitious, whether she was overreaching herself, and Elsa had taken hold of her shoulders, looked her squarely in the eye, and told her there was no such thing, that Nell mustn't limit herself just because she didn't come from a privileged background like so many of her peers.

It was that day in Oxford that Elsa had first confided in Nell about her own upbringing, telling Nell about her devout Presbyterian parents who had mistaken discipline for piety, and who had filled Elsa's formative years as an only child with scripture in lieu of love, and authoritarianism bordering on cruelty. She had described how she had always craved doing something creative with her hands – woodwork, sculpture, art – but that her parents had prohibited her, believing it unbecoming for a girl to get her hands dirty when they should, instead, be holding a bible. She had relayed how she had left home at sixteen, secured an apprenticeship with a cabinetmaker in Glasgow, rented a room in a shared house, and worked six days a week for five years until she had felt confident in her craft, had moved to London, got the job working for Bill. There had been an expression of quiet resilience on Elsa's face as she had acknowledged that she'd never regretted her decisions in spite of the fact that her parents had refused ever to speak to her again. '*I'm a big believer that if people really want to do something – if they're really determined – they can. I know you have every ounce of determination to achieve whatever you put your mind to, Nell.*' That day had been not only the first time Nell felt she truly understood Elsa – the person she was, the person she had enabled herself to become – but also the first time Elsa had spoken to her as an equal, an adult.

As Nell sits on a stool in what was once her father's workshop, she thinks about how Elsa's encouragement has always been so optimistic, in such stark contrast to her mum's anxiety. Nell has never managed to silence the suspicion that her mum might have been happier had Nell never gone to university, had she got a job closer to home. It isn't that her mum isn't proud of her. Simply that she might have been more content had Nell never left Bromley, like

Clare and Laura. Sometimes Nell wonders whether, if it weren't for Elsa, she would have found the courage to leave at all.

'Is everything okay? You seem a bit . . . I don't know . . . restless.'

It is only when Elsa asks the question that Nell realises what has brought her here. The words have been circulating inside her head for two weeks now, like water in a whirlpool, spinning round and round with nowhere to go. 'Did Dad ever say anything to you about me, about his relationship with me?'

Elsa sips her peppermint tea. 'He used to talk about you all the time. You know that.'

Nell tucks her feet behind the bottom strut of the stool, clasps her hands in her lap. 'No, I don't mean like that. I mean . . . More broadly, more generally.'

Elsa tips her head to one side. 'What's wrong?'

Nell takes a deep breath, knows she cannot hold on to her dad's declaration any longer, knows Elsa is the only person to whom she would entrust it. 'The day before Dad died, when I went to see him in the hospital, he said something I can't make any sense of.' She pauses, summoning the courage. 'He said that he'd always loved me even though I was never really his to love. I don't understand what he meant. It's been plaguing me ever since.' Colour bleeds into her cheeks and she looks down, picks at a piece of wood shaving that has stuck to her leggings.

Elsa takes hold of Nell's hand. 'He'd have been on so much morphine in those last few hours, I doubt he really knew what he was saying.' Her voice is apologetic, as though she does not want to take away from Nell anything from that final conversation she might yet want to hold on to.

'But don't you think it's a weird thing to say? I mean, even on morphine, that thought still had to come from somewhere.' Nell recalls the urgency in his voice, cannot convince herself it was simply the effects of the medication.

Elsa doesn't say anything for a few seconds. 'Your dad was devoted to you, you know that. But perhaps . . . I don't know. Maybe there was a bit of guilt about how much he loved you – about how grateful both your mum and dad were for you – after what happened with Danny. Maybe that's what he meant.'

It takes a few seconds for Elsa's suggestion to sink in. 'Who's Danny?'

Confusion studs Elsa's forehead. 'You don't know?'

Elsa's voice is low, anxious, and Nell feels the hairs on her arms stand on end. 'I don't know who you're talking about.'

Deep ridges appear at the bridge of Elsa's nose. She does not say anything for a few seconds, and when she does, her words are steady, deliberate, as though only by slowing them down can she minimise their impact. 'Your mum and dad had a baby before you were born. After Clare and Laura. He died when he was five weeks old. You really didn't know?'

Nell is aware of shaking her head though she is not conscious of controlling the movement. Elsa's explanation rings in her ears and she tries to make sense of it, but it is a collection of jumbled words that she cannot organise into meaning. 'When? What happened?'

'It was about a year before you were born – a bit longer, actually. He died of cot death. I'm so sorry, Nell, I had no idea you didn't know.'

Nell can feel Elsa's eyes on her but does not look up, is not yet ready to meet her gaze.

'Are you okay?'

Nell nods even though it is a lie. In her mind, the tapestry of her family history begins to unstitch, the fabric loosening at the seams. 'Why has no one ever told me?'

Elsa frowns. 'I don't know. Maybe they thought it was kinder on you. Perhaps they thought it would be hard growing up, knowing there'd been a baby brother who hadn't survived.'

'But Clare and Laura – they must know. Why haven't either of them ever mentioned it?'

Elsa shakes her head. 'You'd have to ask them. But it wasn't something your dad ever talked about, not after the initial shock. Maybe it was one of those tragedies that was just too painful to have out in the open. I really am sorry, Nell. I'd never have just dropped it into conversation like that if I'd known. All these years I just assumed you didn't want to talk about it, and that was fine. I never for a second imagined that you hadn't been told.'

From the main road outside there is the rumble of a heavy vehicle passing by.

'It's not your fault. It wasn't your job to tell me. Of course you'd think I already knew.' Nell's voice sounds strange in her ears, as though her tongue, her lips and her mouth are speaking without the rest of her body's awareness. She tries to untangle the knotted threads of story in her head, finds that she cannot hold on to one end long enough to follow it through to the other. She thinks of her family, all these years, harbouring such a momentous secret, a chapter in their shared history she has not known about until now. She tries to imagine her mum bearing that kind of grief, surviving that kind of loss, cannot envisage how she has coped all this time. She remembers her dad's final words to her in the hospital and wonders if Elsa is right: whether the explanation is hidden in the grief for a child that Nell had never even known existed.

From the phone holder strapped to her arm, Nell's mobile rings, and she scrambles to silence it. Glancing at the screen, she looks apologetically towards Elsa. 'Sorry, it's Clare. I'd better take it.' By the time she has lifted the phone to her cheek, her sister is already barking into her ear.

'Where the hell are you? You literally can't be trusted with anything, can you? You need to get back here right now.'

THEN

Annie yanks open a drawer, pulls out babygrows, vests, a bag of nappies, a pair of blue mittens, stretches her hand right to the back, but it is not there. She opens the drawer below, snatches at folded blankets, shakes them loose, discarding them on the floor when she does not find what she is looking for. Her eyes dart around the room, past the white wooden cot, past the Peter Rabbit mobile, past the collection of stuffed animals, panic snaking between her ribs, but it is nowhere to be seen. Crouching on all fours she scans the floor, tugs at each corner of the rug, slides onto her stomach and reaches under the cot, sweeps an arm across the dusty carpet but her hand finds only a crumpled tissue, a ball of Blu Tack, a safety pin.

'Mum, what are you doing?'

She turns her head, sees Clare standing in the doorway in her school uniform, coat still buttoned up, rucksack slung over one shoulder. Her brain scrambles to make sense of Clare's presence but her mind is claggy. 'Why are you home from school so early? What's wrong?' Annie hauls herself onto her knees, peels a tendril of hair from her face where it has stuck to her cheek.

'It's not early. It's the usual time. You didn't come to collect us so we walked home by ourselves.'

Annie looks down to her wrist where her watch should be, but there is only the sleeve of her dressing gown over the thin cotton of her nightie. 'What time is it?'

'About half past three.'

Annie turns to the window, sees that the light is already beginning to fade in the late January sky. 'How did you get home?'

'I just said. We walked.'

'On your own?'

Clare nods, nibbling at her bottom lip.

Annie tries to untangle the jumble of thoughts in her head but she cannot unwind them into separate threads. She remembers Bill leaving with the girls this morning, remembers lying in bed feeling the day stretch inexorably before her, but she cannot account for the seven hours since.

'Where's Laura?'

'Downstairs.'

Annie looks back out of the window and then down at the frayed hem of her dressing gown. She wants to be able to offer Clare an explanation, but cannot think what it might be.

'What are you doing?' There is a hint of accusation in Clare's voice and Annie feels her cheeks redden. Her family do not know how much time she spends in Danny's room when they are absent from the house. In the seven weeks since Danny died, Bill has told Annie many times, in the gentle voice he usually reserves for the girls when one of them has argued with a friend at school, that he does not think it is good for her to spend so much time in Danny's room. He does not think it is helping her to recover from their loss. Annie has listened without speaking, has allowed Bill to believe there is tacit agreement in her silence. Nobody in her family knows that every morning she waits until she has heard the click of the front door, and then she crawls out of bed and into Danny's room, lies on the floor next to his cot and tries to remember the feel of him, the smell of him, the sound of him. Some days she thinks it is the only thing keeping her sane. Other days she is no longer sure where her sanity ends and her grief begins.

'Why are you in here?'

Annie remembers suddenly, panic flooding her veins. 'Danny's blanket. Have you seen it?'

'What blanket?'

Impatience taps at Annie's wrists. *How can you not know?* she wants to scream. *How can you not remember? It's only been seven weeks, for God's sake.* She forces a deep breath, reminds herself that Clare is only eleven, that it is not her responsibility to remember. And yet the need to find Danny's blanket, to hold it in her hands, to lift it to her nose, to breathe in the smell of him, is an urge she cannot control. 'Danny's favourite. The blue one with the elephant on it.'

Clare shakes her head. 'I haven't seen it. What's for tea?'

Annie turns away, lifts Danny's mattress from the cot's wooden slats, searches each of the four corners and then the middle, but it is not there.

'Mum, what are we having for tea?'

Annie cannot think about tea. She needs Danny's blanket, cannot focus on anything else until she has it. 'Are you sure you haven't seen it? It's got to be somewhere. Could it be in your room? Maybe you or Laura took it by accident?' She rushes past Clare, into the bedroom her daughters share. Flinging back Laura's duvet from the bottom bunk bed, she searches under the pillow, thrusts her hand between the wall and the bed's wooden frame to see if it is wedged in the space, but there is nothing. Clambering off the bed, she lifts the lid from Laura's toy box, seizes item after item – a Rubik's cube, boxes of Lego, Hungry Hippo – and casts them aside until it is empty. Turning to the chest of drawers on top of which Clare keeps a hotchpotch of decorative boxes filled with hair bobbles and costume jewellery, she begins rooting through them, opening one and then the next until their contents are splayed across the pine surface.

'What are you doing? Mum . . . stop it. It's not in here. You're messing everything up.'

Annie jerks open the top drawer. 'It's got to be here somewhere. It can't just have disappeared.' The panic is hot in the back of her throat. She has to have it, she has to find Danny's blanket.

'It's not in here. Maybe Dad put it in with the washing this morning.'

A cold trickle of dread inches along Annie's spine. She races down the stairs and into the kitchen, unlatches the door of the washing machine, pulls out piles of wet shirts, sports kits, pants and socks, casts them aside, hoping that Clare is wrong. Wet washing sprawls across the kitchen floor, lino she has not washed for weeks covered in grit and grime, but Annie cannot think about that, all she can think about is finding the blanket, the one that had been tucked at the end of Danny's cot every single night of his short life. And just as she is pulling out the last of Bill's shirts, just as she begins to believe that Clare is wrong, that it must be hiding somewhere else, she sees it, lying at the bottom of the metal drum. Snatching it out, she brings the damp material to her face, sniffs it, is aware of something compressing in her chest. There is nothing of Danny left. There is no longer the scent of his skin, his hair, the sweet smell of his gummy lips. There is no longer the essence of him ingrained in the fleecy material. There is only detergent, chemicals, neutrality. All traces of Danny have been rinsed, washed, spun out of it until there is nothing left of him at all.

Annie sinks her body against the wooden cabinets in the corner of the kitchen, clutches the blanket to her cheek, waves of grief dragging her under, carrying her along on their current until her lungs are full and she cannot breathe. She is sobbing – big, heaving sobs – and she can sense Clare standing in the doorway, watching her, but she cannot lift her head from her hands, cannot excavate herself from the deep trench of mourning in which she is being buried.

She does not know how long she sits there, curled in a corner of the kitchen, Danny's blanket pressed against her face, howls erupting from her throat. But then Bill is there, crouching in front of her, his hands on her shoulders, telling her that it is going to be alright, that it is all going to be okay, pulling her into his arms, holding on to her as though he knows she is at risk of drifting away, reassuring her again and again that it is going to get better, in time. But Annie knows it is an empty platitude, that there is no amount of time that can ever heal this grief, that time cannot reverse itself, cannot deliver Danny back to her.

'You washed his blanket. You washed Danny's blanket.' The words are slurred, as though she is drunk on grief or fatigue, she is not sure which, and Bill holds her tighter, saying he is sorry, it was a stupid mistake, he's so very, very sorry. And she knows he means it and she does not want to punish him any more than they have both already been punished, but she does not know how she will ever be able to forgive him, not just for the blanket but for failing to save Danny, failing to breathe enough air into their son's lungs to bring him back to life. And yet somewhere deep inside of her she knows it is not Bill who needs forgiveness, not Bill or the paramedics or the doctors at whom she silently rages for not having been able to save her son. The person at whom she is most angry is herself.

'I just want him back. I just want Danny back.' She does not know how many times she has said these words over the past seven weeks but there is still a part of her that believes if she says them enough, with sufficient conviction, perhaps there will be a way to undo what has been done, perhaps she will be allowed to wake up and discover that it has all been a terrible dream.

Bill breathes into her hair, his head resting on hers, telling her that he knows, of course he knows, he wishes it could happen more than anything too. But Annie suspects he does not feel it as she does: he does not feel it in his muscles, his bones, in every stretch of sinew running through his body. He does not – cannot – feel the loss of Danny as viscerally as she does: deep inside her pelvis where once her baby lay.

The absence of Danny is suddenly so fierce, so acute, that she is speaking before the thought is fully formed in her mind. 'I want another baby. I need to have another baby.' Her voice does not sound like her own and yet she knows these words belong to her, even though they have crept up on her and out through her lips without any preparation.

Bill continues to hold her, rocking her gently back and forth, saying he knows how hard this is for her, but she can hear it, unmistakeable, in his voice: he is comforting her as he might a small child, but he does not believe what she says.

Pulling herself free of his embrace, she keeps hold of Danny's washed blanket. 'You don't understand. I mean it, I want to have another baby. I need to, before it's too late.' The words tumble from her mouth and she is not even sure she has said them in the right order but she knows from the drumming inside her chest that they are true.

Bill looks at her and there is kindness in his eyes but she can see the scepticism too. 'It's too soon even to be thinking of that, Annie. We're still so raw. Neither of us can think straight about anything right now.'

Annie tightens her grip on Danny's blanket, feels the moisture seep through the cracks between her fingers. Bill is staring at her but she cannot meet his gaze, cannot be near him when he does not understand the urgency of her feelings. She scrambles to her feet and out of the kitchen, ignoring Bill's voice trailing behind her, past Clare and Laura loitering in the hallway, up the stairs and back into Danny's room. Slamming the door behind her she lies down next to his cot, the damp blanket that no longer smells of her little boy clutched in her hand, and tries to breathe slowly against the tempest raging behind the wall of her chest.

NOW

The front door has not closed behind Nell before Clare is standing there, obstructing the hallway, her expression caught somewhere between disapproval and triumph.

'Just one thing you're expected to do, and you couldn't even do that. Do you know where I found her? In the front garden, in her dressing gown.'

'I'm sorry. I—'

'Anything could have happened. It's a good job I decided to pop by this morning before work.' Clare folds her arms across her chest, flesh dimpling above her elbows. 'I don't understand why you bothered coming if you can't do even the most basic thing of being here when Mum wakes up.'

Clare's censure is so familiar that another apology readies itself on Nell's lips, as automatic as an arm extending to reach for a falling cup or fingers flinching from a flame. 'I'm sorry. Laura told me Mum never woke up before eight. Where is she? I'll go and see her now.' She moves to walk past Clare, but her sister takes half a step to the left, blocking Nell's path.

'It's always been the same, hasn't it?'

'What?'

'You've always thought you were special, that the same rules didn't apply to you.'

'What are you talking about?'

'Always Little Miss Perfect without ever having to lift a finger.'

Nell breathes deeply, shocked by how quickly it returns, the feeling of being condemned without a trial, a feeling with which she is so wellacquainted it ought to be numbed by familiarity, but isn't. 'I said I'm sorry. What more do you want me to do?'

Clare rolls her eyes. 'I don't *want* you to do anything. If you remember, I told you not to bother coming in the first place. Why don't you just swan around *exercising*' – she looks Nell up and down, the word spiking like barbed wire from her lips – 'while I clear out the kitchen cupboards, make endless trips to the dump and then get to work for my shift, how about that?'

Nell's heart thuds as if operating on its own muscle memory, recalling all the countless conflicts with Clare in the past. 'You don't need to do the dump runs. I've already told Laura I'll do those.'

Clare raises a sceptical eyebrow. 'Are you sure you can manage that? It won't interrupt whatever else you've got planned for the day?'

Nell shakes her head, curses under her breath, brushes past Clare and into the sitting room. Her mum is sitting at the elm wood dining table that looks out onto the back garden, still in her dressing gown, burgundy slippers hugging her heavily veined feet, their backs trodden down where she has not managed to pull them on properly on successive occasions. Her hands are wrapped round an empty mug painted with the *Keep Calm and Carry On* logo that had at one time been so ubiquitous. Her eyes seem fixed at a point on the wall where once had hung a cheap reproduction of Constable's 'The Hay Wain' but where now there is nothing but a clean square of paint, highlighting the grubbiness around it, soiled with decades of accumulated living. Her mum does not appear to hear Nell come in, does not turn around.

'Mum, can I make you another cup of tea?'

Her mum's head turns slowly, like a sloth on the branch of a tree. 'Nell? When did you get here? Clare didn't tell me you were coming.'

Nell crouches down beside her, places a hand on her arm, feels the rough weave of a dressing gown that has been through the washing machine too many times. 'I stayed here last night, remember? I've come to help sort out the house.' She winces at the euphemism, wonders how much her mum remembers from one minute to the next about how her life is being slowly dismantled, about where she will be living in two days' time.

'I'll make Mum's tea. I need to get her breakfast anyway.' Clare prises the mug from their mum's hand before Nell has a chance to object, sweeping away into the kitchen and calling through the serving hatch as she fills the kettle. 'If you're actually going to do some trips to the dump, you can start with the boxes in mine and Laura's old room. There's half a dozen in there that need shifting.'

Through the serving hatch, Nell sees Clare take a box of eggs from the fridge, crack two into a Pyrex bowl, beat them vigorously with a fork. Nell kisses the top of her mum's head, waits for a reaction, feels something inside her snag when none comes. Slipping a finger into the instep of her mum's slipper, she brings the material over her heel, repeats the same action with the other foot. Her mum stares straight ahead, the muscles around her lips twitching as though she is preparing to speak, but no sound emerges. Nell studies her face, wonders what has happened to the version of her mum she has loved all her life, where she has gone, whether they will be afforded many glimmers of her again. It seems so unnecessarily cruel to Nell, this theft of a person's personality, memories, connections. As though ageing isn't painful enough without dementia killing off so much of what makes a person themselves long before their body surrenders. She is aware of a soft swell of panic rising up through her stomach and into her chest, the realisation that her mum is forever changed. All her life, Nell has depended on her mother's presence for love, support, stability, and now she is being stolen from her by an illness Nell is powerless to stop.

Holding her mum's hand, she looks into her eyes, tries to find some trace of the trauma she suffered thirtyseven years ago. There is so much she wishes her mum could remember and yet Danny's death is the one thing she hopes dementia will allow her to forget. She tries to imagine how her mum must have coped with the death of a child, what internal strength she must have needed to survive such a loss, but something closes down on Nell's thoughts like a metal shutter lowering over the glass window of a shop. Tracing a finger over the liver spots flecked across the back of her mum's hand like a child's dottodot pattern, she wonders what story they would tell if she were able to join them together, uncover the picture. 'Are you sure I can't get you anything?'

Her mum turns to her, a fractional smile upending her lips. 'You be a good girl, won't you? No dallying after school. You come straight home.' She pats Nell's hand and Nell nods, swallowing against the stone lodged in her throat.

She leaves her mum overlooking the garden, leaves Clare scrambling eggs in a saucepan, heads out of the room and up the stairs, towards the bedroom her sisters once shared. Standing at the threshold she is aware of an ingrained sense of transgression: the knowledge that this is not her territory, that she has, historically, not been permitted to enter. From downstairs in the kitchen she can hear her sister's voice, a phlegmatic monologue about the long list of things she needs to do today, and Nell suppresses her childlike reticence, pushes open the door and steps inside. Instead of bunk beds and George Michael posters there is now a narrow single bed pushed up against one wall and a collection of cardboard boxes advertising cereal brands, cleaning products and lime cordial filled with an array of clothes and shoes, scarves and hats, the past crammed into boxes as though it has no need to be remembered.

Her eyes fall on the open cardboard box sitting alone on the bed, sheaves of paper rising to the surface and threatening to spill over the sides of the torn lid. Her hand reaches for one of the leaflets – its paper yellowing, its edges tattered – and she sees it is an old bus timetable. She picks up a recipe card for mushroom risotto, a dish she is almost certain her mother has never cooked, and unfolds a quote from an electrician for rewiring the house, dated three years earlier, though no such work ever took place.

And then her eyes land on it, as if it has been waiting patiently for her to discover it.

It is crinkled as though it may once have been screwed into a ball. The main word across the front is in bold white font against a bright orange background, below which is a photograph of six smiling children standing in a playground. They are dressed in clothes that belong to another era: shiny tracksuits, denim dungarees, oversized tshirts. Nell studies the single word on the front, knows what it says, is aware what its eight letters spell out, and yet is unable to fully grasp its meaning.

Picking up the slender leaflet, she sees that it is nothing more than a sheet of matte A4 paper folded vertically to make a trifold brochure, and wonders how it can possibly contain all the necessary information about the topic emblazoned across its cover.

Opening it, she has to train her eyes on the words, force them to focus, in order to read the opening sentence.

> *Adoption provides a family for children who are unable to live with their birth parents. It is a lifelong commitment and one that should only be entered upon after serious thought and consideration.*

Nell is aware of her breath accelerating, and she presses the flat of her free hand against her chest to try to steady it. Her eyes skim the rest of the first page, the words swimming in front of her, slipping from her grasp. Turning it over, she registers the bold heading – *FAQs* – and the list of ten sections underneath, questions and answers she reads but is not able to absorb. Her mind races, thoughts speeding ahead of her as though they are eager to hit a finishing line Nell is yet to see. Questions burrow in her head like Japanese knotweed, their roots entwined so that she cannot separate one from the other, a tangle of thoughts and feelings she is unable to unravel. Her dad's words from a fortnight before hum in her head like an earworm she cannot silence: *You need to know that I've always loved you even though you were never really mine to love.*

She stares at the leaflet, and then down at the cardboard box, the only one perched high on the bed, as if demanding attention. She thinks of Clare's suggestion just minutes earlier to deal with the boxes in this room and a thought begins to unfurl in her head like a paper snowflake cut from a pleated circle, the pattern emerging only once it has been unfolded: Clare meant her to find it. Clare wanted her to find it. Perhaps – whether out of spite or kindness, Nell does not know – Clare is trying to tell her something no one else has ever dared.

THEN

Bill stands in front of where Annie is sitting on the edge of the bed, holding out a leaflet that she has no intention of taking from him, even less intention of reading. From downstairs she can hear Clare and Laura making pancakes for breakfast, their favourite Sunday morning treat, which Annie would once have presided over, but now she cannot find the energy to pull the nightie over her head, step into the shower, get dressed, let alone whisk eggs, milk and flour into a batter and heat it over a hot pan.

'Will you at least take a look, please?'

Annie does not answer. She does not know whether it is disquiet or frustration clenching her jaw, but she does not want to see what Bill is trying to show her.

He sits down on the bed next to her, and there is a flash of static where the acrylic of his jumper meets the polyester of her dressing gown. She senses the indentation of the mattress, is aware of him by her side, but does not turn to look at him. She is not used to having him so close to her, not used to feeling the heat of his body. Since Danny's death almost five months ago – five months next Thursday – they have been like magnetic figures spinning on top of a child's music box, circling one another's grief, neither able to pull apart nor travel close enough to touch, orbiting in the same field of mourning and yet their paths never converging.

'Annie, please. I'm only trying to help.' Bill takes hold of her hand but his fingers feel hot, charged, and she snatches hers back, buries it in her lap. She cannot remember the last time they held hands, cannot remember when they last shared a moment of affection. These days Annie goes to bed long before Bill, and when she wakes in the early hours, knowing that sleep will elude her until morning, she creeps out of bed and into Danny's room, drags the spare duvet from underneath Danny's cot where it is now stored, and curls up on the floor until daybreak.

'Annie?'

Annie's eyes flit towards the leaflet in Bill's hand and then back towards the net curtains tinged with grey hanging at the window. She breathes through her nose, does not part her lips, does not trust herself to speak. It is as though Danny's death has erected a barrier between them – tall, thick, opaque – and they are not able to reach over or around it, cannot see or hear one another clearly.

It is not that she no longer loves Bill. She does not, in truth, know what it is that she feels. Sometimes she thinks that all her good feelings were anaesthetised the day Danny died, and that she has been waiting for the paralysis to subside ever since.

'Please. Won't you even read it? That's all I'm suggesting.'

Her eyes graze over the leaflet in his hands, at the word blazoned across the front in thick, white lettering against an orange background. Below the writing there is a photograph of children standing in a playground, smiling, laughing, and Annie turns her head away, does not want to see their counterfeit happiness.

She cannot believe he is even suggesting it, that he thinks it may be a solution. A part of her is furious at his insensitivity, his tactlessness, his misunderstanding of the situation. Another part of her is dismayed to discover how little he seems to know her, that he thinks this might be the answer to their problems. She does not understand how it can have happened, this chasm that has opened up between them where once their intimacy had been, but it does not seem possible for either of them to bridge the gap.

'Love, I know how much you want another child. But after everything we've been through, wouldn't it be . . . I just think that perhaps this might be for the best.'

Annie shakes her head without being fully conscious of doing so. She knows he does not have the courage to say the word out loud, because the word does not belong here, in this bedroom, in this house, in this family. But there it is – ADOPTION – shouting at her from the front of the leaflet he has insisted on bringing into their lives.

She does not want to adopt someone else's baby. The only fourth child she wants is her own.

There are times now when those five weeks with Danny feel as though they belong to a parallel universe, as though she had stepped off the travelator of her life for a brief interlude, one in which she was given five weeks to love her child with all her heart before he was taken away from her. And yet she knows that her time with Danny is a part of her now, sewn into the muscles binding her heart as much as Bill, Clare and Laura. Her pregnancy had been so unexpected and yet now when she thinks about it she cannot imagine a version of her life without him. It is inconceivable to talk of replacing Danny with a child that is not biologically hers. She does not understand why Bill would even suggest it, why he could imagine for a moment that it is the stitching with which to repair their frayed family.

She knows that Danny is gone, knows it as a fact in her head, but it is like a mirage of water in the desert that seems to shift out of reach every time she thinks she is nearing it.

She remembers those early weeks after Danny died, when people would tell her they were sorry she had 'lost' her baby, as though she had left Danny in a supermarket aisle by mistake and hadn't been able to locate him since. When they told her Danny was in a better place as though she could ever believe in heaven, in a benevolent God after what has happened. When they tried to share stories about friends, colleagues, neighbours who had suffered similar losses as though there was safety in numbers. But Annie did not mislay her baby. There is no heaven she believes in and even if there were it would be of no comfort, thinking of her baby there, alone, without her to look after him. She has not the space in her heart for other parents' grief. Danny's death was an inexplicable tragedy. He was taken from her by something that no one can explain, no one understands. It is unfathomable to her that doctors can have a name for something they do not comprehend, cannot prevent. Cot death. It is the most monstrous of oxymorons: how can a place of sleep, of sanctuary, of security be, at the same time, a place of death?

She remembers their appointment with the consultant, after the post mortem and the inquest had delivered a verdict of sudden infant death syndrome, how the consultant had told them that it wasn't their fault, there was nothing they could have done, it was simply a terrible tragedy that they would need, somehow, to come to terms with. But Annie does not want to come to terms with it. She does not want it to be a mystery. How can her child dying – how can the fact of his life just disappearing one night while he was sleeping – be simply a tragedy that no one can explain? The death of her son is already incomprehensible to her, and the absence of any medical explanation is an added layer of cruelty, an additional facet to her grief.

'I know you wouldn't want to adopt an older child – not one this age.' Bill raises the leaflet, waves it in front of her. 'But if we could adopt a baby . . . ?' The rest of Bill's question hangs in the air, unsure whether it wants to settle or fly away.

Annie's eyes hover on the leaflet, like moths drawn to a flame. She knows why he is suggesting it. He does not need to articulate it for her to know. Bill has never said anything specific but she is sure that he blames her for what happened to Danny, is certain he thinks it is her fault. The guilt gnawing at her own heart tells her it must be true.

'The last few months – they've been so hard on you. I never want you to go through that again. Wouldn't this . . . I don't know. Wouldn't it be better? Easier?'

Annie curls her fingers into rigid fists, nails digging into the flesh of her palms. She has heard them all talking in whispered voices when they thought she wasn't listening: Bill, Pam, Alan, Denise. She has heard them discussing her state of mind, trading words Annie does not want to hear: *grief, trauma, medical help*. She has felt the injustice stinging her eyes as she has heard Bill confiding in their friends his concerns about Clare and Laura, about the effect of Annie's behaviour on them, as though she would ever – *ever* – do anything to hurt them. She has listened from the top of the stairs when they thought she was asleep as they have debated whether to call a doctor, whether she needs medication, whether it might help for her to talk to someone, a professional, someone who has experience in 'these kinds of things'. But Annie doesn't want to talk to anyone. There is nobody who can change what has happened, nothing that might alter how she feels.

'Annie?'

A strange feeling creeps over Annie. It begins as a gentle thrumming, like the distant beating of a drum, and gradually increases until it lands in her chest and she cannot silence it. 'I couldn't love it.' They are the first words she has spoken all morning and they feel strange in her mouth, tough and unmalleable, like chewing gum that has long since lost its elasticity.

'What?'

She presses her fingers deeper into her palms, repeats herself, barely louder than before. 'I don't want someone else's baby. I couldn't love it.'

There is silence for a few seconds and she raises her eyes, watches Bill digest what she has said, turning it over in his mind like a baker kneading a piece of dough. It is such a familiar sequence of expressions that she feels an urge to wrap her arms around him, try to close the distance between them. But she does not move.

He places a hand on hers and this time she does not pull away. She looks down at his broad fingers: the calloused knuckles and thick gold wedding ring he has been wearing for the past fifteen years, now so deeply embedded in his flesh she suspects it would be impossible to remove.

'You might feel like that now, love, but I'm sure you'd feel differently if we had a baby living with us from soon after it was born. I think we'd be able to love it as one of our own, I really do.'

She feels the squeeze of his hand around her fingers and fears that if they sit there much longer, tears may begin to leak from her eyes. The drum continues to beat loudly in her chest and she tries to shut her mind against Bill's suggestion: it is not a thought – not even a consideration – that she wants inside her head.

The shrill ringing of the telephone on Bill's bedside table pierces the stillness. It rings twice before she hears Clare, in the hallway below, answer it.

'Dad! It's for you! It's Elsa.'

Something buckles beneath Annie's ribs, a feeling she would rather not put a name to.

'Can you tell her I'll call her back?'

Annie hears the murmur of Clare relaying the message, and then she is shouting up the stairs again. 'She says it's urgent.'

Next to her Bill hesitates, and then he is lifting himself from the mattress, laying the leaflet on the duvet beside her, pressing it down with the flat of his hand as though it may otherwise attempt an escape. 'Just have a think about it. You know—' He hesitates, and Annie anticipates the gist of what he is going to say before

121

he speaks, has an urge to put her hands over her ears to stop his words worming their way into her brain. 'Neither of us is getting any younger, and Danny . . . I don't want either of us to have to go through that again.' His voice fractures and Annie wishes she could reach out, find him in the black hole of their grief, cling to him so that neither has to be alone inside it. But her limbs are heavy and she cannot seem to lift her arms from her sides, cannot seem to tense the muscles in her thighs to stand up.

He waits for a reply but when she says nothing, he turns and leaves.

As she hears him hurry down the stairs she knows she should make her way to the bathroom, have a shower, join the girls for pancakes. But instead she stays perfectly still, straining her ears towards one half of a conversation she can hear in the hall downstairs, her skin bristling at the warmth in Bill's voice. Every morning he goes to work alongside Elsa, talks with Elsa about things Annie can only imagine. Every evening he returns home, the rhythm of his daily life unaltered by the tragedy that has befallen them. And every day a voice screams silently at him inside her head: *How can you continue as if nothing has happened? How can you carry on as normal when our lives have been shattered? How can you bear it?*

She manages to lift herself from the bed, moves to the stool by the dressing table, lowers herself onto it. Looking into the mirror she is shocked by her own reflection. Her short hair has gathered in clumps close to her scalp – she cannot remember the last time she pulled a comb through it, or washed it – and dark rings hang beneath her eyes. Her skin is pallid, as though it has been washed at too high a temperature, bleaching all the colour from it, and her lips are cracked at the edges. She looks diminished, as though the mirror is allowing her a glimpse of how small her life has become.

She thinks about the hours ahead: today, tomorrow, next week, next month, next year. There is so little for her to do with any of them. When she winds back her mind to before Danny was born, she can no longer recall how she used to fill her days. She would take the girls to school, collect them again seven hours later, and in her memory she was always busy in between, but now she cannot remember with what. Now the hours seem to stretch interminably before her. Some days she cannot face staying in the house with only the ticking clock for company, and yet neither can she muster the energy to go outside. There is a feeling that time is marching on while she stands still, as though she has forgotten how to move with it. It is a feeling that provokes both panic and inertia simultaneously, and she does not know how to dispel it.

Behind her, in the mirror's reflection, she sees the adoption leaflet on the bed. Later, she thinks, when Bill takes the girls out for a breath of fresh air, she will crumple it into a ball and thrust it somewhere she does not have to look at it. She wants another child – she needs another child – but adoption is not the answer.

She cannot explain it, even to herself, this urge to have another baby of her own. It is not that she is trying to replace Danny: even the thought of it makes her queasy. But her pregnancy had come at a time when she could see on the distant horizon a future in which her girls would grow up and no longer need her. Danny had given her a sense of purpose again. A sense of meaning. And now that he has gone, she does not know what to do. All she knows is that there is something unfinished about her family, like a piece of music that has been halted pages before the end of the score. And she knows – she is certain – that the only way to banish the feeling is with another baby of her own.

NOW

Nell has just got into her car with a bootfull of her parents' possessions ready for the dump, the adoption leaflet tucked safely in her
handbag, when her phone rings. She picks it up from where it is
lying, face down, on the passenger seat, sees Josh's name flash up
on the screen. For a few seconds she hesitates, though she is not
sure why, staring at the screen as though the two of them might be
able to communicate silently without the need for her to answer.

Eventually she swipes a finger across the screen, presses the cool
glass to her cheek.

'Hey. How are you?'

'Much better for a decent night's sleep. How're things there?'

Nell pauses, finds herself oscillating between one version of the
truth and another, unsure where on the spectrum honesty might
sit. 'Fine. Lots to do, but we're getting there.' It is an empty platitude, but she does not know what else to say without veering into
territory she has no desire to enter.

There is a pause on the other end of the line and Nell imagines
Josh sitting in the battered leather armchair by the firstfloor window of his flat overlooking London Fields, a cup of strong black
coffee resting on the arm, rubbing his eyes with the heel of his
palm, a tic she imagines to be a hangover from childhood, a glimpse
of the boy he used to be.

'Are you sure you're okay? You sound . . . I don't know. Pretty beleaguered.'

Nell hesitates, thinks about all that has happened since she arrived at her mum's the previous evening: the tension with Clare, her mum's confusion, the newspaper cuttings, the photograph albums. The revelation about Danny. And now the adoption leaflet. She does not know how she would compile all those incidents into a comprehensible narrative, is not sure whether they hang together as the beginnings of a story or whether they are nothing more than random anomalies. Something shifts in her head, like a cog unilaterally fitting into one spur rather than another, and she is answering before she has had time to decide precisely what it is she wants to say. 'I'm fine. Just woke up early and now have about a hundred trips to the dump to do.' She has tried to inject some levity into her voice but it is still there, at the edges: a strain, like a tootight item of clothing stretched at the seams.

'Why don't I come down and give you a hand? I've got the whole weekend off. If I jump in the shower now I could be there in ninety minutes, two hours tops.'

Something inside Nell baulks, and she does not know whether it is the prospect of her worlds colliding, or whether there is something else, something she cannot identify. She only knows that her head is crammed with things she does not understand, is unsure whether there is anything even in need of understanding or whether her grief and imagination are conspiring to cause a perfect storm of anxiety and confusion. 'Honestly, there's no need. I'm whingeing about nothing, really. We'll get it all done.'

The phone line goes quiet, and Nell imagines Josh running his fingers along the dark stubble lining his jaw.

'Look, I know I haven't met your family yet, and the timing's a bit weird, but I really would like to come and help.'

Nell catches sight of herself in the rearview mirror, sees the lines furrowing along her forehead. 'It's not that – there's just no need. We've got it all in hand.' Her voice is more brusque than she had intended and she winces at the sound of it, wishes Josh could see her expression so he would know she would swallow the words back down if she could. 'I'm sorry, I didn't mean it to come out like that. It's just . . .' She falters, wondering where the root of her ambivalence really lies. What, in truth, it is really all about. 'It just feels like something I need to do with my family. Does that make sense?' It is not, she knows, an entirely honest explanation but she is too unsure of her feelings to offer any greater clarity, to herself or to Josh.

'Course. But the offer's there if you need it.'

Neither of them speaks for a second and it is Nell who fills the silence. 'So what will you do today?' Usually, on weekends Josh is not working at the hospital, they will drive to Hampstead Heath, walk for miles through the woods, head to their favourite pub for a late lunch and a read of the weekend papers, sometimes just the two of them, often with friends or with Josh's brother and sisterinlaw. There is a part of Nell that wishes they were doing that today too, that this weekend of houseclearing was over and that the rhythm of her life could begin the tentative process towards normality.

'I think I'll go for a run and then see who's about. My brother texted earlier, asked if we fancied going for dinner tonight, so I'll probably head over there later.'

'Okay, well, say hi to them from me, won't you?'

'I will. I'll text you later, see how you're getting on.'

They say goodbye and, as Josh rings off, Nell is overcome by a feeling of emptiness, like an acute form of homesickness, though for where, or for whom, she is not quite sure. Sitting alone in her car, phone in her lap, she tries to unpack the conversation that has just taken place, but there is such a welter of conflicting feelings that she does not know how to separate one from the next. The midday sun bleeds through the windows, sweat pooling at the base of her spine, and she thinks about Josh, unsure how to square the fact that she loves him, needs him, wants to see him, with the instinctive rejection of his offer to come and help.

The sound of a car alarm further along the street jolts her back to the present. Glancing at the clock on the dashboard she sees it is almost ten thirty, knows she has to get on with clearing the house, deal with the boxes in the boot. She starts the ignition, begins the drive towards the dump, and it is only when she turns left before the main road, heading along familiar suburban streets, that she realises she is making a detour.

A few minutes later she pulls up in front of a house not dissimilar to her parents': terraced, pebbledashed, three square windows and a front door. The kind of house a child might draw in a picture. She checks her appearance in the mirror, pulls a compact from her bag, dabs powder over her shiny nose and on the dark circles beneath her eyes.

Through the net curtains, she sees the shadow of movement and before she has a chance to reconsider, she is swinging open the metal front gate, walking along the concrete garden path and pressing a finger to the doorbell.

Pam's expression, when she opens the door, begins as surprise but quickly morphs into concern. 'Is everything okay? Is your mum alright?'

'She's fine. I've left her with Clare, having breakfast. I was on my way to the dump and thought it would be nice to pop in. Sorry, is this a bad time?' The explanation is flimsy – she cannot recall ever having popped in alone on Pam before – but Nell does not know what else to say, is not yet ready to ask the questions to which she needs answers.

'Course it's not a bad time. Come in. I've just put the kettle on.' Pam talks as she walks through the narrow hallway, into the kitchen, Nell following behind. 'Alan's down at the allotment. He's promised me a crop of runner beans to have with Sunday lunch.'

It is all just as Nell remembers it. She has not been in this kitchen for fifteen years, perhaps more, but nothing has changed: the same reproduction oak cabinets with their beveledged doors and brass handles; the same floral curtains trapped behind tasselled tiebacks; the same glosspainted serving hatch through to the dining room next door.

'Tea or coffee? I've only got instant, I'm afraid. I bet you've got one of those fancy coffee makers at home.'

For a moment, Nell has a feeling of being caught out. 'Tea's great, thanks.'

'So how did you find your mum last night? I know the move's taking its toll, but I honestly think it's for the best. She can't stay living there by herself.' Pam pours boiling water into a pair of matching blue mugs. 'I know it'll take some getting used to but I've told her I'll go and visit every day. It's only ten minutes on the bus.' Squeezing the excess liquid from the teabags, Pam hands a mug to Nell, gestures for her to follow into the sitting room where a tan leather sofa has replaced the floral one Nell remembers from childhood.

'She's not great, to be honest. She got quite agitated and said some things I didn't quite understand.' Questions line up on Nell's tongue, impatient to be let out. She thinks about the adoption leaflet in her bag, wants to know whether it is a coincidence or something more. She isn't sure whether it is a lack of courage or something else that stops her, but when she begins to speak, her line of enquiry takes her in a different direction. 'Can I ask you something?'

Pam sips her tea. 'Course. What is it?'

Nell shifts on the sofa, the brown leather cushion squeaking beneath her. 'Do you know why my mum and dad chose never to tell me about Danny?' It is only once the question is out that Nell understands how seismic it is, understands the full weight of regret that it is not a question she will ever be able to discuss with her parents.

Pam looks at her quizzically. 'You didn't know?'

Nell shakes her head. 'I had no idea until earlier today.' The words feel tight in her throat, and she wraps her hands around the mug, rests it on her knee, feels the heat of it through the denim of her jeans.

Pam hesitates. 'I don't want to speak out of turn. If your mum and dad didn't tell you, there must be a reason. Maybe they thought it was for the best?'

Nell tries to keep her voice steady even as a sense of agitation creeps across her skin. 'Whatever their reason, I can't ask them now, and you're the only one who might be able to fill in the gaps. Please, Pam.'

She watches the scales tip from one side to the other in Pam's head, weighing up the pros and cons of telling Nell whatever she knows. Pam glances out of the window and Nell wonders if she is hoping Alan might return to rescue her, or whether she is checking he is not about to arrive.

'I honestly don't know why they never told you. It wasn't some-thing your mum ever talked about with me. I always assumed they just wanted to put it behind them.'

Pam smiles kindly, but Nell is not yet ready to accept that this is a dead end. 'Even if she didn't talk to you about it directly, you've always been close to her, you must have seen what was going on. How did it affect her?'

Pam dabs at the corner of her lips with an embroidered cotton handkerchief retrieved from the sleeve of her cardigan, tucks it back in again. 'It was dreadful, of course it was. She was torn apart, any mother would be. It's unimaginable, really . . .' Pam's thoughts seem to drift off somewhere Nell is not invited to follow, and she knows she must get her back on track.

'So what happened? Did she have any help – counselling or anything like that?'

Pam shakes her head. 'She wouldn't hear of it. Believe me, we all tried. Your dad was so worried about her. Got the GP out a few times. Looking back, I suspect she had a touch of depression, though people didn't talk about it then like they do now.' Pam whispers the final sentence as though depression is still not a topic she considers suitable for public consumption.

Nell tries to let the pieces of information settle in her head, but they are like snowflakes on warm concrete. It has been only a few hours since she discovered the death of her brother, and she cannot control the flurry of conflicting thoughts and emotions. There is the knowledge that she would probably not be here had Danny survived, that she owes her life to his death. The awareness that her childhood must have been played out to a soundtrack of grief even though she never heard it. She wonders whether her parents have always watched her progress – from nursery to school to university to work – alongside speculations about what Danny would be doing now had he lived. Just a couple of hours ago she had not known her brother had ever existed, and yet now his ghost sits on her shoulder and she cannot imagine that he will not follow her for the rest of her life.

'What about when I was born? How did that . . . Did it change things?' She cannot bring herself to say the words out loud. *Did they adopt me? Was I never really theirs to love?*

Pam smiles and pats Nell's hand. 'There were times before you came along that I thought Annie would have done anything for another baby. She was so devastated after Danny's death. You were

JEFF
MEG
xxxxxxx1001
2/20/2022
Item: ï¿½2001010104995633 ((book)

just what she needed. And you don't need me to tell you how much she loves you.'

Nell tries to return Pam's smile but her cheeks ache with the effort. A wave of restlessness sweeps over her, a need to be alone with her thoughts. Thanking Pam for the tea and telling her she really ought to get to the dump, she kisses her goodbye, promises to pop in again soon.

It is only when she is in the car, driving away, that she realises the conversation with Pam has raised more questions than it has answered. Because Danny's death does not explain that final, perplexing conversation with her dad at the hospital, or her mum's cryptic remarks the previous evening. It does not explain the folder of newspaper cuttings Nell found in the loft, each originating in the first six months of Nell's life, or the adoption leaflet that had once been screwed into a ball and yet kept all these years.

Driving along familiar roads, from Pam's house to the dump, Nell is unsure whether the disquiet she is feeling is justified, or whether she is merely collecting scraps of chapters from different books and building a narrative that has never really existed.

THEN

Annie runs the flat of her palm against her stomach. It feels the same as it always has: soft rolls of flesh she often wishes didn't exist, but today she does not mind the extra padding. It is reassuring, comforting to know that it is there, an additional layer or two of protection. There is a part of her that wishes she could wrap herself in cotton wool and stay cocooned until March, emerging in spring, ready to stretch her wings, metamorphosed into a mother for the fourth time.

It is still early days. At twelve weeks she is beyond the most treacherous time but she is taking nothing for granted. After all that has happened, she will never take anything for granted again. She knows that the twoinch baby inside her is precious, extraordinary, knows that she will do whatever it takes to safeguard it.

Pulling the single sheet of paper from its envelope, Annie reads it for the umpteenth time, cannot help smiling as she takes it all in, yet again. The letter arrived last week and there is something so reassuring – so tangibly uplifting – about seeing it written in black and white: the date and time for her appointment with the midwife next Thursday. A part of her still cannot believe it. Over the past few weeks she has woken so frequently in the middle of the night fearing that the pregnancy is nothing more than a fantasy condensed into an eighthour dream, and that she is now on the cusp of a rude awakening. But then she has opened her eyes and remembered the euphoric expression on Bill's face when she had told him, and she knows that it is real.

They both understand that this pregnancy is nothing short of a miracle. Neither of them has said it aloud, but Annie imagines Bill must be thinking it too because she has thought of little else. She does not know how they can have been so lucky. Just that one night since Danny died that they have cleaved to one another, just one night that their bodies rediscovered each other in the darkness. Even now, Annie is not sure whether that night had been fuelled by love or loss, by passion or loneliness. She cannot remember what had happened that day, what had prompted her to reach out across the barren landscape of their bedsheets to find Bill's hand, to bring it towards her, to place it on her breast. It had been over quickly, that much she remembers, as though neither of them had dared break whatever spell had temporarily been cast over them, bringing them together for the first time in months. It had been so different from the intimacies they had shared in the past, as though they were two strangers unsure of themselves and each other, as though they had both needed it to happen and yet wanted it to be over. Afterwards they had retreated to their separate sides of the bed, backs facing each other, Annie feeling exposed suddenly as if she were standing in the street without a shred of clothes on. She had lain in the darkness, listening to Bill's deep breaths, in and then out, until she had been sure that he was asleep, before creeping out of bed and into Danny's room to spend the rest of the night wrapped in a duvet on his floor.

But now it is as though the marvel growing inside her has given their marriage a new lease of life. It is tentative, still, the affection between them. But there are echoes of their relationship as it had been before grief silenced their ability to love aloud, and Annie feels quietly optimistic that they are beginning to find their way back to each other.

Tucking the letter safely in the pocket of her apron, she reminds herself to hide it in her bedside drawer before the girls get home from school so that there is no chance of either of them finding it. Clare and Laura do not yet know about the baby: nobody knows except Bill and the GP. Annie has not, historically, been prone to superstition, but she will not take any chances with this pregnancy, will not do anything to put it at risk. Once they have had their appointment next week, then she may feel able to trust that it is real, and to share the news.

Glancing up at the kitchen clock she sees that it is almost half past one: ninety minutes until she needs to collect the girls from school. Her stomach feels full but she forces down the last of her cheeseandpickle sandwich, knows it is important she keeps her strength up. Since Danny's death nine months ago her appetite has shrunk and she has eaten not out of desire but out of necessity. Now she has begun to eat not just for herself but with love for her unborn child.

There have been so many days since Danny died when she has not been able to disentangle one feeling from another: the grief from the guilt, the loss from the longing. Her internal world has felt like a canvas onto which an artist has splattered paint at random, no single, definable shape on display. Bill's patience with her has, in some ways, made things harder. So many times she has wanted to apologise for not being the wife he deserves, for letting him down, but she has not dared open the gates to that conversation for fear of the floodwaters that may come rushing through. Instead, she has kept them private, eddying inside her, waiting for them to subside.

But now things are different. Even though the guilt still hangs inside her like early morning fog suspended over the hills, she finally feels hopeful again.

Nausea churns in her stomach and it is so familiar, so paradoxically comforting, that she hopes it stays with her every day for the next six months. As she pulls on a pair of yellow rubber gloves and prepares to clean out a fridge that has been accumulating dirt for weeks, she is aware of a glint of optimism inside her, like the first rays of sunlight creeping around the edge of a mountain after a long Alaskan winter.

NOW

Nell sinks the dirty dishes into soapy water and wipes the grease from their surface. Next door, her mum watches TV, a comedy with canned laughter with which she does not join in.

Dinner with her mum had been brief, muted. Nell cannot remember the last time they ate supper alone, just the two of them. Since Laura left home when Nell was twelve, there has always been a trio at mealtimes, and her dad's absence tonight was like walking through a room in a museum in which half the display cases are empty. The pieces of grilled chicken and salad had been pushed around her mum's plate: food in search of an appetite. Nell had eaten quickly, her hunger fuelled by a relentless afternoon bringing boxes down from the loft and piling them up in the hallway before ferrying them to the dump. Her mind had not been at dinner with her mum, but in another, imagined place: with her family before her birth, grieving the baby brother who had not made it through his sixth week of life.

All day she has been replaying the movie of her childhood in her mind, viewing it from different angles, in search of clues to her parents' grief she may not have noticed before. The days she would find her mum and dad in a silent embrace in the sitting room, holding each other tightly, and have a sense that she was disturbing something sacred. The Christmas mornings she had walked into the kitchen and found her mum leaning against the sink, glassy eyed, staring out into the garden, a counterfeit smile pulled from her lips when she saw Nell behind her, hugging her with a fierce, protective love. The moments she would sense her mum staring at her with such intensity that Nell would feel like a creature under a microscope, would turn away or make an excuse to leave the room, embarrassed by such acute scrutiny. All those incidents of her mum's overprotection – all that desire to keep Nell close, shielded, safe – that Nell sees, for the first time, through the prism of her mum's heartbreak, of her desire to protect one child when she had already lost another.

All day she has hunted through the archives of her childhood, searching for evidence of any lingering sorrow her mum might have experienced when Nell was little, unsure whether the snapshots she has accrued are proof or merely misapprehension. The Sunday mornings her dad would tell her that her mum was having a lie-in, and the two of them would leave the house early, head off on one of their long walks around Crystal Palace Park or across the South Downs, returning home late in the afternoon. The days her dad would unexpectedly collect her from school, take her to the workshop for the rest of the afternoon, accompanied by excuses about her mum having been waylaid somewhere, explanations Nell had only half listened to at the time and cannot now recall. How, on Nell's birthday, she would so often have the sense of her mum trying too hard to make it special: the smile fixed slightly too wide, the forced exuberance in her voice, the determination to keep the momentum going as though, if she didn't, the day might fall apart. Nell cannot be sure she is not misremembering, that she is not falsely rearranging the past to suit the present, like a lighting director shining a spotlight at the wrong angle. Her memories could be something or they could be nothing.

A rinsed plate slips from her grasp and clatters onto the stainless steel draining board.

'Clare? Is that you?'

'No, Mum, it's only me.' Nell calls over her shoulder, through the open door.

'Who's there? What are you doing?'

She hears the panic in her mum's voice, grabs a towel to wipe her soapy hands, hurries into the sitting room.

Her mum sits upright on the sofa like a meerkat on watch, alarm pinching the skin between her eyebrows. 'Who are you? Why are you here?'

Nell lowers herself onto the sofa, tries not to let distress seep into her voice. 'It's me, Mum. It's Nell.'

Her mum frowns. 'I knew someone once who had a daughter called Nell.'

'Yes, I know, Mum, that's—'

'How could you know? You couldn't have known them.' Her words snap at the air.

'No, I mean, I'm Nell.'

Her mum peers at her through narrowed eyes. 'No, you're not. Nell's just a baby.' She tuts, shakes her head. 'She's beautiful, my Nell. You look nothing like her.' She turns to gaze out of the window, through greying net curtains that have not been washed for months.

Nell swallows hard, tells herself that her mum doesn't mean it, that she does not know what she's saying, but tears threaten to sting her eyes nonetheless.

'She was always my favourite.' Her mum's voice has softened, taken on a distant quality as though it has got lost somewhere, far away, and cannot find its way back. 'You're not supposed to have favourites, but Nell was my special girl. No one else's. Just mine.'

Nell says nothing, watches the twitch of her mum's lips, wonders what words or memories are trapped inside her head, unable to find their way out.

Closing her eyes, Nell coaxes her own memories out of storage: her mum's arm around her shoulder when someone had been mean to her at school; the soft swab of dampened tissue against her knee when she had fallen; the fingers brushed across her forehead as she had lain in bed with a fever; the gentle combing of tangled hair after it had been washed; the patient instructions about tying shoelaces, brushing teeth, boiling kettles, icing cupcakes, catching balls, digging up weeds, plaiting hair; the soft lips against her cheek as she drifted off to sleep. The entire spectrum of maternal love encompassed in such small, quotidian acts.

Nell looks at her mum, knows that somewhere inside her ageing body is the woman who performed all those acts of love even if sometimes, now, it is not always possible to reach her.

Nell rests a hand on top of her mum's. 'Can I get you anything? A cup of tea? Glass of water?'

Her mum turns back to her, runs a tongue over her dry lips. 'When's breakfast?'

Nell allows a beat before she answers, to steady the fissure in her voice. 'We just had dinner, remember? Chicken and salad?' She winces at the slow, steady pattern of her speech, a tone she might use speaking to a recalcitrant child.

Her mum stares at her with disbelief. 'Why would I eat dinner first thing in the morning? I want my breakfast. It's seven o'clock.' She holds up her wrist, taps her watch to prove the point.

'It's seven o'clock in the evening, Mum. You've just had dinner. Laura left some chicken breasts in the fridge and we had them grilled with some salad.'

Her mum's face softens. 'Laura's a good girl. She never caused any trouble.' She stares wistfully, over Nell's shoulder, as though expecting Laura to emerge from another room. 'Where's Bill?' Her head darts from left to right, fingers pulling at a loose thread on the cuff of her cardigan.

Nell keeps hold of her mum's hand, wondering whether this is how it will be from now on: her mum learning the news of Bill's death over and over, like a Groundhog Day of grief. She does not know what to say for the best, knows only that she does not want to cause her mum any more distress. 'He's just gone out. It's only you and me here.' The lie tastes bitter on her tongue and she does not know if it is the right thing to have said, is unsure how to navigate them both through this cruel new world.

Her mum does not reply, turns back to the television set, and after a minute Nell gets up, heads back towards the kitchen to finish the washing up. She is already at the door when she hears her mum's voice behind her. 'I never forgave him. I said I did but I didn't.'

The words are little more than a murmur, just loud enough for Nell to hear. She sits back down, scrutinises her mum's expression, tries to find some clue as to where she might have gone, what she might be thinking, but her face is the same blank canvas as it had been the previous evening. 'Who are you talking about?'

Her mum stares straight ahead, does not acknowledge Nell's question. 'He said it couldn't happen . . . They were gone, there was nothing I could do . . .'

There is agitation in her mum's voice, and Nell senses she should encourage her to stop talking but she needs to hear whatever it is she has to say.

'He wanted to return . . . I wouldn't let him . . .' A frown knots across her forehead and she shakes her head with small, almost imperceptible movements.

'Wanted to return where?' Nell keeps her voice low and calm but inside her head a dozen thoughts jostle for position. She thinks about Danny lying in his cot, about how her mum and dad must have felt when they found him that day, wonders whether that is what her mum is now halfremembering. She thinks about her dad's line to her in the hospital that final evening, still unsure whether it is an enigma to be cracked or simply the confused ramblings of a heavily medicated man.

'I should have been stronger . . . It was all my fault . . .' She clamps her hands together, kneading her knuckles as if grinding them into submission. 'I couldn't let them take another one . . . I wouldn't let it happen again . . .'

A shiver slips across Nell's skin. Speculations snake through her mind, and she has a sense of being tipped off balance, unable to find her footing, not knowing where she will land if she falls.

'He said—' Her mum begins to shake her head, muttering things under her breath that Nell cannot decipher.

Nell doesn't speak, doesn't want to interrupt wherever her mum's train of thought may be leading them.

'Nobody can say I didn't love that child.' The edges of her mum's eyes twitch and for a moment Nell thinks she is about to cry. But then she turns her head towards the window, continues mumbling to herself, and Nell can feel the moment slipping away.

Nell leans forward, tries to keep her voice calm even as her heart thumps in her chest. 'Who are you talking about?'

Her mum says nothing for a few seconds, staring out of the window, murmuring quietly.

'Mum? What are you thinking about?'

She turns towards Nell, a flash of surprise crossing her face. 'Nell? When did you get here? What a lovely surprise.'

Nell allows herself a beat of silence before replying. 'A little while ago. Can I get you anything?'

Her mum smiles and for a moment it is like the sun inching out from behind a black cloud after a lengthy absence. 'Yes, please. I'd love some breakfast.'

Nell forces her lips into a smile, squeezes her mum's shoulder. 'I'll put the kettle on and make some tea.'

THEN

Annie, Pam and Denise sit at Pam's dining table surrounded by rolls of wrapping paper, dispensers of Sellotape and bags of secondhand toys that have been donated to the school Easter fair, which they are preparing for the lucky dip. There is still almost a fortnight until the fete, but with Annie's baby due next week she had not wanted to leave it any longer.

Wrapping some paper around a parcel – a box of Fuzzy Felt that seems to have half the pieces missing – Annie places it carefully into the plastic carrier bag on the floor by her feet, one arm wrapped protectively across her bump as she leans forward. It is not easy, these days, bending down and standing back up again. Her swollen stomach precedes her wherever she goes. She is sure it is bigger than with any of her previous children, as though this baby is determined to make its presence known even before it is born. And Annie is impatient to meet it, wishes that time would stop dragging its feet. Some days, whole hours disappear while she imagines what life will be like when the baby is born. She cannot remember ever feeling so impatient for anything before, cannot think of a time she has ever looked forward to anything with quite so much happiness, quite so much hope. This new baby will be a chance for her and Bill to begin again, and Annie is eager to start this new chapter of their lives.

It is as she looks up that she sees it, in Denise's hand. A piece of material, no more than six inches square, and yet the sight of it makes Annie vertiginous even though she is sitting down. The material is pale blue and soft – the kind of material that begs you to rub it against your cheek – and attached to one corner is the small figure of an elephant.

Annie closes her eyes and the memory is there to greet her. An identical blanket grasped in the fist of her little boy as he lay in his cot. The same pale blue elephant trapped between his gummy jaws as he sat in his bouncy chair. The same blanket Annie now keeps under her pillow, that she holds on to every night, even though it has long since lost the scent of her baby, after Bill mistakenly put it in the washing machine and rinsed any trace of their son from its fibres.

Annie breathes deeply, in and then out again, in and then out. Tears threaten her eyes and she blinks against them. She does not want to cry, not here, not now. Over the past year she has learnt that even with your closest friends, there is a time limit on grief. There is a point at which discomfort creeps around the edges of people's sympathy, a flicker of impatience visible in their eyes. She has learnt to tuck her grief inside a box behind the wall of her chest, to be taken out and handled with care only when she is alone.

Pam is telling Denise about the school play in which Darren, her eightyearold, is cast as a pirate, but Annie cannot concentrate on Pam's story about costumes, singing solos and parental disgruntlement. Instead, her thoughts are fixed on the calendar inside her head that has been tallying the hours, days and weeks for months now.

In three days' time it will be fifteen months since she went into Danny's room and found his lifeless body. To Annie it is inconceivable that it has been that long, that over a year has passed since she last held him in her arms. The memory is still so raw, so visceral, that sometimes it feels like only yesterday.

143

It'll get easier in time. So many people have said it, on so many occasions, that Annie can only imagine none of them have ever grieved for someone they loved with the ferocity that Annie loved Danny. Grief, Annie is discovering, does not follow a neat, linear trajectory. It does not, contrary to popular aphorism, get easier with every day. It does not gradually recede, like a tide that only ebbs but never flows. Instead, it is more like an unpredictable season of tropical storms that can be whipped into a tempest out at sea before crashing onto land, disabling everything in its path, without any warning.

Over the past fifteen months, Annie has seemed to existed in two parallel worlds. There is the tangible world of Bill, Clare and Laura, of shopping and cooking, of the girls' school life and Bill's growing business. The world in which she is carrying a new life inside her, knowing how lucky she is to have been granted this eleventh hour opportunity to become a parent again. It is a world Annie knows is real even though sometimes she seems to be viewing it through a haze, as though her life is a film and somebody has smeared Vaseline on the lens. But separate from the real world is Annie's imaginary existence, a world in which Danny is growing every day, in which she catalogues his every milestone: his first tooth, his first crawl across the carpet, his first tentative steps. It is a world only she and Danny inhabit, a world she chooses not to share with anyone, not even with Bill. Three months ago, on the day they should have been celebrating Danny's first birthday, she had passed the hours as if in a dream, as though the physical world had faded and the colour had been turned up on her imaginary world. Bill had brought home a bunch of yellow roses, had enfolded her in his arms as she had stood at the kitchen sink, washing the dinner plates, their shared grief palpable between them like charged particles. Sometimes she fears that if it were not for the prospect of this new baby to care for, she may have struggled to find motivation enough to continue. This baby, she knows, has saved her before it is even born.

'That's a lovely toy. Why on earth is someone giving that away?' Pam nods at the plastic telephone in Annie's hand. 'Just think, in nine months' time, the three of us will be sitting here wrapping Christmas presents, and you'll be wrapping for the new baby too.' Pam's smile broadens and Annie feels the warmth of expectation deep inside her. She knows how much she has to celebrate, how much she has to be grateful for. And yet sometimes she feels as though, for the people around her, this pregnancy balances the scales: that the tragedy of Danny's death is eliminated by the prospect of this new child. She understands how blessed she is with this pregnancy. But she also knows that she could give birth to a hundred other children and none of them would ever put an end to her grief for Danny.

Denise pulls a packet of Fondant Fancies from her bag and offers them round. Annie takes one, bites the cream off the top, eats the rest in two hungry mouthfuls.

'You know who I saw yesterday evening getting on the bus in the most unbelievable outfit?' Pam allows a beat of silence. 'Elsa. As in Bill's Elsa. You wouldn't believe what she was wearing. A psychedelic floorlength dress with a cream fur jacket over the top. She looked a bit out of place getting on the 208.' Pam laughs, shaking her head.

Bill's Elsa. Annie does not look up, pulls a strip of ribbon between her thumb and the flat of the scissors, curls it into a tight corkscrew.

'I like her taste in clothes. I think she's got style. I wish I had a figure like hers – you can wear anything with a figure like that and get away with it.' Denise sighs. At twentysix, she is three years older than Elsa, and yet it is Elsa who seems to Annie to be the more grown up of the two.

'God, don't you start. Alan's eyes were practically popping out of his head.' Pam laughs again and Annie snaps a piece of Sellotape from the dispenser, sticks it firmly onto the parcel in front of her.

145

Elsa has been working for Bill for almost fifteen months now and is showing no sign of wanting to leave, no indication that she is searching for something bigger or better, even though Bill is always telling Annie how talented she is. Annie can only hope that Elsa's current commitment to Bill's business is a passing fad: she is only twentythree and Annie is convinced that it must just be a matter of time before she moves on.

She is contemplating how to respond to Pam when she feels it. A slow trickle of liquid between her thighs. At first she thinks it is momentary incontinence; it has happened, on occasion, in the years since giving birth to Clare and Laura. But when she clenches her pelvic floor muscles, the seeping continues. It is like a leak in a dam which, now breached, cannot be stopped. This, Annie realises, is not urine. This is not incontinence.

Excitement flutters in her chest, swiftly followed by embarrassment and confusion. Her waters are breaking on Pam's best dining chairs and she does not know what to do. She wishes she could call out telepathically to Bill, that he could arrive as if by magic, could reassure her that this time things will be different, this time their baby will be strong and fit and healthy. But Bill is in his workshop over a mile away and even if Pam telephones him now, it will be ten minutes before he arrives.

The water continues its steady flow and Annie's heart races, both eager to meet her unborn child and anxious that history should not repeat itself.

She turns to Pam, tries to find the words to explain what is happening, to ask her to fetch Bill, but she cannot seem to encourage her mouth to make the right sounds. Instead, a single thought chants silently in her head, somewhere between a wish and an invocation: *Please make this baby okay. Whatever else happens, just please make my baby okay.*

NOW

Nell wakes from a fitful sleep and peels open her eyes. The neon digits on her phone tell her it is 2:47 a.m. Her fingers scrabble for the switch to the bedside light, and there is a split second of panic when it is not where it should be. Activating the torch on her phone, she experiences a moment's discombobulation: there are faded flowery curtains instead of plain cream linen; a mahogany chest of drawers where it should be light oak; a thin polyester duvet rather than duck down.

It takes a few seconds for Nell to remember that she is not at home in north London but fourteen miles south in her parents' house. The realisation fills her with an overwhelming urge to run away, though from what and to where she is not quite sure.

From the bedroom next door she hears the rustle of a duvet and hopes that her mum is sleeping deeply. She finds the switch of the bedside lamp beneath the peach floral shade, turns it on, its glow illuminating the corner of the room. Staring at the heavily artexed ceiling, she is reminded of all the nights during her childhood she would lie in this bed, worrying about the dangers she might encounter the following day.

'*If you hear footsteps behind you, cross to the other side of the street.*'

'*If a stranger tries to talk to you, don't answer them.*'

'*If anyone asks you to get in their car, run away.*'

'*If someone you don't know offers you sweets, always say no.*'

She can hear her mum's voice as clearly as if they were standing opposite one another, her mum buttoning up Nell's coat, placing the Tupperware box with her packed lunch into her rucksack, pulling her hair into a ponytail. So many scenarios, so much vigilance. It is only now, knowing what she knows about the baby her mum was unable to save, that Nell understands where all that caution may have come from.

Nell turns onto her side, knows that if she allows herself to tumble into this warren of memories she will never get back to sleep. But a recollection slips into her head, and it is as if the years are being rewound and she is eight years old again, lying in bed, listening to the whispered conversations of her parents long after they think she has gone to sleep.

'*I don't know how to live with it, Annie. I don't know how to bear the guilt.*'

'*It's the only thing we can do.*'

'*Is it? We didn't have to. We chose to. And every day I wonder if it was the right choice.*'

'*Of course it was. It was the only choice.*'

'*I don't mean for us. For them. You must think about them too?*'

There is a moment's hesitation and Nell holds her breath, does not dare exhale in case she betrays herself.

'*It was the right thing. Could you have lived with what would've happened if we hadn't?*'

There is muffled sound, a stifled sob.

'*You know I couldn't. But—*'

'*It's done now. That's all that matters. We did the only thing we could.*'

Nell opens her eyes, the feeling attached to the memory lingering beneath her ribs. She has not thought of it for years, is not convinced it is a real memory or just a trick her mind is playing on her in the semidarkness.

In the pale orange glow from the streetlamps outside, her eyes catch the framed photograph by the bed. It is the photo that had graced her dad's bedside table for the past fourteen years, which Nell rescued earlier from a cardboard box destined for the dump.

In the centre of the photograph stands Nell in an oversized black gown, mortar board at an angle on her head. On one side of her stands her dad in a charcoal grey suit he had bought especially for the occasion, a royal blue tie Nell had given him for his birthday fastened in a compact knot beneath his Adam's apple. One arm is wrapped around Nell's waist, his grin so wide it stretches across his face. On the other side of Nell is her mum in the navy floral dress she had worn to Laura's wedding six years earlier and kept for best ever since. Her arms are rigid by her side, lips held in a tight smile. Between her eyebrows is a tiny indentation which could be worry or could just be a squint against the sun. Behind them, fellow students pose for similar family photographs, the honeyed stone of the Sheldonian visible in the background.

Nell studies the picture, wonders what thoughts and feelings are hidden in her mum's expression. It is a photo that has always filled Nell with equal doses of pride and sadness. Her dad's unbridled joy seems to accentuate her mum's uncertainty. Even now, all these years later, Nell can feel the weight of her own disappointment that day. All she had wanted at her graduation was for both her parents to be happy, proud, to revel in the ancient traditions of the occasion. But her mum had been fretful, nervy, distracted, her anxiety like a dark cloud in an otherwise blue sky. Now Nell wonders whether her mum's thoughts had been elsewhere that day, whether they had been locked in the past, with the little boy who would not make it to his first day of school, let alone university.

The previous day's events begin to play out in Nell's mind like a film in which the frames have been cut out of sequence so that the story no longer makes sense. There is so much she still doesn't understand: about Danny's death, about her parents' grief, about her mum's garbled memories which may be the missing scenes in her family's past or may just be discarded sequences she has no need to see.

Laura is the person she needs to speak to. She put off talking to her sister yesterday, reeling too much from the shock of what she has learnt. But Laura must be able to tell her something about the events preceding her birth.

Snapping off the bedside light, she closes her eyes. Later today, she thinks, she will go and see Laura, find out what her sister knows, and see if she can help fill the gaps in her patchworked family history.

THEN

It is three months since Annie's waters broke at Pam's dining table. Time has passed in a blur, as if Annie has been watching her life through the window of a speeding train.

Beside her, lying in a wooden crib, the baby begins to cry, shattering the silence.

Annie looks down into the crib, at the baby's crumpled face and scarlet cheeks, at her curled fingers and jerking limbs, and she is aware of her heart clenching like a fist.

Leaning over the crib, she watches as her arms outstretch towards the baby, watches one hand slip under the baby's head, the other beneath the small of its back, watches herself lift the baby out of the cot and glide it through the air towards her body. They are not movements she is conscious of performing: it is as though her limbs are acting on an instinct of their own, born of some other time and place.

She holds the infant against her chest, feels the weight of the child's head against her sternum, its bent knees tucked beneath breasts which have long since dried of milk she has chosen not to offer.

There is a part of her that wishes she could disappear, take nothing with her. It is a weight of yearning so strong, as though something is pressing down hard on her lungs, squeezing the air out of them like the last gasps of a spent balloon.

The baby howls into Annie's ear and the noise is like shards of glass piercing her thoughts. She jiggles the baby up and down, and although she knows this is what she must do, the movement does not seem to belong to her: she has the sensation of having slipped outside her own body, of hovering on the periphery of the scene, watching herself perform this millenniaold act and yet unable to connect to it.

The baby continues to writhe in her arms and Annie feels the heat of anger and frustration bleeding through the thin cotton of her nightdress, does not know whether the heat belongs to her or the child.

Laying the baby down on the bed, she changes its nappy, replaces its white babygrow. Each of these duties she performs as if she has been preprogrammed to do so, as if there is no individual will involved in her actions.

The baby falls silent and in those few brief seconds Annie manages to fill her lungs, to reinhabit her body. But then the baby's forehead furrows into a frown, its lips form a wide gummy circle, and a noise emerges that is so shrill, so demanding, that it penetrates every pore of Annie's skin. She has to stop herself from clamping her palms over her ears to shut it out. Instead, she picks up the baby, puts it back in its crib, tucks a cotton sheet around it. The baby looks up, eyes wide with disbelief that it has been returned to a place it has no desire to be.

Annie and the baby stare at each other, neither of them uttering a sound, but the silence is filled with such need, such desire, that Annie imagines it leaching all the oxygen from the air and suffocating them both.

Love. That is what this child needs. She needs love. And Annie has tried, she has tried so hard. But whatever love she once may have possessed seems to have leaked out of her, like heat from a poorly insulated window, and she does not know how to capture it, bring it back. She does not know whether she will ever be able to love this baby, not as a child ought to be loved. She is doing her best to care for it – she knows she must – but it is a poor facsimile of what a mother's love should be.

The baby sucks in a deep gulley of air and Annie feels her skin prickle in anticipation before the next plaintive wail emerges. She sinks down onto the bed, wraps the duvet around her, pulls a pillow over her head to muffle the sound, trying to shut out the memory of what happened in the hospital three months ago. But she knows it is something she must hold on to, knows that she must cling to the truth of what happened, whatever anyone else might say. She has to. Because only by clinging on to the truth does she keep alive the hope that one day the unforgivable wrong will be put right.

The bedroom door scrapes against the carpet and Annie scrunches her eyes tighter, wishes she could make herself invisible.

'Are you okay?'

Bill's voice is soft, forgiving, but Annie does not want his forgiveness. What she needed from him he failed to provide and now it is he who should be seeking forgiveness, not her.

She hears him pad over to the crib, hears him coo reassurances as he lifts the baby from under the cotton sheet, hears her cries reduce to a gentle whimper. It is a form of magic, this ability he has to stop the baby crying where Annie cannot. It is a type of sorcery Annie had possessed with Clare, with Laura, with Danny, but now it seems to have abandoned her.

'Pam and Alan are downstairs. They've popped round with a lamb stew for dinner. Why don't you come down? They'd love to see you.'

It cannot be almost dinnertime. If it is, the day has passed without her noticing and she has no idea where the lost hours have gone.

She shakes her head, the heels of her hands pressed against her eye sockets.

'Come on. It'd do you good. It's only Pam and Alan. You don't even have to get dressed. Just pop your dressing gown on.'

She does not move, keeps her breaths shallow.

'Annie, please. Clare and Laura are both on sleepovers. It'll just be the four of us. And Nell, of course.'

If she could make herself disappear, she would. She does not want to see Pam and Alan, does not want to see anyone. She just wants to be alone.

'Okay, well I'll take Nell down and give her a bottle. *That's what you want, little one, don't you? You're a hungry Poppet, aren't you?* We'll be downstairs if you want to come down.'

She listens to him leave, whispering endearments into the baby's ear. '*Let's get you some food shall we, sweetheart? Are you a hungry girl?*' There is nothing pointed in Bill's voice but Annie hears the accusations anyway: *Your mummy won't feed you, will she? Your mummy's useless, isn't she? Your mummy can't even get herself dressed, can she?*

The door closes behind them and she listens to the soft tread of Bill's feet on the carpeted stairs, to the diminuendo of his footsteps, wanting to be certain that he isn't coming back. And then she hears muffled exclamations from the lounge below and she imagines Pam stretching out her arms, taking the baby from Bill, gazing down beatifically at it. The thought curls Annie's fingers into hardened balls.

All she wants is silence.

She has seen neither Pam nor Alan since the day her waters broke, has seen no one except Bill and the girls and the hospital staff. She has not wanted to see anyone, is not capable of keeping up the pretence.

The muscles in her stomach push against the wall of her bladder and she propels herself to her feet, onto the pale blue carpet worn through with years of footfall. Treading carefully, she heads for the door and opens it slowly so as not to alert the gathering below. She moves silently towards the bathroom, is level with the top of the stairs when she hears their voices.

'I really think you need to get the doctor to see her.' Pam's voice is hushed but it still drifts through the lounge door, up the stairs and into Annie's ears.

'It's still early days. She's just . . . tired, that's all.' Bill does not sound convincing and Annie does not move, transfixed by a conversation she knows she is not meant to hear.

'But it's not right, being cooped up like this. After being stuck in hospital all that time, you'd think she'd be champing at the bit to get out and about. And the fact that she won't see anyone . . . You must be worried?'

Annie waits for Bill's reply, blood throbbing in her ears. He has promised her that he will not tell anyone the real reason she had to stay in hospital for as long as she did. They have both sworn not to tell a soul. There has been nothing to suggest that he has broken that confidence but now she fears that perhaps he has, or is about to. So many things have happened over the past few months for which she may never be able to forgive Bill, and she does not know how her heart will bear it if he adds another layer of betrayal.

'Leave it, Pam. Bill knows what's best for Annie.' Alan's voice is firm, matter of fact.

'But it's not normal. You can see that, surely? A couple of weeks of feeling a bit down, that's normal. But not this. And after what happened before . . . Aren't you worried the same thing's happening again?'

Annie's head feels light and she does not know if it is provoked by fear or anger.

The same thing's happening again. The words thrum in Annie's ears and she grips the top of the bannister, her knuckles turning white. This is not the same thing. It is not the same thing at all. She is not grieving a death. She is grieving something different, completely different. And she has been rendered powerless by people who will not listen to her. People who keep telling her that it is residual grief for Danny making her have these thoughts, believe these things. But she knows they are wrong. It is not a fantasy. It is the truth.

She does not wait to hear Bill's reply, does not want to know what he says on her behalf, as though she is a ventriloquist's dummy and he the puppeteer. If a doctor is called she will refuse to see them. Nobody can make her. It is not a doctor she needs. Doctors have already proved themselves to be useless, incompetent, unreliable. She does not trust any of them. There is only one thing she needs and they have all proved themselves incapable of giving it to her.

Creeping into the bathroom, she sits on the toilet seat, shuffles her bottom forward so that when the torrent of urine is released it does so silently, hitting the ceramic bowl rather than the water.

Scuttling back into the bedroom she notices how stale the air is, like a box that has been unopened for decades. Climbing into bed, pulling the duvet around her, she hears the cry of the baby downstairs, feels herself flinch in response. Images of the hospital three months ago pierce her thoughts and she scrunches her eyes against them, trying to squeeze them from her mind. And yet she cannot give them up – knows she must not give them up – because she needs them if things are ever to be put right. She knows she will never stop raging at Bill for letting her down, will never stop railing at the doctors and nurses for their catalogue of failures. She will never stop cursing time for not allowing her to rewind it and do things differently. But, above all, she knows she will never forgive herself for failing to fulfil the single most important role any mother has to perform: to safeguard their child, to shield them from danger, and to protect them against every possible harm.

NOW

She has left her mum at home with Denise, drinking tea and watching a Sunday morning cookery programme, having found the remote control in the fridge between a jar of Branston pickle and a half-eaten cucumber. The suburban streets between her parents' house and Laura's are still quiet – it is not yet nine thirty – and it is only as Nell walks past the turning towards Laura's street and on towards the main road, only as she arrives at the twin red-brick pillars and green wrought-iron gates, that she realises where she has come.

The moment she steps inside the cemetery there is an immediate sense of calm. Behind her a bus trundles along the main road, but the graveyard seems to have its own sensory microclimate: restful, peaceful, still.

Walking along the path, the leaves whispering in the breeze overhead, she wanders towards the plot where her grandparents are buried. In the shade of a sycamore tree she finds their shared headstone.

Arthur Ernest Hardy
1915 – 1982
Mabel Winifred Hardy
1918 – 1983
Together in love, life and death

So few words to denote the lives they must have lived, though Nell never knew them. Her eyes cast around the jumble of graves, wondering where her father's ashes will be interred in a few weeks' time. She knows he has a double plot reserved for him and her mum, has always imagined it would be close to his parents, but now she is here she realises she does not know exactly where.

It is as she is walking away that she sees it. Not far from her grandparents' grave is one she has never noticed before. It is not the grave that demands her attention, but the words inscribed on the headstone.

Daniel William Hardy
28 October 1984 – 3 December 1984
Taken from us too soon
We will never stop loving you

A cluster of feelings catch in Nell's throat. Regret that she never had a chance to know her brother. Guilt that she is here only because he did not survive, that she has taken up his rightful place in the world. Sadness that her parents never felt able to discuss his short life with her.

In a vase beneath the inscription is a bunch of fresh sweet peas in a bloom of colours, their scent carrying on the breeze, and Nell wonders who placed them there, and when. She kneels down, runs her fingers along the indentations of the letters in the granite surface, peels a string of moss from inside one of the numbers. She places her hand flat onto the cool stone surface, as if by touching his headstone she can get closer to the brother she never knew.

Her eyes scan the area one last time, making sure she has not missed her father's plot, but she cannot see an obvious space.

Across the cemetery is a light coming from the caretaker's office and Nell makes her way through the twisted avenues of graves towards the small, square redbrick building. The door is ajar and she pushes it fully open, sees a tall, thin man with a wizened face eating a bacon sandwich and reading *The Mirror*. He looks up as she enters, surprise giving way to a welcoming smile.

'I'm sorry to disturb you. I'm just looking for my father's plot. His ashes are due to be interred here but I'm not sure where.' The words feel mechanical in her mouth, as though she is a clockwork doll reciting lines she has been programmed to say.

The man wipes a spot of tomato ketchup from his chin. 'Take a seat, love. What was your father's name?'

Nell lowers herself onto the fraying blue chair next to a tall filing cabinet. 'William Hardy.' Her throat tightens and she wishes there was a way those two words could convey the man he was, the father he had been, the cavern he is leaving behind.

'Ah, name rings a bell. I'm sorry for your loss.' He rummages inside a blue cardboard folder on his desk, pulls out a sheaf of papers attached with a single staple. 'Here we are. I knew I'd seen it recently.'

Nell watches as his eyes roam down one sheet of paper and then the next.

'That's it, I remember now. He's got a double plot reserved in the far corner of the memorial garden.'

'The memorial garden? But I thought it was near his parents. They're not far from the entrance, on the righthand side.'

The caretaker rereads the document before looking across at Nell. 'No, it's definitely the memorial garden.'

Nell scans her memory, searching for a recollection of her dad saying where he wanted to be buried, cannot be sure whether she has just always assumed it would be with his parents or whether it had actually been specified. 'Is that because there isn't room near the entrance?'

The caretaker shakes his head. 'I know it looks crowded there but there's still a bit of space. No, according to this, your dad reserved that plot in the memorial garden – hang on, let me do the maths – over thirty years ago. It's a lovely spot. I can show you, if you like?'

There is kindness in the caretaker's voice but Nell is struggling to make sense of what he has said. 'Over thirty years ago? Are you sure?'

The caretaker nods. 'That's what it says here. Headstone won't be in place for another few weeks, but you're welcome to take a look at the plot now.' His tone is gently encouraging and Nell wonders how many similar conversations he has had over the years.

'Could you point me in the right direction?'

Opening a drawer in his desk, the caretaker takes out a printed map of the cemetery and points at the top righthand corner. 'This is the memorial garden. If you go to this wall here, on the lefthand side, you'll see a wooden bench – almost brand new, you won't miss it. Right in front is where your dad's headstone will be. Any problems finding it, just pop back and I'll show you.'

Nell takes the map. 'Thanks. I'm sure I'll find it.'

Heading back out into the cemetery, she follows the path down a lefthand fork. There is a moment's disorientation as she enters the memorial garden, upright headstones being replaced with polished plaques lying flush with the earth. It does not take her long to find the bench the caretaker referred to: it is clean and fresh in light ash, and the brass plate on it tells her that it is dedicated to a woman called Eleanor Lively, who died only this year, and Nell wonders, as she sits down, whether Eleanor lived her life according to her name.

Across the memorial garden are row upon row of plaques in dark marble or granite, each with a slender vase attached to the top, some filled with fresh flowers, others noticeably empty. In front of her, on the end of a row, is a small square of grass, the empty plot where, she assumes, her father's ashes will be interred.

She looks around the garden with its welltended flowerbeds skating the perimeter, fallen magnolia blossom carpeting the grass, the closely cropped lawn in between rows of plaques. Nell wonders what made her father choose this as his final resting place rather than next door with his parents, with Danny. It doesn't make any sense that he should have buried his son with his parents and yet chosen a different location for himself.

She wonders whether he visited this exact spot, picked out the precise patch of earth as his own. She tries to imagine him making enquiries, seeking out availability, submitting his application, but something closes in her mind, like curtains being pulled shut against her thoughts.

The sun heats her scalp even though it is still early. Her eyes meander across the inscriptions chiselled into shiny black surfaces: short, elliptical epitaphs to encapsulate lives lived, leaving so much unsaid.

Ruth Charlotte Hazelmere
Devoted Wife to Ted, Loving Mother to Sarah and
Martin.
You will never be forgotten.

Thomas James Marsh
July 1949 – December 1991
Husband, Father, Brother, Son. We will miss you,
always.

Amy Imogen Whitworth
Two years on earth but forever in our hearts.
Sleep peacefully, angel.

Edith Edna Collins
1893 – 1992
Beloved member of church and community.

Nell reads the abbreviated biographies of those with whom her father will share his final resting place, wishing that tears would fall to articulate the depth of her loss, but it is as though her grief has been locked in a box and she does not know where to find the key.

From the back pocket of her jeans, her phone vibrates and she pulls it out, sees Josh's name, swipes a finger across the screen to answer it.

'Hey.'

'Hey, how are you doing?'

Nell looks around the memorial garden, wonders what the honest answer is to Josh's question. 'I'm okay. I'm at the cemetery, where my dad's headstone's going to be.'

There is the thinnest sliver of a pause and Nell can hear Josh's sympathy in his intake of breath. 'God, I'm sorry. That must be hard.'

Nell nods before remembering he cannot see her. 'I think . . . I just needed to see it.'

Neither of them says anything for a moment and it is almost as if Nell can sense the processing of Josh's thoughts before he begins to speak.

'Are you sure you're okay? I'm worried about you. I know how much you're grieving, and I can only imagine how hard it must be, having to move your mum into a home. But it feels like you're bottling it all up, and I think it might do you good to talk about it.'

Nell shifts to the far end of the bench, beneath the shade of a horse chestnut tree, wonders what she is actually doing there, why she has come. 'I'm fine, honestly. I'm sorry if I'm a bit distracted.'

'You don't need to apologise. You're allowed to be distracted, the amount you're going through. I just feel . . . Maybe I'm totally off the mark here, but it feels as though there's something you're not telling me, something you're holding back on.'

Nell picks at a thin smear of dirt on the thigh of her jeans, thinks about everything that has happened over the past thirty-six hours. A part of her cannot believe it has been less than two days since she arrived at her mum's, time during which her understanding of her family's history has shifted onto a different axis. And yet, even as she tries to make sense of all that has happened, she knows she is not yet ready to share it: to try to articulate it to someone else – even to Josh – would be to acknowledge a dissonance in her family she is not yet able to comprehend.

'I'm not. I know my head's all over the place, but I just need to get through this weekend, that's all.'

'You're back tonight though, aren't you? How about I come over, cook us both dinner? We can talk or we can just veg in front of the TV. Whatever you want.'

She hears the generosity in his voice, the care in his suggestion, and a part of her wants to reach out, grab it with both hands, immerse herself in it and not emerge until the darkness has passed, like a creature hibernating for winter. But there is the knowledge that if she were to see Josh, face-to-face, she would not be able to conceal from him the sea of confusion she is swimming in, would not be able to hold on any longer to the secret of what her dad said to her in the hospital that night. And it is still too raw, too unsettling to share with him.

'That's a really nice thought, but I think I'll be late back, and I'll be shattered when I am. I won't be good for much except collapsing into bed.' She laughs but it sounds strained, as though the noise is being dragged from her throat.

There is a pause on the other end of the line. 'Just know that I'm here for you. You don't need to shut me out.'

Words snap from Nell's lips before she has a chance to stop them. 'For God's sake, stop saying I'm shutting you out. I'm not. I've just got a lot on, that's all.' The line goes quiet and heat throbs in Nell's cheeks. 'Josh, I'm sorry—'

'It's fine.'

'Not, it's not—'

'It is. I hear you. Why don't you get through this weekend and give me a call when your head's a bit clearer?'

'I really am sorry—'

'Stop apologising. I get it. Honestly, I understand. Look, I'd better go. Jamie's just turned up and we're supposed to be meeting the uni gang for a game of football. I'll text you later, okay?'

There isn't time for Nell to apologise again before she hears a muffled greeting from somewhere inside Josh's flat, and the line goes dead.

Hugging her knees to her chest, she berates herself for her snappiness, her secrecy, for her inability to confide in Josh. She wishes she could explain, tell him it is not about him, that there is no one to whom she could convey the fears that are taking shape in her head. Fears that may be something or nothing, but which to voice out loud would be to give them a legitimacy – a weight, a significance – she is not yet ready to acknowledge.

Her phone bleeps with a text message and she scrabbles to answer it, assumes it will be Josh, clearing the air. But instead it is Laura asking what time she is popping round.

Looking at the time, Nell sees it is gone ten o'clock already. She has been at the cemetery longer than she realised. Taking one last glance at the plot into which both her parents' ashes will one day be interred, she carries herself away from the bench and out of the memorial garden, towards the exit, aware that she cannot delay any longer the conversation with her sister she knows she must have.

THEN

Annie does not hear the click of the front door, her thoughts too focussed on what is in front of her, her ears not paying attention to the world around her while her eyes are doing so much work. It is only when she hears his voice behind her that she realises she is not alone.

'What are you doing?'

Whipping her head around, she leans forward instinctively, spreads her arms across the table to cover up the pieces of paper she has been studying all morning, but there are too many for her to conceal.

Bill walks around to the side of the table and she sees the changing expression on his face as he looks down, notices what is laid out there. He picks up one piece of paper, then another, deep indentations forming at the bridge of his nose as his eyes survey the photographs, studying one and then the next. She sees the cloud pass across his face, the ridges of crows' feet deepening at the edges of his eyes.

'What's all this?'

Annie follows his gaze to the collection of newspaper cuttings on the table in front of her. It is only now, looking at them with Bill, that she registers how many there are, sprawled across the elm wood table, does not know whether it is shame or indignation causing her cheeks to blaze.

'Annie?'

She shakes her head, begins gathering up the pieces of newspaper, scooping them into her arms, trying to shuffle them into a pile, but they are all different shapes, different sizes, and they will not form a neat group. Some are getting bent at the corner, others creased along the middle, and her hands tremble as she tries to coax them into an orderly stack.

Bill pulls out the chair next to her, sits down, tries to place a hand on top of hers, but Annie shakes him off. She needs to finish the task, needs to get all the cuttings back into the pale green cardboard folder, where they belong. They have been out too long already, have been seen by more eyes than they should. It is as though he has already stolen some of their secrets from her.

'Annie, talk to me, please. What's going on?'

She does not reply, blinks against the threat of tears. She manages to get the first pile safely back into the folder, starts to gather up the rest, wants both to hurry and to take her time, cannot bear the risk of crumpling any of those sweet, innocent faces.

'Are these what I think they are?'

Annie brushes a hand across her face, sweeps the hair from her eyes. Bill was never supposed to see this, was never supposed to know. It is her thing, *hers*, and she knows it will never be the same now that he has witnessed it.

'Where did they all come from? They're not all local. How on earth did you get hold of them?'

She does not look up as she continues to assemble the cuttings into a pile. So many faces she has collected over the past two months, so many hours she has spent studying them, searching for something she fears she may never find but knows she will never give up seeking. She cannot tell him where she has got them from, cannot bear to see the judgement and disappointment on his face. There is no way she can confess to all the mornings she has spent in the public library, scouring newspapers from across the country, a pair of scissors in her pocket, the baby asleep in the pram beside her, surreptitiously cutting out every relevant article she finds and slipping it into her handbag to study properly later at home. She would not know how to tell him about the dozens of futile trips she has undertaken, when she has scanned every newspaper and been unable to find a single article – a single photograph – worth cutting out and keeping. There are no words to convey the necessity of this task, or how it has become the cornerstone of her days. And even if there were words, she is not sure she would want to share them with him.

The last of the cuttings make their way into the folder and she tucks the flap inside to keep them safe, thinks that next time she will have to be more careful. Next time she will look at them upstairs, in the bedroom, so that she will have more chance to hear any intruders before they discover what she is doing.

It is only when Bill's hand begins moving across the table top that she realises what his fingers are reaching for. She snatches the folder from his grasp, clutches it to her chest. He will not take it from her. After all she has lost already, she will not let him have this too.

'Annie, please. You must see that this isn't good for you, not good for any of us, especially not Nell. Give it to me, please.'

Annie presses the folder more firmly against her body. She thinks about Nell, five months old, asleep in her cot upstairs, and a quiet fury snakes between her ribs. Bill does not understand, he does not understand a thing. This is not a betrayal of Nell. She is doing this for Nell, for all of them.

Bill's hand continues to stretch out towards her and then his fingers curl around the edge of the folder and he is pulling it away from her chest, but Annie clings on to it, her last vestige of the truth. He is tugging at the corner and she is clutching it ever tighter, panicked that he may rip it – may rip everything inside – if he pulls any harder.

'We don't need this. Let me take it, please.'

Bill's hands are now either side of the folder and she knows she will not be able to hold on to it much longer without damaging what's inside.

'Don't throw it away. *Please*. It's mine, I need it.' Her throat fills with the heat of desperation and she is aware of tears spilling from her eyes.

Bill retracts his hands and Annie sees the shock on his face but she doesn't care, it doesn't matter, all that matters is that he does not throw her cuttings away.

'Okay, love. Just take some deep breaths.'

But Annie cannot breathe properly because the air is pummelling in and out of her lungs, and her shoulders are heaving, and tears are falling down her cheeks.

'It's okay. I'm not going to take anything away.' Bill places an arm around her shoulder as Annie continues to hug the folder to her chest. 'That's it. Just try to breathe. It's all going to be okay.'

Annie knows that it is a lie, that nothing will be okay until mistakes have been rectified, not just hers and Bill's, but other people's too. But Bill's voice is gentle, soothing, and she lets him rub her back, feels her shallow breaths begin to lengthen, allows her body to regulate itself towards some semblance of calm.

'I just want to help, love. I'm worried about you, that's all.'

Annie shakes her head, though she does not know if it is the help or the concern she is rejecting.

'You're not sleeping, you're not eating. You're not seeing anyone. Pam phoned last week and she said you haven't seen her or Denise since Nell was born. She said every time she rings there's no answer and whenever she pops round you're out. But you're not out, are you?'

Annie does not reply. There is no point talking to him. He knows what is wrong and has chosen to ignore her, has told her she is mistaken. But Annie knows she is not mistaken. She knows the truth even if everyone else is denying it.

'Think about Clare and Laura, how confusing this is for them. I know you didn't mean to snap at Clare last night, and if it was the first time I wouldn't mention it. But she was really upset, even this morning on the way to school. She said she doesn't know what she's done wrong, why you're so quiet one minute and shouting the next. And I didn't know what to tell her because I don't understand it either.'

Guilt reaches around Annie's throat. She had not meant to shout at Clare, last night or any of the other times, cannot remember now what had provoked her. It is like a monster inside her, this anger. For hours it lies dormant, heavy and leaden, so that even the most mundane tasks – getting dressed, feeding Nell, walking to the library – are a struggle. And then, without warning, it will wake and a fury erupts from her, and there is nothing she can do to stop it. Clare or Laura suffering is the very last thing she wants but she does not seem able to control it.

'I know how hard the last eighteen months have been for you, and I know that having Nell must have brought it all back. But Nell's strong and healthy. Nothing bad's going to happen to her.'

Annie scrunches her eyes closed, wishing she could shut down all of her senses in one go. Fury drums against her ribs that Bill should have it got it so wrong, that he should understand so little. Her grief for Danny is not something that disappeared with pregnancy, only to be recalled once Nell was born. What she is going through now is not the fear that history might repeat itself. It is the knowledge that a different tragedy has already occurred. And the fact that Bill will not listen to her – that no one will believe her – has left her no option but to hold on to it herself, however she can.

'Me and the girls – we need you. And so does Nell. We all need you.'

Bill pauses his monologue, waiting for Annie to respond. But Annie has nothing to say that she has not said before, that he has already chosen to ignore.

He places a hand over hers, her arms still hugging the folder to her chest. 'I know you've been adamant that you don't need any help, but I'm going to call the GP, get him to come round and see you.'

A flurry of panic skims over Annie's skin.

'I just want you to get better, that's all. That's all any of us want. Now, I know you want to keep all these cuttings, so how about I put the folder up in the loft, for safekeeping?' He places his hands gently on either side of the cardboard, not tugging or pulling, just making his intentions clear.

She knows what he is doing. He thinks that by putting the folder in the loft, it will be out of sight and out of mind. He does not understand that it is on her mind every second of every day: it is the last thing she thinks about before she goes to sleep, the first thing she thinks about when she wakes up, and in between it populates her dreams. But it does not matter to her if he puts it in the loft. Wherever he puts it, she will find it.

Releasing her hold on the folder, she lets him take it from her. He leans forward, kisses the top of her head. 'It's going to be okay. We'll get the GP to come and see you and it'll all get better, I promise.'

He hovers next to her, waiting for a reply, but she does not speak. She knows it is not going to get better – how can it when the facts remain the same? – but she does not want to prolong an interaction she wishes had never begun.

'Right, well, I'll just put this up in the loft then. I expect Nell will be waking from her nap soon. I only popped home to collect some invoices I left in the kitchen. I'll be back in a minute.' He says it in a voice that suggests he thinks she might run away before he has time to return.

She listens to his footsteps on the stairs, to the soft screech of the loft ladder as he pulls it down. She closes her eyes and strains her ears to hear the direction of his tread on the plywood boards across the loft floor, to determine where he might be hiding the folder, but he is too far away. It doesn't matter. Later, when Bill has left and Nell has her afternoon nap, she will extend the retractable loft ladder, make her way under the eaves, and search for the folder until she finds it. She will study its contents up there where she is less likely to be discovered, tuck it back where she found it after each visit, so that Bill will never know. She needs to believe that the answer will be there because if she no longer believes in that, she does not know how she will continue getting up every day and masquerading as the mother she knows she once was and fears she may never be again.

NOW

Nell follows Laura into the hallway of a house she visits rarely, wonders why she and Laura never get together outside of wider family gatherings. There have never been weekend lunches, just the two of them, never a postwork drink or a Saturday morning coffee. Nearly all their meetings for the past fifteen years have taken place at their childhood home, with their parents. It is their mum and dad who have hosted every Christmas and Easter, who have cooked Sunday lunches, summer barbecues, birthday dinners. Their parents have been the central star around which the rest of them have orbited for so long that Nell cannot imagine what will happen now they are no longer able to do that.

'Oh, God, he's forgotten it again. I'd better just call him and check he's got his spare.' Laura holds up an asthma inhaler, rolls her eyes, picks up her phone. 'He's out playing football this morning so he can't be without one. Sorry, won't be a sec.' She jabs at the phone's screen, holds it to her ear. 'Hey, love . . . Yes, I know . . . No, I just wanted to check you had an inhaler with you . . . Are you sure? . . . Do you just want to—? . . . Okay . . . Hope the match goes well . . . Love you.'

She puts the phone face down on the work surface. 'Honestly, kids. You never stop worrying about them. Coffee? I've just boiled the kettle.'

'That'd be great, thanks.'

Laura tips two teaspoons of instant coffee granules into a pair of spotty mugs, pours boiling water over the top. 'Do you take sugar?'

Nell shakes her head.

'Me neither, I've been weaning myself off it. Trying to lose weight – fat lot of good it's doing me. Not that you've ever had a problem on that front. You've always been skinny.' She picks up the two mugs, hands one to Nell. They stand facing each other, leaning against work surfaces on opposite sides of the kitchen.

'I popped in to see Elsa yesterday morning.' The words spring from Nell's lips before she has readied herself to say them, and although it is the subject she has come to discuss, she still feels unprepared for them.

'How is she? I haven't seen her since the funeral.'

Nell sets her coffee down on the work surface behind her, slips her hands into the back pockets of her jeans.

'She's fine. Good. Busy.' From the street outside, a car alarm begins to shriek, three or four seconds of wailing before it is silenced. 'The thing is, she told me some things that . . . well, that have thrown me a bit, to be honest.'

'What things?' There is nothing unusual in Laura's voice, nothing to suggest that Nell is heading into unchartered territory.

Nell bites her bottom lip, tugs at a piece of skin with her teeth, feels a sharp sting as it pulls free. 'She told me about Danny. She didn't mean to. She just assumed I already knew.' The words feel like treacle in her mouth. 'Why did no one ever tell me?'

The colour drains from Laura's face. 'I don't know.' Her voice is small suddenly, like a child concealed in a den who does not want to be found.

'But it's crazy. I had a brother I never even knew about. Everyone else in the family knew – all our friends knew – but for some reason I've never been told. Don't you think that's weird?' The frustration of the past thirtysix hours seeps from her voice and she does not try to stop it.

'I don't think anyone deliberately kept it from you. It's just . . .'

'Just what?'

A series of deep grooves plough across Laura's forehead. 'It wasn't as if everyone was discussing it behind your back. It was just never talked about.'

Nell tries to imagine the reality of what Laura is saying, finds she cannot. 'That doesn't make any sense. Mum and Dad can't just never have talked about him?'

Laura takes in a deep breath, lets it out again. 'Well, they didn't. One day we had a little brother. The next we didn't. And after a few months no one ever really talked about him again.'

'But didn't you ask? Didn't *you* want to talk about him? Surely you—'

'For God's sake, Nell, I was seven years old. I didn't have a clue what was going on.'

Nell hears the crack in Laura's voice, watches her gulp from her cup of coffee. 'I'm sorry. I didn't mean it to sound like an accusation.'

Laura shakes her head, a small, almost invisible movement, as though she is not sure she wants it to be seen. 'You've no idea what it was like. Mum was . . . I don't even know how to describe it. Devastated doesn't even come close. She was completely traumatised, for months. It wasn't until she got pregnant with you that things started to go back to normal. And that didn't exactly last long.'

Something in Laura's voice – a trace of bitterness like a hint of spice you cannot quite identify – prompts the question before Nell is aware of needing to ask it. 'Why not? What happened?'

Laura wraps her arms across her chest, bites the inside of her cheek. 'Mum had a bit of a . . . I don't know . . . a relapse, I suppose, after you were born.' Laura's eyes flick briefly upwards, meet Nell's, cast themselves to one side again. 'No one really told us what was going on. But it was really hard on me and Clare. That month she was in the hospital with you after you were born, when we weren't allowed to go and visit her . . .' Laura swallows. 'I'd convinced myself she was dead and we'd never see her again.'

The words hit Nell as though she has been physically slapped. 'Mum stayed in hospital for a month after I was born and you weren't allowed to visit her? Why?'

Laura shrugs. 'Dad said she'd lost some blood – had a haemorrhage, I found out later – and that you'd had some breathing difficulties, but that you were both fine. He said you both just needed to be kept in for observation. He kept trying to reassure us everything was okay but it was hard to believe when we couldn't actually see her. And then—' Laura stops abruptly, turns away, busies herself tidying a row of tea and coffee jars that were already neatly lined up.

'What is it? Come on, I'm thirtyfive years old. Whatever it is, please just tell me.' *You need to know that I've always loved you even though you were never really mine to love.* She almost blurts it out, almost tells her sister about her dad's dying words, but she is not yet ready to share them, fears too much where they might lead.

Laura stops, hand clutched around a damp Jcloth, turns to Nell. 'When Mum came home from the hospital, it was like she wasn't really the same person any more. I don't know whether it was postnatal depression, or that your birth brought up difficult feelings about Danny, but it was horrible. It was as if our mum had gone into hospital and a complete stranger had returned in her place.'

Nell senses a hollowing out deep inside her, and even though she fears what may come next, she cannot stop herself from asking the question, like a voyeur to a car crash who wishes only later they had not witnessed it. 'How long did it go on for? Mum's depression?' Her voice is thin, reedy, as though it is being squeezed through too narrow a gap in her throat.

'Ages. Months.'

'Months?' Nell hears the incredulity in her voice, feels as though she is drunk, stumbling, unable to fully grasp what is going on.

Laura pauses, eyebrows pinched. 'It was awful. One minute she'd be locked away in the bedroom and the next she'd be angry and shouting for no reason. Dad looked after us most of the time. I don't really know how he managed, running the business and being there for us. I guess Elsa must have held the fort at work but still . . .' Her voice trails off and this time Nell does not try to follow it.

Instead, she replays Laura's explanation in her head, tries to mould it against what she already knows, but it is awkward, illfitting.

'It wasn't your fault, Nell. She wasn't well. Millions of women get postnatal depression.'

She knows her sister is trying to console her but she feels like a character in a ChooseYourOwnAdventure book who has just been sent back to the beginning of the story to start again on a different path. 'I'm sorry. It must have been hard for you. And Clare. Really hard.'

Laura attempts a smile but it snags at the corners of her lips. 'I think the worst thing was how guilty I felt.'

'What about?'

'That I couldn't make her better. That I didn't know what was wrong with her. That perhaps it was my fault she was like that.' Laura fiddles with a piece of lint on the cuff of her cardigan. 'When she started getting better, I remember this huge feeling of relief.

It was like we'd all been living in darkness and then someone had switched on the light. But then—' Laura stops abruptly.

'What? Come on, it can't be any worse than telling me Mum was depressed for months after I was born.' Nell has attempted to inject some humour into her voice but can hear her hunger for information.

Laura wraps the Jcloth around her hand, pulls hard, the tips of her fingers turning red. 'Then you ended up being Mum's favourite. You were the one she always loved the most.' There is a strain in Laura's voice, like a spring that has been coiled too tight. 'You've always been the one she loved best, you know you have—'

'Laura—'

'It's fine, I'm a grownup, I can handle it now. But it wasn't easy when we were younger, knowing how besotted she was with you. It was like she was obsessed. She just wanted you with her all the time. Clare and I barely got a lookin.' There is something out of kilter in Laura's voice and it takes a few seconds for Nell to understand what it is: Laura is trying to be kind but her resentment has trickled through like blood seeping into a thin piece of gauze. 'It wasn't your fault. You were just a baby. To be honest, I think Clare found it harder than I did.' Laura pauses, meets Nell's eye, looks away again quickly. 'I have sometimes wondered whether Clare would've got pregnant so young if things had been different at home.'

It takes a few seconds for the implication to take shape in Nell's mind and when it does, it is as though she is holding a shell against each ear and all she can hear is the distant swell of the sea. She thinks of Clare's short, unhappy marriage, all her years as a single parent, and the thought that she is inadvertently responsible is like a leaden weight deep in her stomach.

'I'm sorry, Nell. That was a shitty thing to say. Clare was an adult, she was old enough to take responsibility for her own decisions.'

Nell shakes her head, her mind scrambling to put everything she has heard into coherent order, but her thoughts are a tangled ball and will not be untwined. 'I'd better get back to Mum's. There's so much to do.' She picks up her bag, slings it over her shoulder.

'Please don't rush off. I shouldn't have said that. I'm sorry.'

Nell twists the keyring of her mum's house keys around her finger, lets it dig into her skin. 'I pushed you to tell me. I wanted to know.' Her voice is higher than usual, as though her vocal cords are being stretched by invisible hands. She turns and walks out of the kitchen, into the hall, Laura following closely on her heels.

'If you give me ten minutes, I'll come with you. I need to sort out the last of the lounge anyway.'

Nell puts a hand on the front door lock, pulls it open. 'Honestly, don't worry. I'll see you later.' She doesn't wait for a reply as she turns and walks down the short garden path.

As she hurries away, theories clamour in her head like clues to a puzzle she does not know how to solve. And loudest of all she hears her dad's voice, eighteen words that continue to echo in her ears: *You need to know that I've always loved you even though you were never really mine to love.* They are like a bruise on her memory that will not heal and as she arrives outside her parents' house, she knows what it is she must do. There is only one way to answer the question that otherwise may never be silenced.

THEN

The doorbell rings and Annie leaves Nell on her playmat, walks into the hall, glancing at the clock on her way. Ten thirty. They are right on time.

When she opens the door, Denise and Pam stand smiling at her. Melissa is asleep in the pushchair, head lolled to one side.

There is a moment's hesitation, an awkwardness born of unfamiliarity. It is eight months since the three of them were last together, and Annie does not know how to close the gap for which she is responsible. But then Pam bundles the pushchair into the narrow hallway, throws an arm around Annie's shoulder and squeezes tightly.

'We come bearing gifts.' From underneath the pushchair she retrieves a square cardboard cake box. 'I'll get some plates, shall I, put the kettle on?' She doesn't wait for a reply before breezing into the kitchen, and Annie is grateful for her informality.

Denise hugs her, heads into the lounge, makes a beeline for Nell. 'Oh my God, she's adorable. Those eyes! She's just gorgeous.' Denise sits crosslegged on the floor beside Nell, picks up a fluffy bunny, bounces it along the playmat, Nell laughing in response. 'I can't believe how big she is.'

There is no censure in Denise's voice, but Annie feels it nonetheless: the months she has allowed to go by without seeing her friends, without letting her friends see her baby.

'Right, where shall I put this? The kettle's on.' Pam carries a tray with cakes, paper napkins, and a stack of side plates. Leaving it on the dining table, she joins Denise on the floor, tells Nell what a pretty girl she is, and Annie feels a rush of relief that her friends are making things so normal, that there are none of the tacit recriminations she has been dreading.

It is three months since Bill came home and found Annie with her collection of newspaper cuttings. Three months since he called Dr Lewis, who came to visit Annie the next day when the girls were at school, and talked to her in his kindly, avuncular manner about the way she was feeling and what might be causing it. At first she had not wanted to listen, had refused to answer any of his questions, but he had returned a second time, and then a third, and it was on the third visit that he managed to persuade her to try a course of antidepressants, just to see if they might help regulate her feelings. For the first few weeks she had felt nothing, had thought it a waste of time. But then she had noticed how the edge had been taken off her feelings: anger diluted to irritation; panic abated; the heaviness of her limbs lightened. There had been headaches at first but they had eased in time. Now there is a strange sense of distance where once her heightened emotions had been, and Annie is not yet sure whether she likes the way the medication clouds her thoughts and feelings, rendering them slightly out of reach. She has told this to Bill and Dr Lewis, and they have both raised the same point: whether this slight distance from her feelings is not preferable to the amplified emotions she had been experiencing before.

Since starting the medication, she has been seeing Dr Lewis every week, late on a Wednesday afternoon, while Bill looks after the girls. The doctor has sought to reassure her that it is not uncommon, what she has experienced: postnatal depression is surprisingly widespread, he has said, and given what she has already been through with Danny, he does not seem surprised that Nell's birth caused a recurrence of the melancholy she had suffered then. Grief, Dr Lewis has told her, can manifest itself in a multitude of ways.

'Is she hitting all her development milestones okay?' Pam runs a finger along Nell's hairline where dark curls cling to her scalp.

As if on cue, Nell points a chubby finger towards Annie. 'Ma! Ma!' Annie beams with pride as Pam and Denise burst out laughing.

'Just the odd sound like that. And she's crawling everywhere. I have to watch her like a hawk.' Annie crouches down, scoops Nell into her arms, sits her on her lap and hands her the clothbound book she picked up in the charity shop last week.

'That's incredible at eight months. None of mine tried to speak before their first birthday.'

Annie turns the pages of the book, pointing at various animals as she says their names aloud, kisses Nell's cheek, her daughter's porcelain skin as soft as silk.

It has taken time – more time, Annie knows, than it ever should – but between Bill, Dr Lewis and the antidepressants, she has begun to accept that what happened in those months after Nell's birth was a symptom of her illness. That it was hormones and historical trauma that had made her imagine such terrible things. It is still early days, but now when she holds Nell in her arms, she is aware of something swelling inside her chest: the love she ought to have felt from the outset that has finally begun to take root inside her now.

From the hallway comes the squawk of a child, and Pam goes to fetch Melissa. They return a few moments later, Melissa clutching Pam's fingers in one hand, a toy penguin in the other. She burrows her face into Pam's thigh when she sees Annie, and Annie feels a stab of guilt that Melissa – now almost three and a half – no longer recognises her after an eightmonth absence. 'Come and say hello to Nell. She's got some lovely toys you can play with.'

Melissa buries her head further into Pam's leg, who lifts her into her arms and sits down with her on the floor. 'You're still a bit sleepy, aren't you, sweetie?'

As the three women talk about the council's refusal to renovate the playground, about the supermarket opening up in town, about Pam's new nextdoor neighbours, the butterflies that had been flitting inside Annie's stomach since she got up this morning begin to settle, and she is aware of a feeling she has not experienced in a very long time: a feeling of normality. After months of darkness, there is a glimmer of light at the end of the tunnel, and she can finally see the possibility of a happy future for her family.

NOW

She has only just closed the front door behind her when she hears a voice calling out.

'Laura, is that you?'

Nell curses under her breath, annoyed with herself for not realising Clare might be there.

'It's me. I've just got to get something.'

Clare strides into the hall, stands in front of Nell like a sentry on duty. 'Where have you been? Denise said you left ages ago, that you were only popping out to get some bread and milk.' She looks down at Nell's empty hands.

Nell opens her mouth to defend herself, thinks of all the boxes she has lugged down from the loft, all the rubbish she has transported to the dump, all the cupboards she has emptied and the clothes she has taken to the charity shop. But then she looks at Clare's tight expression, at the patch of eczema in the crook of her elbow, and thinks about all that Laura has just told her, all that Clare has been through without Nell ever knowing. 'I'm sorry. I got totally distracted. I can pop out now to get some bread and milk?'

Clare shakes her head with exaggerated vigour. 'Don't bother. I'll get Laura to pick some up on her way over.'

Clare tuts and Nell feels it immediately: the pull towards conflict that has been their default position for as long as she can remember. It happens so quickly, as if they are both operating on autopilot, but today she does not want to take Clare's bait. Today she has no intention of allowing them both to fall into that same, familiar trap.

'I really am sorry I was so long. I know this is hard for all of us – you and Laura especially, doing the lion's share of it – but I just needed to clear my head for a bit.' She looks at Clare expectantly, waits for her sister's impatience to make itself known, is nonplussed when it is not forthcoming.

A series of imagined scenes slip into Nell's head: Clare, aged eleven, watching her mother fall apart after the death of her child; Clare, aged thirteen, anxiously awaiting the return of her mum from the hospital; Clare sensing her mother's love pivot to her baby sister and being unable to win back her attention; Clare, aged eighteen, falling pregnant, getting married, escaping a household in which the centre of gravity has shifted, relocating her from the nucleus to the periphery.

Nell reaches out a hand, places it on the flesh of Clare's arm, just below the elbow. Clare flinches almost infinitesimally, but Nell keeps it there. 'Mum's so lucky to have you around. Dad was too. I don't know what either of them would have done without you.'

There is a moment's stillness, like the hesitation before a breath, like the darkness before dawn, and it seems to Nell that she and Clare are balancing on the braided wire of a tightrope, waiting to see which way they will fall, whether they will be caught.

Eventually Clare looks up, meets Nell's gaze. 'Thanks. It's not just me. Laura obviously does a lot too.' There is none of the usual corrosiveness in Clare's voice and Nell allows her hand to rest on her sister's arm a moment longer before Clare turns around, calls over her shoulder. 'I'd better get back to the kitchen cupboards. You wouldn't believe how much grime there is in them.'

Nell watches her disappear behind the kitchen door. The moment she is gone the flutter of adrenaline returns, and she is reminded what she has come for, where she needs to go.

Heading up the stairs, two at a time, she turns left into her bedroom and grabs her overnight bag before heading back across the landing and into the bathroom. Locking the door behind her, she opens the white cabinet above the sink, where pill bottles fight for space with tweezers, nail scissors, scrunched up plastic shower caps. On her mum's shelf she sees what she is looking for amidst half-fused tubs of face cream, a tattered blue washbag with a broken zip, and a bottle of talcum powder yellowed with age. She pulls it out and puts it down on the toilet lid before reaching up on tiptoes to search through her dad's shelf. She takes out a bottle of cod liver oil way past its expiry date, a stick of deodorant, a bottle of aftershave from which she lifts the lid, inhales deeply, letting the smell fill her nose. But she puts that aside too, continues to rummage through the clutter with her fingers until she finds what she is looking for lying flat on the shelf. She takes it out, places it next to her mum's on the seat of the toilet, looks at them side by side.

Her mum's black Denham hair brush.

Her dad's brown tortoiseshell comb.

Staring at them both, she wonders if she really has the courage to do this.

There is a clatter from the kitchen downstairs and Nell's heart leaps. Pulling off a long strip of toilet paper, she wraps it around her father's comb until it is completely secure, places it carefully in the inside pocket of her overnight bag. With a second sheaf of paper, she prises a handful of hairs from her mum's brush, folds the paper around them, winding it in every direction so as to seal any gaps, before opening the zip of her purse and placing it inside as gently as if lowering a baby into its crib.

She is careful to watch her tread as she heads back down the stairs, careful to avoid the creaking fourth step. Opening the front door, she clicks down the Yale lock slowly so as not to make a sound, closing it softly behind her, muting the snap of the lock back into its cylinder. Getting into her car, she texts a joint apology to Laura and Clare, tells them that something has come up at work, that she has to leave but will be back soon. She knows it is a flimsy excuse. But she also knows that she has to do this. If she doesn't do it now, she may never find the courage.

THEN

Birthday cards are lined up on the mantelpiece, like pictures in an art gallery awaiting inspection.

Happy 2nd Birthday!
To A Super 2YearOld!
You're 2!

Annie's eyes travel along the cards, and then down to the lounge floor where Nell is pushing pieces of wood through the holes of a shape sorter.

How can two years have passed? she thinks. How can it be two years since she had lain in that hospital bed, feeling her world turn upside down, thinking such dark, terrible thoughts?

'Mama! You take! You push dem dare!'

Nell points to the shape sorter with a chubby finger and Annie kneels down on the carpet next to her, picks up a red star. 'This one?'

Nell nods. Annie makes a pantomime of trying to fit it into the circular hole, and then the square. 'I'm not very good at this, am I? Why don't you have a go?' She passes the wooden shape back to Nell who finds the right hole immediately, twiddles it with a dexterous hand, pushes it through.

'Me do it!'

Annie wraps her arms around Nell, hugs her tightly. 'Well done, angel, you clever girl.' She kisses the top of Nell's head where a mass of dark curls cling to her scalp as if wary of straying too far from her head. People keep telling Annie they're just baby curls, that they will disappear with her first haircut, never to be replaced, but Annie refuses to believe them. She has never seen such beautiful hair on a child. It is so unlike her own mousey hair, so unlike Clare's and Laura's; they have hair so fine it refuses to be styled. Annie has always kept the older girls' hair short as a result, but Nell's hair she imagines tumbling down her back like a character in a period drama.

'Me do dat jigsaw.' Nell points to some jigsaws on top of the mahogany sideboard.

'Which one? The world jigsaw or the alphabet one?'

'Da world!'

Annie laughs and leans across to the sideboard, prises the box from beneath a pile of other toys, puts it on the floor. Lifting the lid, she takes out the chunky wooden frame, arranges the individual pieces in a random formation on the playmat. Nell's eyes scan the choice of brightly coloured continents decorated with animals and buildings, before picking up the jagged South American triangle and slotting it correctly into place. Asia, Africa and North America follow. Europe is a trickier fit where the edges abut Asia, and Nell wiggles it from side to side, trying to make it go in, but her angle is slightly skewed and it will not comply. She looks up at Annie, frustration puckering the skin across her forehead, and Annie resists the urge to dive in and do it for her. 'You can do it. Just turn it round a bit and it'll fit. You just have to keep trying.' Nell focuses back on the jigsaw, eyes narrowed with concentration, and after a few seconds Europe slips into place.

'Look, Mama! Me do it!' Nell beams up at her, pride shining from her eyes.

'Well done. Now can you find Antarctica?'

Nell identifies it correctly, fits it into its rightful slot, before doing the same with Oceania. Her eyes roam over the remaining twenty pieces, the countries that fit on top of their continents, and Annie watches in silence as Nell picks up Argentina, Russia, India, Germany and slots them into place.

When Elsa had given Nell the jigsaw puzzle at her second birthday party a fortnight ago, Annie had rolled her eyes at Pam, bemused that someone should have so little conception of a two-yearold's capabilities, bringing her a present clearly way beyond her years. Pam had laughed and the pair of them had shared a moment's silent agreement that Elsa, at twentyfive, would inevitably choose an inappropriate gift.

But later that afternoon, when the other children were beginning to tire, after the sugar rush from slices of Victoria sponge and chocolate fingers was beginning to wear off, Annie had watched as Elsa had huddled in a corner of the lounge with Nell, taken the jigsaw from its box, and sat beside her as Nell had experimented putting different pieces in each slot. Annie had watched the unwavering concentration on Nell's face, her complete fixation on the task, not distracted for a second by the other children's shouts or squeals. Nell and Elsa had sat together for fifteen minutes, oblivious to the rest of the party, until suddenly Nell had clambered to her feet, run over to where Bill was chatting to Alan and pulled on his hand. '*Look, Dada, look!*' Her voice had been so excitable, so filled with wonder, that they had all turned to look at the completed jigsaw in the corner of the room. Bill had kept hold of Nell's hand, allowed himself to be dragged over to inspect it more closely. '*Did she really do that by herself?*

Elsa had nodded, smiling, and something had churned in Annie's stomach. '*I gave her a tiny bit of help, but not much. I had a feeling she'd like it. I used to love jigsaws at her age.*'

Annie had not known whether the feeling pressing down heavily on her chest was pride in Nell's ability or envy that Elsa had been the one to discover it.

Now, a fortnight later, it is as though Nell has memorised all the pieces, where they go, how they fit together. There is no way, Annie knows, that Clare or Laura would have been able to manage it at a similar age.

'All done!'

Annie looks at the completed jigsaw and pulls Nell onto her lap, holds her close, breathes her in: the honeyscented shampoo from her newly washed hair; the cheese, bread and banana Nell had for lunch; the unidentifiable smell that Annie cannot name but which belongs uniquely to her daughter.

Nell rubs her eye with a balledup fist.

'Are you tired?' Annie glances at her watch, sees that it is almost half past one. 'Mummy's made you late for your nap, hasn't she? It's because we've been having such a nice time playing. Shall we take you upstairs?'

Nell rests her head against Annie's clavicle. Her cheek is warm and there is a weight to it that conveys a need for imminent sleep. Annie gets to her feet, carries Nell upstairs to her bedroom where she pulls down the blind, closes the curtains. She lays Nell down in her cot, covers her with a WinniethePooh blanket, a birthday gift from Pam and Alan, which has already become a favourite. Standing over the cot, smoothing fingers across her daughter's forehead, she is certain it will not be long before Nell drifts off to sleep.

'Sing a song, Mama.' Nell gazes up at her with bright blue eyes, a small triangle of light reflected in each of them from where the sun is sneaking in through a gap at the edge of the blackout blind.

'What song would you like?'

Nell stares up at the ceiling as though there is a songbook hidden in the coving. Her dark curls splay out on the white pillow like coiled pencil shavings on paper. In the silence, Annie can almost hear the cogs whirring in Nell's brain. 'Da sunshine song!'

Annie smiles. It is invariably Nell's choice. Annie has lost count of the times she has sung it over the past year. 'Okay, but you have to close your eyes.'

Nell dutifully scrunches her eyes shut, the skin on her nose crinkling. Annie begins to sing the chorus of 'You Are My Sunshine', lyrics she knows so well they are etched onto her memory. Her fingers brush gently across Nell's forehead as she repeats the same four lines over and over until Nell's eyelids relax, her breathing deepens.

Looking down at Nell sleeping, Annie knows she will never tire of this: watching Nell's eyelids flutter as she enters a parallel universe filled with stories of her own making. The way her lips part gradually, admitting a stream of air beneath the Cupid's bow of her top lip. The way her breaths lengthen incrementally, until they settle into a regular, hypnotic rhythm that Annie could listen to for hours. Even as she watches her now, she feels a stab of preemptive regret that one day in some distant, unknown future, when Nell is grown up, she will no longer be able to do this. Gazing down at her sleeping daughter, her chest fills with guilt that she had, once upon a time, struggled so much to love her.

Nell pivots onto her side, one arm tucked beneath her, the other bent at the elbow, her hand resting against her chin as if recreating Rodin's 'The Thinker'. Annie watches her flickering eyelids, wondering where her dreams are taking her.

It is unthinkable to her now, looking at Nell, that the first six months of her daughter's life were dominated by such different feelings. Such dangerous feelings. Those events in the months after Nell's birth are like a bad dream that Annie has no wish to remember. It never did anyone any good, she thinks, to dwell on the past. But occasionally, in moments when she is least expecting it, the memories will creep out of hiding and she will know that, for the time being at least, there is no way to be free of them.

She feels them now, inching out of the darkness, and knows that even if she were to leave the bedroom, the feelings would come with her. It is one thing she has learnt over the past two years: there is no escape from her guilt, however deeply she tries to bury it. Part of her wonders if it is some sort of punishment, her recompense for having failed to give Nell what she needed for the first six months of her life.

She remembers very little about the daytoday events of that time. Her memories are like an abstract painting: a swirl of emotions, a sensory impression. When she looks back now, she envisages a dark cloud descending on her, funnelling into her lungs, seeping through her skin and into her blood, like a phantom in a horror film. It is as though she had been inhabited by a golem that had taken control of her feelings, making her think things, say things that were out of her control. All those wild thoughts that had taken up residence in her brain. All those delusional feelings that had threatened to engulf her. All those impossible scenarios she had been so convinced were true.

Now, when she looks back, she can offer no explanation other than that she had been the victim of a temporary madness. Almost six months of her life – six months of Nell's life – in which she had not been in her right mind.

When she thinks back now to some of the outrageous things she had asserted, she cannot understand how she had ever believed them. They are to her now like a lingering faith in childhood fantasies about fairies, unicorns, Easter bunnies and Father Christmas: once so fervently believed in and yet nothing short of absurd. She looks down at Nell and guilt rests like a leaden weight in her chest that she had ever allowed such thoughts to overpower her.

It is almost five months since Dr Lewis weaned her off the antidepressants, and she has never felt better. It is as though she lost herself somewhere between Danny's death and Nell's birth and now, finally, she has found herself again.

For the past year and a half she has tried to be the mother Nell needs and deserves, has done everything she can to make up for those initial months of failure. Sometimes, though, she cannot help fearing what the effect on Nell may have been, cannot help worrying that there will be consequences, that something inside of Nell will be stunted forever like a sapling denied sufficient light and water.

The letterbox clatters and Annie freezes. She lifts her hand from Nell's forehead, holds her breath in her chest. If Nell wakes now she will not get back to sleep and the rest of the afternoon will be spoilt by tiredness. She does not move as Nell shifts onto her tummy, slides her arms at right angles to her head as if acquiescing to an arrest, and snuffles gently. Gradually her breaths deepen and Annie tiptoes out of the room, closes the door behind her and heads down the stairs.

On the front doormat she finds the culprit of the noise: this week's local newspaper. She picks it up and carries it into the kitchen to make herself a cup of tea. Her eyes scan the front page as she waits for the kettle to boil, a story about a local charity worker embezzling funds. With the tea made, she decides to allow herself five minutes on the sofa before getting on with tonight's chicken and leek pie. Settling down in the front room, she flicks through the newspaper, knowing she has at least an hour before Nell is likely to stir.

It is on the fifth page that she sees it. A photograph staring at her as if it is there just for her to see. She hears the sharp intake of her own breath and closes the paper, her heart thudding, telling herself that her eyes are playing tricks on her. Dr Lewis has warned her that things like this might happen: that she may be prone to occasional relapses, that the paranoid fantasies might try to take hold again. She breathes slowly, in and then out, reminding herself that she has been here before, that these ideas have poisoned her mind once before. She closes her eyes, tries to remember all the things Dr Lewis has told her, about how she has to resist the thoughts when they come knocking. About how seductive they can be, how persistent. How strenuously they will try to convince her that they are right and she is wrong. She tries to conjure up Dr Lewis's voice, to hear his sensible reassurances in her ear. It is not until she has rounded up the dangerous thoughts, put them in the box Dr Lewis has taught her to imagine, and turned the invisible key, that she dares open her eyes.

She knows that she should put the newspaper straight in the bin, that she should avoid the temptation. To look again would be to feed suspicions she does not want inside her head. Dr Lewis's voice is telling her to stand up, go out of the back door and into the garden, put the paper in the dustbin, thrust it down among the rotting vegetable peel and sodden tea bags so that she will not be tempted to look again. But something stops her. There is another voice, not louder than the first but more compelling, more insistent, telling her that she needs to look, just one more time, that she needs to check what she thinks she has seen. It is a clever voice, wily, trying to convince her that it only wants to reassure her that she was wrong. But she knows it is lying. She knows it does not really think she was wrong. She knows that it wants her to check because it wants to prove to her that the dark thoughts are right.

For a few moments she sits, immobile, listening to the two voices inside her head vying for attention. She knows what she should do – what Dr Lewis and Bill would want her to do – but the other voice is so seductive, so persuasive.

Before she has a chance to stop herself, she opens the newspaper again at the same page, her eyes drawn back to the photograph, to the hazel eyes staring out at her, as if challenging her to look away. But Annie does not look away. She cannot. It is as if her eyes are locked with those in the photograph, as though she and the photo are holding one another's gaze and she will never be able to tear herself away. She is aware of a uterine tug pulling deep within her, of the bad voice in her head saying *I told you so*. She stares at the picture and it stares back, and however much she tries to tell herself that her mind is playing tricks on her, that her grief is finding ways to harm her, she cannot convince herself that it is true. Certainty and doubt begin to slip in her mind until she can no longer tell one from the other.

She stares at the photograph, its image throbbing at her temples. A part of her brain is telling her that it cannot be so, that please God she has got it wrong. But then there is a second photograph and it is another onslaught, another confirmation of what she does not want to be true.

Her eyes move to the text beside the pictures, but the words swim in front of her and she cannot catch hold of them long enough for them to make any sense. She scrunches her eyes shut, counts to five, opens them again, and there it is, the headline, its bold, black letters shouting at her, telling her something she does not want to know, something she cannot bear to know, but it is there, in front of her, and she cannot unsee it. Her eyes sprint across line after line of the article beneath, darting from one paragraph to the next, every word a new assault, every sentence a fresh attack. She tries to breathe but something is lodged in her chest and she cannot fill her lungs.

And then she reaches the final line, and she reads it, and reads it again, and any hope that she might have been wrong drains out of her as if all the blood is being leached from her veins. The voice in her head telling her it is not true gets fainter and she does not encourage it back. She knows that she is looking at confirmation of the suspicions she harboured for such a long time, suspicions she has allowed herself to be convinced were false. But as she rereads that final line, as she looks at the main photograph, again and again, she knows that she was right all along. She has never been more certain of anything in her life.

Her stomach lurches and she runs to the kitchen, leans over the sink just as the muscles contract, retches into the stainless steel bowl, streaks of saliva hanging from her lips, and she grabs a piece of kitchen roll, wipes her mouth, but her stomach heaves, again and again, and every time she closes her eyes it is there in her mind, staring at her: the photograph that is squeezing her heart in its fist, an injury from which she knows she can never recover.

When there is nothing left in her stomach to purge, she ignores the bitter taste in her mouth, staggers back to the lounge, picks up the paper. There is still a part of her that thinks perhaps when she looks this time, it will be different, the face will have changed, and she will discover it was just a figment of her imagination. But when she looks at the photograph again, it is just as it was before. Panic grips her throat and she does not know how she will get through the next minute, the next hour, the next day. She does not know how it will be possible to go on.

She thinks about Bill and a hot fury surges through her veins. She told him. She *told* him. And he wouldn't listen. And now . . . Sharp, jagged breaths judder in and out of her body, and a chasm opens up inside her, a vast, empty space into which plummets everything she thought she knew, everything she has ever loved, trusted, understood.

She falls onto the sofa, wraps her arms across her body, tries to hold herself together even as she begins to fall apart.

And then she thinks about Nell upstairs, asleep in her cot, and her world tips onto a different axis, spins out of control. Her skin crawls with the terror of what will happen now. Scenarios race through her mind, each more appalling than the last. Panic throbs in her veins, both urging her to act and simultaneously paralysing her. She does not know what to do, where to turn, who to trust. The walls begin to close in on her and it is all she can do to curl into a foetal ball as a deep, primitive grief ruptures her heart.

NOW

Nell sits in the empty laboratory, staring at the piece of paper in her hand. She knows what it means, but cannot make sense of it. Her head spins, thoughts refusing to settle.

The corridor outside is silent: there will be no sign of her colleagues until tomorrow morning. She had known the lab would be empty on a Sunday afternoon, does not know if she is grateful for the silence or is being crushed beneath its weight.

She tries to swallow but her mouth is dry. Her head feels light, as though everything she has ever known has evaporated, and she closes her eyes, tries to grab hold of a thought long enough to discover where it leads, but it disappears as soon as she nears it, like a wisp of smoke that cannot be caught.

In her hand is a piece of paper with a collection of letters and numbers that to most people would look like nothing more than a random assembly of meaningless figures, but which to Nell is a sequence upending her entire life. A code that encapsulates her biological truth, which reveals the secret of where she comes from, to whom she belongs. To whom she does not belong.

It tells her that her mother is not her mother.

Her father is not her father.

It tells her that everything she thought she knew about herself – about her family, about her identity – is untrue.

In front of her, the numbers and letters stare at her in defiant black type, daring her to refute them. But she knows it is incontrovertible proof. These twentyfour loci tell her she is related to neither of the people she has spent the past thirtyfive years believing to be her parents. You cannot, she knows, argue with DNA.

Staring at the alphanumerics, the paper shaking in her hand, she has a sense of being untethered, like a heliumfilled balloon that has been cut free, with no idea where she is floating, where she may end up. There is just a profound sense of loneliness: a sudden, abrupt dislocation.

All the moisture seems to have evaporated from her mouth, and when she prises open her dry lips, she is aware of a small piece of skin pulling itself free, knows that it should sting but feels nothing.

She thinks, suddenly, of Clare and Laura, and her stomach churns at the realisation that they are not her sisters. They are no more her sisters than her colleagues at work. They are biological strangers, as separate from her genetically as each of the other seven billion people on the planet.

She leans forward, presses the heels of her hands against her eyes.

The shrill ringing of her mobile phone makes her jump and she scrabbles in her bag to find it, to stop the noise shrieking into the silence, betraying her unlawful presence, even though she knows there is no one here to find her. Laura's number flashes on the screen and she presses a finger to silence it, switches off the phone. She is not yet ready to speak to anyone, cannot imagine telling anyone what she knows: to do so would be to render it permanent, immutable.

Speculations hurtle through her mind like competitors in a race she has no desire to run. She thinks about the adoption leaflet tossed so carelessly on top of a cardboard box. She imagines her mum's grief after Danny's death, and the gaping hole he must have left behind. She wonders what levels of desperation her mum might have gone to for a third child, a replacement for the one who died, but the thought is too dangerous, like a hand hovering too close to a flame.

Sitting alone in the lab, she is unsure whether she wants to silence the clamouring thoughts and feelings or turn up their volume. She does not know if she dares unravel this tangled web of deception, whether she is brave enough to find her way back to the beginning.

Dusk turns into night, and night morphs into dawn, and it is only when she sees the break of day through the lab's glass windows that she realises it is morning, that she has passed the whole night there alone.

A part of her wants to drive straight to her parents' house, confront her mum, try to uncover the truth, whatever it may be. But another part of her is paralysed by the dread of what she may learn, wants to stay in this land of halfknowledge for as long as she can. And she cannot imagine that her mum, with her memory as it is, will be able to give her the answers she needs.

There is only one person, she realises, whom she wants to see, whom she dares to tell. And it is the thought of them that suddenly brings a new possibility into Nell's mind, one that has perhaps been there all night but which she is only now daring to look at. And as she thinks of confiding in them – as a new theory opens up in her thoughts – she does not know whether it is hope or fear that skitters across her skin. The suspicion is preposterous and yet, somehow, it seems to make sense.

Grabbing her phone from her bag and switching it on, she ignores the sequence of missed calls that greet her. Instead she taps out a single message, watches her finger hesitate before pressing down hard on the 'Send' button: *Can you go into work late this morning? There's something I really need to talk to you about.*

THEN

Annie watches the colour drain from Bill's face. He looks down at the newspaper, up at Annie, down again at the printed words. Such flimsy recycled paper, such cheap ink, and yet a story they cannot possibly erase from their lives now they both know it.

Her jaw is clenched so tightly it aches. The clock ticks loudly on the mantelpiece, hammering each second into the silence while, standing rigid behind the table, knuckles white where her hands are gripping the back of a dining chair, Annie waits for him to speak.

Bill looks at her and she sees the panic in his eyes, the shock studding his forehead. 'I . . . I don't understand . . . How can it . . . ?' His eyes scan her face, searching for answers.

Annie turns away, looks out of the window, folding her arms across her chest to conceal her trembling hands. She does not trust herself to speak, cannot guarantee that the cauldron of rage and anguish that has been bubbling inside her since she opened the newspaper will not erupt if she dares open her mouth. For the past few hours she has not known what to do with herself, has not known how to carry this Sisyphean boulder. There has been no room in her head for her thoughts to find sufficient space. All her feelings have been engulfed by a panic that is strangling her and yet she knows it is crucial she remains vigilant. She has survived the afternoon in a daze: making the girls' tea, chivvying them to complete their homework, getting them to bed. Now, with all the children asleep, and the newspaper finally in Bill's hands, she fears that if she were to try to speak, the only thing to emerge would be a primitive howl filled with grief, recrimination and the unshakeable knowledge that this can never be repaired.

It's your fault. This is all your doing. The words scream silently in her head but she does not let them out.

'It must just be a coincidence.' There is doubt in his tone and Annie is furious he is even entertaining the possibility.

'Look at it. *Look at it.* Are you really telling me that's a coincidence?' There is venom in her voice and she does not try to contain it.

'But . . . It doesn't make any sense.'

It takes all of Annie's selfrestraint not to pummel him with her fists. 'Look at the dates. I told you. I *told* you, but you wouldn't listen.' Her voice threatens to crack and she presses her lips together, stares down at the floor.

Neither of them speaks, the only sound the gurgle of water in the radiators where they are beginning to cool for the night.

'I'm sorry, Annie. I'm so sorry. I . . .' His voice breaks and she can feel the laceration of his grief, as though his heart has been gouged from his chest and all that is left is a gaping, open wound. But there is nothing she can do to alleviate his suffering, not when her own grief is so raw, so urgent, so allconsuming.

'What are we going to do?' Bill's voice bleeds alarm, and Annie does not want to hear it, cannot deal with his panic on top of her own. She hears him suck in a deep breath. 'We have to tell them.'

Annie stares at him for a moment in silent disbelief. 'Don't be ridiculous. We can't.' The words hiss from her lips, but beneath the ferocity she can hear the edge of desperation. She cannot let him do that. To confess would be to destroy her life not once but twice.

203

Bill lifts the newspaper, shakes it in her direction as if perhaps she has not yet understood what it says. 'We can't keep something like this a secret.'

Her hands ball into tight fists. After all she has been through, after all that has happened, it is preposterous, what he is suggesting. 'We have to.' Her voice is fierce, though with anger or fear she is not sure.

'Think about it, Annie. How would you feel if it was the other way around? We can't keep it to ourselves.'

The words are gluey in Annie's ears. She does not want to think about that, cannot bear to contemplate it. She can only think about what she has already been through, about what needs to happen next in order to protect her family. 'You know what'll happen if we say something. You can't want that. You *can't*.' Her body is shaking and she does not seem able to bring it under control.

Bill moves next to her, puts his hands on her arms. 'You're in shock. We both are. But we can't hold on to something like this. It's not right.'

Panic swells in Annie's chest. She swings her arms, shakes him off. She cannot bear for him to touch her, not when he is saying such things. 'What about what's right for our family? What about what's right for me?' Her voice begins to fracture and she clamps shut her jaw, will not let her vulnerability roam free.

'So what are you suggesting? We just carry on as if nothing's happened?'

Exasperation leaks from Bill's voice and Annie turns away, does not trust the fury boiling in her veins not to scorch them both. 'We'll have to move.'

There is a heartbeat of silence. 'Move house? We can't. Where would we go?'

Anywhere, Annie thinks. *Anywhere as far away from here as possible.*

'What about my business? And the girls? And school? We can't just up sticks. You're not thinking straight.'

It's the girls we'd be doing it for, Annie thinks. *How can you not see that?*

'Please, Annie. I know you're angry with me. But don't you think my heart's broken too? Don't you think I'm in pieces as much as you?' She hears the splinter in his voice but still cannot turn to face him.

There is a cry from the baby monitor and the sound is like a jolt of electricity running across Annie's skin.

'I'll go.'

Annie whips her ahead around. 'No. I'll go. You stay there.' She glares at Bill, gripped by an overwhelming physical urge to see Nell, to hold her. Bill opens his mouth to speak and then closes it again, tears pooling in his eyes and slipping down his cheeks. Annie cannot bear to see it, turns away, heads out of the room and towards the stairs.

She finds Nell standing in her cot, fingers clutching the white wooden bars, cheeks red with indignation at having to wait for half a minute. Annie lifts her into the air, balances her on her hip, holds her close. She rests her lips against Nell's head, breathes her in, makes soothing noises until her cries have quietened. And as she stands in the darkness, cleaving Nell to her body, she knows she will never give in to what Bill is suggesting. Whatever happens, whatever it takes, she will protect Nell, keep her close at all times. She will keep her safe from impossible truths none of them should ever have had to bear.

NOW

Nell sits at Elsa's kitchen table, wonders if it is only she who can hear the thudding of her heart.

'What's wrong? What's happened?'

Nell looks at Elsa, searches in her expression for the answer she is seeking, does not know whether it is there, in front of her, or whether she is inventing an explanation simply because she wants it to be true.

'You can tell me, whatever it is.'

Nell shakes her head, does not think there are any words to convey what she needs to ask. She looks out of the bifold doors, onto the garden where she spent so many hours as a child helping Elsa pot bedding plants, build the rockery, tend the herb garden. It was at this table that she had completed endless practice papers for the elevenplus, to this house she had come to discuss her desire to apply to Oxbridge. So many times she has relied on Elsa's support, judgement, advice, and every time Elsa has given it without question. It is only now, knowing what she knows, that Nell wonders why Elsa may have done that, why she has always been there for her. Because it doesn't make sense to her that a woman she knows only by virtue of being her father's business partner should have taken such an interest in her all these years.

'Nell, please. Is it something to do with your mum?'

There is no simple way to answer the question. It is everything to do with her mum and yet so much more.

Tendrils of memory weave through her mind. She remembers sitting on her bed, the door ajar, her parents' hushed conversation from the sitting room below just audible if she held her breath so as not to make a sound.

'*I don't like her going there all the time. Why can't she do her homework here?*'

'*Because she likes going to Elsa's. Honestly, love, I can't see the harm in it.*'

'*Can't you? Really?*'

'*Nothing's going to happen—*'

'*You can say that for certain, can you? Just like you were so certain in the hospital that day.*'

'*Annie—*'

'*No. I don't like Nell going there and nothing you say is going to change my mind.*'

The conversation returns to her as clearly as if it were taking place right now in the room next door. And yet, in spite of her mum's reservations, she had continued to visit Elsa, had continued to treat Elsa's house as her second home, right up until she went to university. Many times since leaving home she has visited Elsa in Dulwich without travelling the extra five miles to see her parents in the same trip.

She looks across to Elsa, at the loose white tshirt and skinny jeans, at the makeshift bun and delicate features, studies Elsa's face, trying to find her own reflection in it, wonders if a resemblance is just in her imagination.

The seconds tick by loudly in her ears but still language fails her. She knows she cannot sit here in silence forever, but to voice her suspicions is to open the door onto a foreign land without any idea what she might find.

'Would it help if I made some tea?'

Nell shakes her head. She does not want Elsa bustling around the kitchen. She needs quiet in order to hear her thoughts.

And then, suddenly, the words are there and she knows, as soon as they emerge, that once she has said them she can never take them back. 'Are you my mum?'

There is a moment's silence into which tumble a thousand permutations of what may happen next.

'What?'

Nell cannot tell whether it is shock or fear creasing Elsa's forehead.

'Nell, what made you ask that?'

She does not know where to begin. Whether to start at the end with the DNA test and its unequivocal proof. Or whether she should start further back, with the interest Elsa has taken in her for as long as Nell can remember. Or if she should start somewhere else entirely, somewhere in the middle, though she is not sure where that might be. 'Please, Elsa, I need to know. Are you my mum?'

Elsa reaches across the table, takes hold of Nell's hand. The seconds lengthen and stretch as though they are in no hurry for a response, and into the space between them falls all the possible versions of the truth Nell fears may never be uncovered.

'No, sweetheart, of course I'm not. Annie's your mum. What's going on?'

Something empties in Nell's chest and she feels as though all the atoms from which she is made are drifting into the ether and will never be conjoined again. It is such a profound feeling of loneliness that tears begin rolling down her cheeks, and then Elsa is sitting by her side, wrapping her arms round her, rocking her gently back and forth.

She does not know how long she sits there, in Elsa's arms, letting the confusion and uncertainty pour out of her, does not know whether it is disappointment or despair that is making her cry. But it is only when she has regained her breath that she is finally able to tell Elsa the whole story: all the things she has found, all the things she has heard, the DNA test with its conclusive proof.

Elsa says nothing for a moment, the silence charged with a thousand unanswered questions. 'You're absolutely sure it couldn't be a mistake?'

The facts churn in Nell's stomach. 'There's no way. I did the test myself.'

'But I don't understand. I saw your mum throughout her pregnancy with you. I saw her a few days before she went into hospital. She *looked* pregnant.'

Speculations turn in Nell's head like acrobats on a highwire but she cannot make sense of any of them, does not have any explanations to offer.

'I just can't believe it. I can't imagine Bill and Annie keeping something like that from you all these years.' Elsa speaks quickly, as though her words understand how difficult it is for Nell to hear them.

Nell wipes a tissue across her damp cheeks. 'Dad really never said anything to you – about me not being theirs?'

Elsa shakes her head. 'Honestly, I'd tell you if he had, I promise. He never even hinted at it. I'm so sorry, Nell. You must be in terrible shock.' She takes hold of Nell's hand, clasps it tightly, as if in doing so she might be able to hold Nell together. 'But . . . what made you think I might be your mum?'

Heat bleeds into Nell's cheeks. It is only now, hearing Elsa say it aloud, that she recognises what a childish fantasy it is. 'I don't know. I suppose I just thought . . . You've always been so good to me, like a second mum. I couldn't understand why you'd do that if you're not related to me.'

Elsa pauses and it is as if Nell can hear her turning the question over in her mind, considering it from different angles, wondering how best to answer. 'You know what kind of an upbringing I had. I learnt a long time ago that the people you're related to by blood aren't always those you're closest to. Sometimes you have to find your own version of love, your own version of family. I worked with Bill my whole adult life. I've known you since you were born. I may not be your mum but that doesn't mean I can't have maternal feelings towards you. I've always thought of you and Bill as family. Better, actually – at least I got to choose you.' Elsa smiles, squeezes Nell's hand.

Nell crumples the sodden tissue into a ball. 'Can I ask you something?' The question revolves around her mind, testing whether it is appropriate to ask. 'Why didn't you ever get married, have children of your own?' The memory of her mum's cycle of criticism over the years echoes inside Nell's head. '*Elsa's an odd one. It's not normal, wanting to live on your own like she does.*'

Elsa stands up, fills the kettle, pulls a pair of matching V&A mugs from the pale blue cupboard next to the sink. 'I just never felt the urge. I'd worked so hard to be independent, I suppose I didn't want to give it up. Or maybe I was scared of imposing my will on another person the way my parents had on me.' She picks some mint leaves from a plant on the windowsill, drops them into a transparent teapot.

Nell thinks about her own childhood, about the woman she has spent her life calling Mum. She knows she should be at the nursing home this morning, should be helping her mum move in, but she is not yet ready to face her. 'Do you know why my mum never liked me spending time with you?' The question springs from her lips before she has a chance to stop it.

'I honestly don't.' The kettle boils and Elsa pours hot water into the teapot, watches it turn green. 'I'd always assumed it was because of what happened with Danny, that it made her overprotective of you. But now . . . If she's not your biological mother, maybe that's more of an explanation.' She brings the mugs and the teapot to the table, places them down on coasters on its wooden surface. 'If you were adopted – although I still don't understand how that could have happened, because your mum was definitely pregnant – maybe that's why she felt threatened by other people getting close to you.' She pours a steady stream of mint tea first into Nell's cup, then her own. 'I should have backed off really. But Bill always encouraged it, and I suppose . . . I was being selfish. I enjoyed your company too much to discourage you, and—' Elsa stops abruptly as though a voice in her ear has told her to shush. There is a pause while she studies Nell's face, as if searching for the solution to a quandary. 'I think perhaps I thought I could see a bit of myself in you.'

'In what way?'

Elsa wraps her hands around her mug, and Nell notices the series of calluses across the tops of her knuckles. 'I know our situations are very different, but my parents had a fixed idea of what they wanted me to be and they were desperate to keep me close to them, close to home. I always got the sense that your mum was similar in some way, that she was scared of you spreading your wings and finding your own path, especially if that took you away from her. I haven't really thought about it before, but maybe I didn't want you having your wings clipped in the way that my parents had tried to clip mine.'

Nell is not able to speak for a moment. For years she has not wanted to acknowledge the ramifications of her mum's overprotection. Now, for the first time, someone else is suggesting that perhaps her mum has never felt entirely comfortable with the path Nell has chosen for herself.

Elsa reaches across the smooth grain of the wooden table, takes Nell's hand. 'I'm sorry. The last thing I want is to upset you any more.'

'You haven't, honestly. It's just . . . I don't know what I'm supposed to do with all of this.'

Elsa leans forward and when she begins to speak, there is a soft urgency to her voice. 'You know how much Bill and Annie have always loved you. Whatever the DNA test says, nothing changes that. No parent is perfect, biological or otherwise, but never doubt how much they loved you. You need to talk to your mum. It's the only thing you can do.'

Nell sips her mint tea, wishing it would soothe away the lump in her throat. 'I can't. She doesn't even know who I am half the time.'

'You have to try, for your own peace of mind as much as anything.'

Nell looks out into the garden, at the wooden bench against the fence at the far end of the lawn that catches the early evening sun. The bench on which she spent so many childhood afternoons drinking lemonade with Elsa, has spent so many adult evenings sharing a bottle of wine. She knows Elsa is right. She cannot ask her sisters. For all she knows they are as much in the dark as she is, and it is not fair to load this burden onto them. Her mum is the only person who might be able to tell her the truth.

Finishing her tea, she hugs Elsa goodbye, promises to call her later. Getting back into her car, she tries to picture how the next few hours will play out, but her imagination fails her: she cannot see beyond the moment of coming face to face with her mum. There is still so much she doesn't know and, even now, as she switches on the ignition and pulls away, she cannot envisage how she might feel when she finds out.

THEN

For the past four weeks, Annie has barely dared leave the house. Instead she has stayed indoors with Nell, playing games, doing jigsaws, baking cakes. Both Pam and Denise have been fobbed off on the telephone with excuses of colds, headaches, bad nights' sleep. Twice she has even pretended to be out when Pam has called round, has held a finger to her lips to signal the need for silence to Nell, has pretended it is all just a game. But it is not a game. The situation they find themselves in could not be further from a game.

And all this time, she and Bill have been engaged in a silent war of attrition. The discovery has lodged itself between them like a pile of rubble neither of them have the power, or perhaps the inclination, to shift. There have been moments when Bill has taken hold of Annie's hand, implored her in an urgent whisper to think again about what she is doing, but each time Annie has shaken him off, told him it is not up for discussion. She is aware that as more time passes, the legitimacy of her argument grows, and she has no intention of giving him the upper hand. And she knows, deep down, that Bill hates the thought of what he is advocating almost as much as she does, even if he has always been one to do things by the rules. But there are no rules for the nightmare in which they find themselves. There is no obvious precedent for what is happening. All they can do is improvise.

The house is empty save for Nell, sitting on the floor building towers from her coloured plastic blocks. Laura has cookery club after school and Clare is at a friend's house supposedly revising for her exams but Annie suspects there is very little revision actually taking place.

Nell cries out in dismay as the tower she has been building topples towards her. Annie knows the blocks are harmless, that Nell's reaction is one of disappointment rather than pain, but she scoops her into her arms nonetheless. 'You're okay, little one. Mummy'll kiss it better.'

Nell rubs the place on her knee where the blocks landed, looks at her hand, and then turns towards Annie, smiling triumphantly. 'All gone!' She shows her palm to Annie as if it holds evidence of the pain she has rubbed away.

A surge of love sweeps through Annie and she hugs Nell tightly as if trying to fuse their bodies together. *I will never allow any harm to come to you, whatever it takes*. The words repeat in her head like a silent invocation. There is no one she will allow to come between her and Nell. It is fierce, this love she has for her daughter: protective, visceral, acute.

Taking hold of Nell's hand, she studies each of the four fingers and thumb in turn, marvelling at the perfect pale nails, the miniature pink halfmoons, the softness of her skin. She lifts Nell's hand to her lips, kisses the tips of her fingers, and there is a split second when she envisages a parallel world in which there is a different woman holding Nell, a different house in which this scene is taking place. She shuts her eyes, tries to squeeze the image out of her mind, but she knows it will come back to haunt her. Over the past few weeks her dreams have become painfully vivid and there is no respite from her worst imaginings.

'Make a castle with me, Mama!' Nell scrambles out of Annie's arms and back to her plastic blocks, out of which she begins to construct a sixstorey square with coloursymmetrical towers at each corner. Annie watches her in wonder, knowing that every parent believes their child to be special, but wondering in this case whether it might actually be true.

A key turns in the front door and Annie looks around to see Bill walking into the hall. Nell greets him with delight as Annie glances up at the clock: it is just gone a quarter to five, ninety minutes before he would usually return from work. Annie is aware of her pulse racing, of the tension that has been building between them pulling taut in her chest, and she holds her breath, braces herself for the news she is dreading. She cannot bear it, if it is to be so.

Bill lowers himself onto the sofa and she senses it immediately: his air of urgency. A part of her wants to get it over with quickly, like the swift ripping of a plaster, but another part wants him to stay silent, to allow her the fantasy that it will all be okay. Her head feels light, as though she has been placed suddenly at too high an altitude, and she is aware of her heart drumming beneath her ribs.

'They're leaving. They're moving away.'

The words swim in Annie's ears like darting minnows that refuse to be caught.

'Did you hear me? They're going.'

She looks at him, searching in his eyes for any hint that she has misunderstood. 'How do you know?' Her voice is barely more than a whisper. She does not yet trust what she has heard, does not dare believe what he is saying.

There is a fractional twitch of Bill's left eyebrow, a sign Annie knows too well to ignore. 'What is it? What aren't you telling me?'

Bill shakes his head and panic grips at Annie's wrists. 'What did you do?'

He looks across at her and she sees it immediately: the guilt in his eyes. 'I just wanted to see where they lived . . .'

He does not need to finish the sentence for her to understand. 'What happened?' Her voice is low, calm, nothing to betray the torrent raging inside her.

'I was just going to drive past. But then . . .' He lowers his head into his hands. 'I saw a For Sale sign outside and I . . . I just needed to see it for myself.'

Blood throbs at Annie's temples. 'You went inside?'

Bill nods. 'I'm sorry. But it was fine, nothing happened. They weren't even home. The estate agent told me they'd already accepted an offer, he was just doing a few more viewings to see if he could get them a higher one.'

Annie seems to hear and not hear at the same time. There is so much she wants to ask but does not dare. She wants to know what it felt like, stepping over that threshold, entering a space when he knew what a risk it posed. She wants to know what it was like walking through their belongings, brushing past their sofa, their dining table, the edges of their duvet. She wants to know if there were photographs on the mantelpiece, whether he has committed details of them to memory, so that one day he will be able to describe them to her as if she were seeing them for herself. She wants to know what hung on the walls, what rugs were on the floor, what toys were on the shelves. She wants to know if it felt like a happy home, whether it had once been filled with love, laughter, joy, care. But even as the questions bolt through her mind, she knows she cannot ask them. They are too painful, too raw. To ask would be to open the floodgates on thoughts and speculations she knows – for the sake of her sanity, for the sake of Nell playing on the carpet beside her – she must keep locked away.

'The agent told me they'd taken the first offer they got. They just want to be gone.'

Annie cannot find any words to respond. There is the fury that he has been so foolish, that he has taken such a risk, has put all of their futures in jeopardy. There is the envy that he has been there, that he has seen with his own eyes things she knows she will never be permitted to see. There is the relief that they are leaving, that they will soon be gone. Thoughts trip over one another inside her head as she tries to decipher what she is feeling. 'So it's over?' Her voice is small, as though it fears jinxing the answer.

Bill looks across at Annie with a pained expression. 'It won't ever be over.'

Annie tries to steady her voice. 'No one ever needs to know.'

'*We'll* know. We'll always know. Do you really think we can live with that?'

Annie looks across to where Nell is placing an extra block on each corner of her castle. There is so much she has had to bear in the past three and a half years, so much shock and trauma and heartbreak, and yet she has survived. There is only one thing now she could not endure.

'There are things I want to ask them. Things I want to know. You must have them too?'

Annie does not answer. She cannot believe he is even asking her. There is a gulf of longing where her knowledge should be. But she is aware that all the questions in the world would not fill the gaping hole inside her, would not repair the loss. What has been broken cannot be fixed with questions and answers. And in order to ask them, she would have to give up the one thing she won't ever surrender.

'This isn't just about you. What about how I feel? Don't I get a say?'

Annie jerks her head towards him. 'You had your chance for a say two years ago and you did nothing. You said nothing. So, no, you don't get a say now.' Heat blazes her cheeks. 'I'll never forgive you if you say anything now. I mean it. If you tell them, we'll lose everything.' She scoops Nell into her arms, carries her out of the room and up the stairs in spite of Nell's protestations at being removed from her game. Walking into the bedroom, she slams the door behind her, slumps onto the edge of the double bed, lets Nell go free beside her.

The others are moving away. She and Bill should be united in their relief. She doesn't understand why he is not more pleased, why he insists on making things more difficult than they need to be.

They are moving away. It is the only thing she needs to focus on. She watches Nell bounce up and down on the bed, waiting to be told off, hesitant when no remonstration is forthcoming.

They are moving away. There is no need for anyone ever to find out. Annie forces her lips into a smile as she takes hold of Nell's hands, helps her to bounce higher, blinking back the tears as she watches her daughter squeal with delight.

NOW

It is late afternoon by the time she pulls into the car park of the care home. She has spent the day deferring this moment – walking through Dulwich Park, wandering around the picture gallery, browsing the bookshop, all while she should have been at work – but now she is here and she knows she cannot postpone the conversation any longer.

The care home smells of overcooked vegetables and regurgitated air. A member of staff directs her to a door at the end of the corridor.

'Have you spoken to Laura today?' The care assistant speaks with an easy familiarity although Nell has never met her before. She is young – early twenties, Nell guesses – with an Eastern European slant to her voice, and Nell wonders what – or whom – she has left behind in order to come here. 'You've only just missed her. Your mum has been quite agitated since she arrived. We find it happens a lot with dementia patients – the move unsettles them and they often get worse for a few days. Don't be surprised if she seems more confused than usual.'

Nell nods, relieved to discover that Laura has already left. She does not know what she would have said had they seen each other.

They arrive at a white glosspainted door onto which is screwed a small, square metal frame. A piece of paper has been slipped inside, typed with her mum's name, and Nell wonders how often they get changed, how often these rooms are vacated.

She thanks the care assistant and waits until the young woman has reached the end of the corridor before raising a hand and knocking.

When there is no answer, she twists the handle and opens the door.

Her mum is sitting in a floral armchair wedged between a narrow single bed and the wall, does not turn her head from where she is looking out of the thirdfloor window as Nell steps inside, closes the door behind her.

The room is smaller than Nell had anticipated. Aside from the bed and the armchair, the sole piece of furniture is a pine chest of drawers, above which hangs a television, its screen a mute, black rectangle. An open internal door reveals a bathroom just big enough to turn around in.

In the armchair, her mum fiddles with the clasp of her gold watch. Click, snap, click, snap.

'Mum?' The moniker feels strange on Nell's tongue, simultaneously familiar and fraudulent. 'Can I talk to you about something?'

Her mum does not look up.

Nell walks towards her, sits on the edge of the bed, keeps her voice low. 'Can I ask you a few things, about when I was little?' The question is deliberately vague but Nell does not know how to be more specific without sending shockwaves through them both.

Her mum continues to stare out of the window where the early evening sun is reflected in the windows of the flats next door.

'I just want to find out . . .' Nell's voice trails off and she cannot summon the courage to chase it back.

Her mum turns to her and the vacant expression vanishes, replaced by fear and horror. 'What are you doing here? You can't take my baby away, I won't let you.' She begins to whimper under her breath, knitting her fingers together, grinding her knuckles with such force Nell fears she may hurt herself.

'It's only me, Mum. It's Nell. There's nothing to be scared of. Nobody's taking your baby away.'

Nell reaches for her hand but her mum yanks it free, holds it tight inside the other, fixes Nell with an expression she has never seen before: something between ferocity and terror. 'Leave me alone. Leave us all alone. I won't let you have her. Nell's mine.'

An icy draught tiptoes along Nell's spine, spreads out across her ribs. 'Who's trying to take Nell away from you?'

'You won't get away with it. I won't let you.'

Nell feels her body tense. She waits for her mum to say more, but her lips are pursed and Nell pushes gently into the silence, trying to keep her voice neutral. 'Who do you think I am?'

Her mum shrinks away, folds her body against the wooden armrest of the chair, her face an expression of abject horror. 'I know who you are. Just go away and leave us all alone.'

There is panic in her voice and Nell wonders if she should leave, if she should summon one of the care assistants, seek help in calming her mum down. But it feels as though something is edging its way over the horizon and only if she is patient enough will she witness what it is. 'Who am I? What's my name?'

Her mum's face begins to crumble. 'Please, I'm begging you, don't do this. It was a mistake, I knew it was a mistake, but nobody would listen.'

Nell's heart is racing but she manages to keep her voice calm. 'I believe you. I'm listening. Tell me who I am, and then we can talk it all through, okay?'

There is a split second of silence, speculations spiralling in the void. And then her mum stares at her, eyes filling with tears. 'You're Jane Whitworth. You've come to take Nell away. You can't have her. Please don't take her.'

Nell leans forward, takes hold of her mum's hand. 'Nobody's going to take Nell away, I promise. Why do you think someone wants to take her from you?' She waits for an answer but her mum is sobbing gently, tears falling from her bowed head onto the pale blue cotton of her trousers, darkened circles expanding on the material where they fall. 'Who is she? Who's Jane Whitworth?'

Her mum begins to murmur under her breath, words Nell cannot decipher, and the events of the past seventytwo hours throb inside Nell's head. There is a part of her that wishes she could rewind the clock to the time before her dad had given her any cause for suspicion. But she knows, deep down, watching her mum pull a tissue from the sleeve of her cardigan, watching her wipe the tears from her cheeks, that somehow it has always been there, lurking in the basement of her family history: the awareness that she has been treated differently from her sisters, the sense that her mum's overprotection of her was excessive.

A minute passes, and then another, while Nell tries to order the chaos of her thoughts, and her mum cries quietly in the armchair.

And then the idea comes to her and she pulls her phone from her bag, opens Google, types in the name her mum has just mentioned. In less than a second, there is a long list of Jane Whitworths on her screen. Her finger scrolls down, wondering if there is any chance that one of them might be the Jane Whitworth to whom her mum is referring. And then she reaches a horizontal line of images – a random collection of faces united by their name – and it is as she scrolls sideways, reaches the fourth picture, that she feels her breath catch in her throat.

She stares at the photograph, thinking her eyes must be playing tricks on her. With her finger and thumb she increases the size of the picture, but it loses definition in the expansion, the features becoming grainy, pixelated. She clicks on the photo and the page it redirects her to causes her head to spin as though she has just stepped off a rollercoaster.

It is a webpage for a Cambridge University college, belonging to a professor in Evolutionary Biology. The photograph is bigger here and Nell's eyes devour it, one half of her brain telling her that she is mistaken, that she is deluding herself, that it is nothing more than a symptom of her emotional disarray. But as her eyes stare at the picture, she cannot silence the voice in her head highlighting the contour of the eyebrows, the delicate point of the chin, the slender nose. There is even a tiny mole to the right of her lips and Nell instinctively raises her hand, feels her own mole in an identical position, as if to check it is there, to check it is not just a figment of her imagination.

Her eyes scan the text, taking in the short precis of Jane Whitworth's career: a career spent mostly at Cambridge bar a brief stint at Imperial. She opens a new page, types *Professor Jane Whitworth Cambridge* and clicks on the 'Images' tab. Dozens of photographs greet her of the same face in a variety of settings: in front of a lectern, sitting on a stage, against a bookcase, at the front of a lecture hall, shaking the hand of a student in a graduation cap, standing on the Mathematical Bridge over the Cam, leaning against a backdrop of leaded light windows and pale red brickwork. Dozens and dozens of photographs.

Nell closes her eyes, imploring them not to fool her into thinking there is something where in fact there is nothing. But when she opens them again, it is there, in every photo she clicks on: a clear echo of her own reflection.

Next to her, her mum continues to murmur quietly. Nell's head reels and it is as though a part of her is in a parallel world, hurtling forward in time, to a point at which she is being told the end of the story, but the rest of her cannot catch up, however fast her mind sprints. 'Mum, who is this?'

She holds her phone face out. Annie looks at the photograph and turns away quickly, shaking her head, fresh tears weaving across her corrugated skin. 'It wasn't my fault. I told them and they wouldn't listen. Nobody would believe me.'

Nell keeps her eyes trained on her mum and for the briefest moment thinks there might be a spark of recognition. But then it vanishes, as quickly as it had arrived, and in her mum's face, a curtain is pulled shut. The light behind her eyes fades and her features take on the distant expression that Nell has seen so many times over the past few weeks. Sitting by her side, she watches her mum disappear into a labyrinth of memories, knowing there is no way for her to follow.

THEN

Annie halfopens her eyes and squints into the bright light streaming through the curtainless windows. It is the noises that have woken her: a man, whistling; crockery rattling; wheels squeaking. From somewhere in the middle distance she can hear female voices in conversation, a pop song playing on the radio, a baby crying.

Her eyes snap fully open. A baby is crying. She tries to pull herself into a sitting position but a burst of pain shoots through her lower abdomen, so intense it almost makes her retch. Slowly, tentatively, she lifts herself onto her elbows, drags her body along the stiff white hospital sheets, until the small of her back is resting on the two firm pillows, her head against the metal bed frame.

She turns to reach for the orange cord with a buzzer attached to the end, but another searing pain tears through her stomach. She has never known agony like it, has not been warned that it could feel like this. It crosses her mind that perhaps something has gone wrong, perhaps there has been a rupture during the night of which she is not yet aware. Gingerly, she lifts the sheet, inch by inch, half expecting to see a pool of blood. But there is nothing. Making a discreet tent around herself, she tugs at the hem of her nightie, pulls it up over her thighs, bunches it beneath her breasts. And there it is: the thick strip of bandage just above the line of her pubic hair.

No blood, no oozing fluids, nothing to suggest the wound isn't as it should be.

Gritting her teeth, she swivels onto her side, breathes against the blistering spasms, manages to press the buzzer.

Easing her head back onto the pillows, she looks around the ward at the five other beds. In four of them, women are sitting up, babies in their arms, smiling rapturously in spite of the rings under their eyes, the unbrushed hair, the makeupfree faces. The bed opposite Annie is empty though she is sure it had been occupied when she had arrived on the ward the previous evening. Annie does not know exactly how long she has been sleeping: only that dusk had yet to fall as she had closed her eyes, and now morning seems to be in full swing. She has never had a general anaesthetic before, had not realised that it would make her feel so groggy.

The two women in beds either side of Annie are engrossed in bottlefeeding their babies. The woman in the far corner is cradling her child, seemingly oblivious to the clatter of noise coming from the corridor outside. The final woman is breastfeeding, running her fingers across her baby's head as it sucks at her nipple.

Annie's own breasts ache in response, hormones making them feel twice their usual size. Her eyes find the clock on the wall and a wave of panic cascades through her: it is just gone a quarter past eight. The liquid morphine one of the midwives gave her when she arrived on the ward yesterday afternoon – fighting back tears springing from the pain of her emergency Csection – must have knocked her out cold.

With all the strength she can muster, she leans over and presses the buzzer again, experiences a visceral need to be reunited with her baby.

'What's all this? You only need to ring once.' A midwife in her fifties with a lilting Scottish accent and plump rolls of flesh around her arms smiles kindly at her. Her voice reminds Annie of Elsa but that is where the similarity ends. 'How are you feeling? I heard your little one made quite the dramatic entrance yesterday. But you'll both be as right as rain in no time.'

Annie scratches her skin, feels as though dozens of microscopic insects are crawling across her flesh. She watches a deep red rash bloom on her arm, streaks of white rising up like miniature mountains.

'That's quite normal, for your skin to itch after a blood transfusion. We can give you some antihistamine if it gets any worse.'

It is only when the midwife says it that Annie remembers. The blood cascading out of her. The surgeon's latex gloves turning from white to red. The scarlet pool seeping across the theatre floor. She remembers it spattering onto the surgeon's shoes, and wanting to apologise for having caused such a mess, but her head had been emptying, the words floating away from her before she could grab hold of them. She remembers the second cannula, in the back of her left hand, the doctor telling her that they were going to have to put her to sleep to find the cause of the bleeding. She recalls someone calling for a nurse to fetch a pack of blood and the anaesthetist telling her to count backwards from ten.

'You might have a bit of a headache too. Nothing that a couple of paracetamol won't fix. Just let me know if you need some?'

Annie nods, but it is not her head or her skin or even the wound across her stomach that is preoccupying her. 'How's Nell? Is she okay?'

The midwife places a hand on Annie's arm. 'She's fine. Her breathing's completely stabilised. Nothing to be concerned about at all. She's been kicking away since I came on my shift this morning. Think you've got a lively one there.'

Relief washes over Annie. 'Can I see her?'

The midwife smiles. 'I'll get her and bring her to you now, okay?'

As the midwife walks back out of the room, Annie lifts herself higher onto the pillows, ignoring the pain where she was sliced open and stitched up again less than twentyfour hours earlier. She manages to sit up, buoyed by the prospect of seeing her baby girl, whom she held for only a matter of minutes before breathing complications meant that Nell was whisked away to the special care baby unit, before Annie's haemorrhage turned the operating theatre into a place of drama.

The midwife returns, cradling a bundle swaddled in a white crochet hospital blanket. 'She's a beauty.' She places the baby in Annie's arms, stands back, grins at them both.

Annie looks down at the swaddled infant in her arms, only the child's face and hairline showing. There is a moment's dislocation, Annie's stomach somersaulting as if she has just driven very fast over a large hump in the road. She looks up at the midwife and down again at the baby, and this time she is sure. 'This isn't my baby.'

'Don't be silly. Of course it is.'

Annie looks down again at the child, doubting herself in the face of the midwife's certainty. But still the feeling churns in her stomach. 'No, it's not. She's not mine.'

The midwife's smile flattens into a horizontal line and she sighs as though she cannot believe her day is getting off to such an irritating start. She leans forward, unwraps the blanket, frees the baby's leg and lifts her glasses onto her nose from the string around her neck. She reads the plastic label around the baby's ankle, turns back to Annie, eyebrows raised. 'Look, there, you see: Baby Hardy. Born March third.' The smile returns to the midwife's voice, as though the awkwardness of an embarrassing mistake has been successfully avoided.

Annie fingers the plastic tag around the baby's ankle. It is secured by a metal popper which, singlehanded, she manages to release and then fasten again.

She studies the baby's face. It is a pretty baby – wide blue eyes staring up at her, a delicate nose, a smattering of dark hair pressed against her scalp – but it is not her baby. She closes her eyes, pictures the real Nell in her arms when she had held her yesterday. Her baby's hair is lighter, just like Clare's and Laura's was when they were born. Her lips are not so full as this child's, with its pronounced Cupid's bow: her baby's top lip had protruded slightly over the bottom and Annie remembers it so clearly because it had reminded her of an old blackandwhite photograph of her own mum – Nell's maternal grandmother – from when she was a toddler. It is a top lip both Clare and Laura have inherited. A top lip Danny had inherited too.

She looks up again at the midwife, holds out her arms, offers the baby back to her. 'She's not mine. I know my baby. That's not her.'

The midwife tuts, a ridge of frustration pleating across her forehead. She glides Annie's arms gently back, pushes the baby closer to Annie's chest until their bodies are touching. 'Now, come on, let's not have any hysterics. You've had a very traumatic time. It's no surprise you're feeling a bit strange. Happens to lots of mothers for a few days, especially when they've been through a difficult labour. Why don't we try breastfeeding little Nell? She's had some formula already, but I bet she can't wait to have a feed from Mum.'

The midwife's hand is still on Annie's arm and it feels heavy, oppressive. Annie's heart begins to accelerate – a gentle trot at first, and then a canter – and she swallows hard, can feel the alarm creeping into her voice. 'Really, you have to believe me. This isn't my baby. My baby has hazel eyes. This baby's eyes are blue. I'm not going to breastfeed a baby that isn't mine.'

For a few seconds there is silence, the midwife studying Annie as though she is a specimen in a curio cabinet. 'Mrs Hardy, you've had a difficult birth, and it's understandable that you might be feeling a bit confused today. You barely saw little Nell yesterday before they had to give you a general anaesthetic, did you?' It is a rhetorical question, Annie knows, designed to prove a point. 'It can sometimes be a bit more difficult, bonding with a baby, when you've been separated at the outset. But trust me: give it an hour or so with little Nell and I promise you'll feel much better.' She smiles again but the warmth has vanished from her eyes.

Annie shakes her head, blood throbbing in her ears. 'This isn't Nell.'

The midwife hesitates. And then she takes the baby from Annie's arms, and there is a rush of relief that the midwife believes her. But when Annie looks up, the midwife has cocked her head to one side, is nodding towards the door. 'Okay. If this baby isn't yours, why don't we go to the special care baby unit, and you can tell me which one is.'

Annie stares at her, wondering if the midwife really means for her to get out of bed and walk along the corridor or whether it is a test, to see how much Annie believes what she is saying. It seems to have become a battle of wills, this conversation, and Annie does not want a battle. She doesn't have the strength for a battle. All she wants is her baby.

The midwife does not blink, and then she steps towards Annie again, holds out her arms to give the baby back.

Annie feels herself flinch, her body shrinking back against the pillows. 'No!' The word blurts from her mouth and she sees shock flit across the midwife's face. She senses four pairs of eyes swivel towards her. 'I want to go to the special care baby unit.'

Annoyance twitches at the edge of the midwife's mouth but Annie holds her gaze, unblinking.

'Very well then.' The words are clipped but Annie no longer cares what this midwife thinks of her. She just wants to find her baby.

Clamping shut her jaw, Annie slides her legs over the side of the mattress, pain slicing across her lower abdomen. She grits her teeth, determined that the midwife shouldn't see how much pain she is in lest she confines her to bed. All she needs to do is walk along the corridor and find her child.

As her legs take the burden of her weight, she feels them buckle beneath her and she stretches out a hand to steady herself. When she turns around, the midwife is already halfway towards the door.

Annie follows her out of the room with small, shuffled steps: nothing too sudden that might cause the severed muscles across her stomach to contract in response. She is aware of the other mothers' eyes trained on her as she leaves, is certain that were she to turn around suddenly, like in a game of What's the Time, Mr Wolf?, she would find them exchanging knowing glances behind her back.

They turn left out of the ward and she hobbles along the corridor behind the midwife's brisk steps, a singular refrain circulating in her head like a windup toy on repeat: *This is all a mistake. There's just been a mixup. It's all going to be fine.*

The midwife looks over her shoulder briefly to check that Annie is following, her face a picture of forbearance. Annie knows that she is being humoured, that this midwife does not believe for a second that the baby she has been given isn't hers. But she doesn't care. She doesn't need the midwife to believe her. All she needs is to find Nell and be reunited with her child.

They arrive at the glass window which looks onto the special care baby unit and the midwife stands next to Annie, still holding the other baby in her arms. Annie can feel the midwife staring at her, but she ignores her, scans the ten beds inside the small room. Five of them are incubators housing babies so small it is hard to believe that modern science is keeping them alive. Of the other five beds, only two are occupied. Annie studies the faces of both babies but neither of them bear any resemblance to her child.

Panic catches in her throat like a sharp wind. 'She's not there. None of those are my baby. Where's Nell?'

The midwife rolls her eyes. 'Come on now, Mrs Hardy. Of course your baby's not there because she's right here in my arms. Now, let's get you and Nell back to bed, shall we?' She tucks the baby that isn't Annie's into the crook of one arm and with her free hand takes hold of Annie's elbow, tries to steer her back towards the ward.

A fierce, febrile terror winds its way around Annie's throat. 'I'm not going back to the ward until I've found my baby.' Her head darts from left to right, past rooms identical to the one she has just left, each filled with mothers nursing babies they know to be theirs because their babies have not been taken away, have not been put in a separate unit and mixed up in some dreadful, terrible mistake.

The midwife studies her through narrowed eyes, sighs heavily and then turns and walks away, the baby that is not Annie's still in her arms.

Annie leans against the wall, looks through the glass panels into the special care baby unit, examines the faces again, willing one of them to be hers. But their eyes are too wideset, their cheeks too round, their lips too aligned.

Glancing along the corridor to the nurses' station, she sees the midwife talking to a colleague, sees them both look in her direction and then turn away quickly. They talk in muted voices, heads bent, and then the second midwife takes out a fat beige cardboard folder from a pile on the desk, leafs through sheets of paper, stops to read something. Annie watches her expression shift, sees impatience replaced by concern. She says a few words to the first midwife before closing the folder, placing it back on the desk, and walking towards Annie.

'Mrs Hardy? I'm Patricia Sherwood, the matron here. Eileen tells me you're a bit upset. Do you want to tell me what's wrong?'

The woman in front of her is about Annie's age – forty – and there is no sign of impatience in her voice. A ripple of relief rises into Annie's chest that here at last is someone in charge, someone sensible, someone who will take her seriously and help find her baby.

'There's been a mixup. I had a haemorrhage yesterday, and my baby had some breathing difficulties so she was brought here. The baby I've just been given – she's not mine. I know I only got to hold Nell for a little while, but . . . I know my baby.' The explanation tumbles from her mouth and she leans against the glass wall, tries to breathe slowly against her spinning head.

'Let me get you a chair. You can't be very comfortable after what you went through yesterday.' The matron walks into the room directly opposite, emerges with two blue plastic visitor chairs. She puts them against the wall, facing each other, and gestures for Annie to sit down.

Annie does not want to sit down – she wants to scour the ward, turn it upside down and inside out until her baby has been found – but she senses that this is the woman she needs on her side to expedite the search. She lowers herself into the chair, heat piercing her wound. The matron waits until Annie is seated before leaning forward and speaking slowly, in the kind of tone Annie might use with Clare or Laura when explaining why they have to do their homework or eat all their vegetables.

'I know you've had a very difficult time, Mrs Hardy. I've just been reading your notes, and I know about the loss of little Danny. I can only imagine how traumatic that was for you, and you have my full sympathy. It must have been terrible.'

Annie nods, blindsided by the sudden mention of Danny. She has been trying so hard not to think about him, not to dwell on the past, when she knows she has so much to be grateful for.

The matron shuffles forward on the edge of her chair, clasps her hands in her lap. 'It's understandable that having another child might bring up some painful memories. And I can see from your notes that you experienced some difficulties – emotionally – after Danny died. I completely understand that there may be some conflicted feelings today.'

Annie does not know whether she is supposed to respond, but before she has a chance, the matron continues.

'Childbirth can be incredibly disruptive to a woman's hormones. It can happen to anyone, but given all you've been through, it's really not surprising that you might feel a bit out of sorts. I understand that it must have been traumatic for you, handing Nell over to the midwives so soon after she was born, and then heading into surgery yourself. But I can assure you that we've taken exemplary care of her.'

A renewed sense of panic grips Annie's throat. She can hear in this matron's tone where the conversation is heading. This one doesn't believe her either. None of them believe her.

The matron carries on speaking as though there is no need to leave any space for Annie's thoughts, Annie's feelings, Annie's knowledge. 'Every baby is given a tag around their ankle the moment they're born. Nell was no different. There was probably so much going on that you didn't notice. And Eileen showed you the tag around Nell's ankle, didn't she? That's how we know who each baby belongs to. That's how we know that the baby Eileen brought you is Nell.'

This matron is speaking in such a calm, measured way that Annie wants to scream into her face just to try to jolt some urgency into her. 'The tag must have come off. It must have got swapped with another baby.'

The matron shakes her head with determined authority. 'That simply doesn't happen. The tags are very secure. They have to be to avoid exactly the kind of mixup you're describing.'

A tornado of frustration rages inside Annie. 'They're not secure. I unpopped the one on that baby with one hand. It could easily have fallen off.' She hears the desperation in her voice, wishes the matron would hear it too, would start to act rather than sitting here, doing nothing.

Matron pauses, sucking in a slow stream of air. 'They *are* secure, Mrs Hardy. They're very secure. Now, as you can see for yourself, the babies are lying in cots a good foot apart, so even if their tags *did* fall off – which they wouldn't – their own tag would be easily reattached without it ever going near another child. What you're suggesting is that *two* babies' tags fell off, and somehow those tags got taken out of the cots and reattached to the wrong child. I do understand that you're feeling agitated but you must be able to see that it's impossible?'

A thin shaft of doubt begins to creep around the closed door of Annie's certainty. From the nurses' station further along the corridor she can sense the other midwives watching her, whispering, exchanging glances. She knows that the matron is waiting for her to respond, waiting for her to agree, but there are too many thoughts whipping around her head to be able to grasp any of them properly.

She sees the matron gesture behind her and then suddenly there is the first midwife, holding out the baby they are insisting is hers, and before she has a chance to object, the midwife has placed the child back in her arms.

Annie looks down at the baby, studies its fragile features, tries to see in its face the child she held for five minutes in the early hours of yesterday morning. Matron's incredulity rings in her ears – '*you must be able to see that it's impossible?*' – and uncertainty weaves between her ribs. She closes her eyes, pictures the baby she had held in her arms the day before, and it is as if somewhere in her mind she had taken a series of snapshots that she can see as clearly now as if someone was presenting her with an album of photographs:

her baby gazing up at her, eyes wide open, drinking in the sight of this strange new world; her baby blinking up at the fluorescent strip lighting overhead; her baby yawning – mouth stretched wide open – as though the effort of her birth had exhausted her.

Annie opens her eyes, looks down at the child in her arms, and a wave of nausea rises into her throat. She thrusts the baby back towards the matron, shakes her head so violently, the air whistles in her ears. 'It's not mine. I don't care what you say. I *know* that baby isn't mine. She hasn't even got the right colour eyes. She looks nothing like my baby.' She sits, holding out the baby like an offering to the gods, and it seems that minutes pass, and then hours, before the matron and the midwife share a look of consternation and the midwife takes the baby from her.

'Mrs Hardy, please. You must see that what you're suggesting is preposterous. This *is* your baby. I think if we can just get you back to bed, perhaps we can give you something to help calm you down, and everything will seem a lot clearer.'

Annie knows what they're doing, what they're implying. They think she's mad. They think she's delusional, that she's making it all up. They are using the fact of her depression after Danny died to suggest she's not in her right mind now. But they're wrong. They're completely wrong. This has nothing to do with Danny. Nothing whatsoever. This is about Nell, her baby, the baby who is no longer here in her arms where she should be. She is not mad. She has lost her mind before and it is not like this. This is not depression, or madness. This is fear.

'Please, I'm not making it up. I know my baby. I'm her mother. This baby isn't mine.' Her voice cracks and she blinks hard against the tears; she will not play into their scepticism.

'If you're so sure this baby isn't yours, then where is she? All the other mothers have their babies, and you yourself have said that none of the babies in the special care unit are yours. Your baby can't just have vanished into thin air.' The expression in Matron's eyes is not unkind but her eyebrows have inched fractionally up her forehead.

Annie does not have an answer and yet she knows – instinctively, primevally – that the baby the midwife is holding is not hers. The pounding of her heart is so strong, so loud, that she thinks they must surely be able to hear it, cannot understand why they are not responding with the requisite urgency.

She feels a hand take hold of her elbow, feels herself being helped up from the chair and led back down the corridor, in the direction of the ward where she spent the night, but it is as if her head is no longer attached to her body, as if she is watching herself from above. All her mental energy is focussed on trying to find an answer to the matron's assertion: '*Your baby can't just have vanished into thin air.*'

As she is led back towards her bed, sandwiched between Matron holding her elbow on one side and the midwife holding the baby on the other, four pairs of eyes look up at her. Annie wants to howl into the unforgiving air, wants to scream until her throat is hoarse and her lungs are empty, until someone believes that she is not mad. She just needs one person to believe that she is telling the truth.

She does not look at the other new mothers – does not want to see the pity or embarrassment in their eyes – but as she allows herself to be led across the room, one slippered foot shuffling in front of the other, something looms into the periphery of her vision, as though determined to make itself seen.

Annie's head swings around and there it is: the empty bed opposite hers.

She stops in her tracks, turns to the matron. 'That empty bed. Who was in it? There was someone there yesterday. Where have they gone?'

Matron and the midwife exchange a glance of professional forbearance. 'They've gone home.'

Images begin to take shape in Annie's head, forming a picture she almost dare not view. 'She must have my baby. That woman's gone home with the wrong baby. You have to get her back.'

Matron's grip strengthens on Annie's elbow as she tries to turn her away from the vacated bed and towards her own. 'Nobody's gone home with the wrong child. Now, let's get you back to bed before you upset the other babies, shall we?' As if on cue, there is a burst of wailing from the bed beside the window, but Annie does not move.

'*Stop* trying to put me back in bed. You asked where my baby's gone. There's your answer. You have to get that woman to bring my baby back.' Tears sting her eyes but she blinks them away, cannot afford to give the midwives any more cause to think she is being hysterical.

'Mrs Hardy, no one's calling anyone back. I can assure you that babies do not get sent home with the wrong mothers. Now, really, you need to calm down. We can't have the whole ward being upset like this.'

Matron's words are glutinous in Annie's ears, explanations jostling for position in her head. 'That woman's baby. Was it in the special care baby unit too?'

Matron hesitates, her eyes darting towards the midwife and back again, and in that sliver of time, Annie sees the answer to her question.

'I can't answer that. It's confidential information.'

The hesitation emboldens Annie, her certainty growing with every passing second. 'Was it a boy or a girl? It was a girl, wasn't it?'

'You know I'm not going to answer that. Now, please, will you get back into bed. You must be in pain. Let's give you something to take that away, shall we?'

Annie shakes her head. She is no longer aware of any pain in her wound. All she can feel is the panic flooding her veins and a burning sensation in her chest, though she does not know whether it is fear or anger, grief or horror. 'I don't need anything. I just want my baby.' She will not allow them to pour more liquid morphine into her mouth, will not allow them to sedate her, silence her for a second time.

Next to her bed, she spies the black holdall containing all the things she had been advised to pack for the hospital: nappies, baby clothes, spare pyjamas, sanitary towels. Pulling herself free of Matron's clutches, she walks over to the bed. With one hand she leans on the mattress, stretches towards the floor, reaches for the holdall.

'What are you doing?'

'I'm discharging myself.' She can hear the mania in her voice, knows they think she is deranged, but she doesn't care. She has to find that woman and get her baby back.

'Don't be silly. You can't leave. You've had surgery, you've had significant blood loss, and you need to stay here, where we can look after you.'

Annie shakes her head, fire in her throat. 'I'm not staying here. You can't expect me to sit here and do nothing. My baby's missing. Why won't anyone listen to me?'

Matron steps towards her, so close Annie can feel her breath on her cheek, can smell the residue of garlic in it. 'Mrs Hardy, we can't let you leave. I'm going to get someone to come and have a chat with you, someone who can help with how you're feeling.'

Matron's voice is quiet but firm, and she does not need to be any more specific. They are sending for a psychiatrist. The veiled threat is loud and clear: if you try to leave, we will make sure you cannot.

Annie leans her weight on the bed, clenched hands pressed against the rough canvas of her overnight bag, unsure where her fear ends and her panic begins.

Behind her comes the sound of squeaking wheels, and out of the corner of her eye she sees the midwife wheeling a transparent plastic baby cot towards her, complete with a child Annie knows is not hers. The midwife parks the crib next to the bed so that Annie has no choice but to look at the child lying awake inside. For a split second she allows herself to hope that perhaps she has been mistaken, perhaps the nurses are right, perhaps this whole episode has been nothing more than postpartum confusion. But as her eyes rest on the delicate features of the baby in the cot – on the dark hair and bright blue eyes, on the wrong lips, the wrong cheeks, the wrong nose, the wrong chin – she knows without a doubt that she is not mistaken.

Matron takes hold of her arm. 'Only half an hour until visiting time. Is your husband coming this morning? I expect you'll feel much better once he's here.'

Bill. It is the first time Annie has thought of him, and now that she does she cannot believe she has been so foolish. 'You have to get Bill here now. He saw Nell yesterday, he'll know there's been a mistake. He'll be able to tell you this is all wrong.' Hope surges in Annie's mind. Bill will know she is telling the truth. He will be able to see that this baby isn't theirs. They will not be able to accuse Bill of postpartum mania, will not be able to confine him to the ward, threaten him with a psychiatrist. He will be able to speak to someone higher up in the hospital, someone more senior, someone with authority who will have to take him seriously. And if the hospital won't listen, he can go to the police. The police will have to do something. Her baby cannot have gone far. Bill will know what to do. He will know how to get Nell back.

'Visiting hours begin in thirty minutes. Your husband is welcome to come then, with all the other fathers. Now, please get back into bed.'

Annie cannot believe these women are being so obstructive, so intransigent. 'But Bill will know I'm right. You have to get him here now.'

Matron whispers something into the midwife's ear, and Annie wants to scream at them for their stupidity, their deafness, their refusal to take her seriously.

'Let's get you something to eat, and hopefully that will make you feel better. If not, we can give you a little injection of something to help calm you down.'

This time the threat is not even veiled. They want to sedate her and she cannot allow that to happen. Every minute lost is another moment without her child. She tries to pull her expression into something resembling compliance, lowers herself onto the bed. She allows the midwife to lift her legs onto the mattress, plump the pillows behind her head, pull the heavy sheets back over her body, all under the watchful eye of the matron.

'There, that's better, isn't it? Now, something to eat? You slept through breakfast but I'm sure we can rustle you up some toast.' Matron's voice is firm, redoubtable, as though she is speaking to a small child returning from a lengthy punishment.

Annie does not say anything. She cannot think of eating. Her mouth is dry, she knows she would not be able to swallow, but she daren't contradict the matron, daren't do anything to risk having medication pumped into her, disabling her from thinking straight.

'Good. Anything you need, you know where we are. Meanwhile, I suggest you spend some time with your lovely little girl. I expect she's ready for a cuddle with Mum.'

Matron glances one last time at the baby in the plastic crib before both she and the midwife turn and leave, Matron looking back over her shoulder at Annie as though checking she is not trying to escape.

From beside the bed, Annie hears the baby gurgling, and she turns her back to it, tries to shut out the sound. Her breasts ache with yearning for her newborn child and there is fear inside her, like a rock lodged in her stomach.

Scrunching shut her eyes, she tries to remember what the woman in the bed opposite looked like, but there is nothing more than a vague impression, like a face seen through mottled glass: dark brown hair in a mass of curls, pale skin, younger than Annie by a decade or so. Annie squints, trying to pull the image into focus, but it is as though the harder she concentrates, the more oblique it becomes.

In place of recall comes an imagined picture that burns behind her eyes and sears itself onto her heart: an image of that anonymous woman, right now, at home with Annie's baby, cradling her in her arms, offering Annie's child her breast, watching with unconditional love as a child she mistakenly believes to be hers suckles at her nipple. She imagines that unknown woman leaning forward and kissing the top of Nell's head, breathing in the smell of her, believing it is a smell they share even though it is as foreign as if she were holding a newborn baby from the other side of the world. She imagines this woman kissing each of Nell's toes, holding Nell naked against her bare skin, singing gently into Nell's ear, holding out her finger to let Nell wrap her wrinkled fist around it.

The imagined scenes blaze inside her mind. She reminds herself that Bill will be here soon, he will know what to do. She just has to get through the next thirty minutes. She will have her baby back soon. It is a belief she has to cling to because if she doesn't she fears the panic will engulf her.

The long hand clicks to a vertical position and Annie's eyes gaze hungrily at the door, waiting for Bill to walk through it.

For the past thirty minutes she has sat motionless on the bed, watching the clock, interested only in the progression of time until Bill arrives. She has ignored the tea and toast the midwife put on the bedside cabinet, ignored the snuffling of the baby in the cot beside her. She has shut her ears against suggestions that she feed the baby, paid no attention as the midwife fetched a bottle of formula and fed the child herself. All she has wanted is for time to speed up, so that Bill will arrive and help find their baby.

Men begin to stride through the door, simultaneously eager and hesitant, as though they know this hallowed space is not really their domain. Two hold enormous bouquets of flowers in pinks, whites, yellows. One is clutching an oversized blue teddy bear under his arm. Another holds the hand of a little boy halfhiding behind his father's leg.

Annie looks beyond them, over their shoulders, in search of Bill. But only four men have entered and Bill is not among them. Behind the four fathers, the doorway is empty.

Panic needles her skin, her mind racing with thoughts as to where he might be. She wonders if there has been an emergency in the workshop, though Annie cannot imagine what could be so urgent that he cannot leave it for an hour to visit her, cannot allow Elsa to hold the fort. Her mind speeds on, to Clare and Laura, to whether anything might have happened to either of them to prevent Bill from visiting. But they will be at school and she trusts that if anything untoward had occurred, he would have telephoned the hospital to let her know.

In the cubicle next to hers, a father sits down on a blue plastic chair, his baby clad in a pink babygrow asleep on his chest while he studies each of her fingers in turn. Behind her she can hear the toddler asking his mummy how long it will be before the baby learns to talk. Diagonally opposite, a man has taken off his shoes and is lying on the bed next to his wife, their baby in his arms, both of them staring down at the child as though unable to unpeel their eyes. Annie lies alone, watching, listening, waiting, trying to visualise the circumstances that could have kept Bill from coming.

And then, suddenly, he is there, walking through the large square doorway, a bunch of daffodils and crocuses he has picked from the garden wrapped in brown paper. He is smiling but she sees it immediately: the stiff lips, tight cheeks, worried eyes. They have got to him first. The midwives have already told him what has happened, have already poisoned his mind against her with their fabricated side of the story. They are the reason he is late.

He arrives at the bed, bends down, kisses her cheek, and it is only then that she realises how clammy her skin is: how strands of hair have stuck to her forehead, how the pillow is damp beneath her. He walks around to the far side where the cot is stationed. She does not turn, does not follow him with her eyes. But then he is back, with the baby in his arms, smiling at her with desperate encouragement.

'She's beautiful, love. Completely beautiful. She looks just like you.'

Annie winces at his insincerity. The baby looks nothing like her. It is the other baby – the one that has disappeared – who looks like Annie. It is that baby – her real baby – who is the spitting image of Clare and Laura and Danny when they were born.

'Just wait till we get her home. The girls were so excited when I told them they had a little sister. How are you feeling?' Bill sits down on the chair beside the bed, cradling a baby he has been duped into believing is his own.

Anxiety churns in Annie's stomach and she reaches out, grabs his elbow, pulls him towards her. From his startled expression she can see she has taken him by surprise, perhaps is gripping him too tightly. But she does not let go, pulls him closer until his face is near enough for her to whisper without anyone else hearing. 'She's not our baby. Look at her. Just *look at her*. She looks nothing like our baby. They've given our baby to someone else. They won't admit it, but I know they have. We've got to find her. *You've* got to find her.'

Bill gently wrestles his arm free from Annie's hand and she sees the quartet of thin short lines imprinted on his skin where her nails have dug into the flesh like the markings of a seam on a dressmaking pattern.

He drags the chair closer to the bed, the baby still lying against his chest, unfeasibly small next to his big, broad frame, and Annie thinks to herself that her three other children never looked like that in Bill's arms, never looked so out of place.

He leans in close, smiles at her in a way he might if she had flu and he was bringing her a cup of hot honey and lemon, but he cannot hide the concern in his eyes. 'Annie, love, I know yesterday was really hard, and I'm so proud of you for getting through it. I know it's been an upsetting morning, but what you're saying, about this baby not being ours: the midwives have explained it's impossible. Things like that just don't happen.'

He speaks softly, fervently, and there is a quiet, urgent desperation in his voice that she should listen, take in his reassurance. She knows he believes he is speaking the truth. But she also knows he is wrong and somehow she has to make him see it. Pulling herself up on her elbows, her wound protests at the sudden movement, but she ignores the pain, tries to speak as calmly as she can while making him understand the necessity for him to act. 'But it *has* happened. It has. I know my own baby.'

In an adjacent bay, an infant cries. Bill edges forward on his chair. 'You've had a really traumatic twentyfour hours, and it might have . . . You must be exhausted.'

She wipes the hair from her forehead where it is sticking to her skin. 'I'm *not* exhausted. Someone else has our baby and you're all just sitting around doing nothing. They won't let me go and look for her, but you can. You can leave. You have to find someone to talk to, someone higher up, someone who'll listen.' Annie's fingers ache where she is clutching the starched white sheet in both hands.

'What would I say if I found someone?'

'You'd tell them there's been a mistake. That the tag on our baby has been swapped somehow. That someone else has gone home with our child. It's the woman in the bed opposite, I know it is. They won't admit it, but I know I'm right.' She gestures towards the empty bed and Bill follows the direction of her eyes, turns back to Annie, deep creases lining his forehead. 'She's out there somewhere, Bill, I just know it. You've got to find her and bring her back.' Her voice cracks and she knows she sounds frenzied but she doesn't care because all she cares about is finding the real Nell.

Bill takes a deep breath, holds the baby with one hand against his chest, places his free hand on the bare skin of Annie's arm. 'I know you're upset, but you have to listen. The hospital wouldn't have let that happen. This *is* our baby.' He turns the baby round to face her but Annie will not look, stares so hard at the diamond pattern on the cubicle curtain that the shapes begin to blur. Thoughts scramble in her head, trying to find the words to make him believe her.

'This is her, Annie. Our beautiful Nell.'

She whips her head back round. 'That is *not* Nell. *Look at her.* She's nothing like Clare or Laura. Or Danny. The baby I gave birth to yesterday was the spitting image of them when they were born. That's not the baby I gave birth to. She's *not* our daughter.' She hisses the words at him, cannot understand how her love for this man, how their seventeen years of marriage, are not sufficient to make him see that she is telling the truth.

'Love, I know it must be hard, having a new baby after what happened. I'm thinking a lot about Danny too. It's only natural that we would.'

'This has nothing to do with Danny. It's about Nell.'

Bill continues as though she hasn't spoken. 'We have to try and separate the two. It's not fair on Nell if we don't. Of course we're never going to forget Danny, but we need to try and look forward now, to our life with Nell.'

Annie shakes her head. 'Someone else has our baby. Why won't anyone believe me?' Tears spring from her eyes and she does not know whether they come from a place of frustration or fear.

Bill looks at her and she sees her own anxiety reflected back, and for a second she thinks she has managed to convince him.

'Annie, listen to me.' His voice is quiet, almost a whisper, but there is a hint of warning in it. 'They're getting a psychiatrist to come and see you. They think you're having some kind of psychotic episode and you won't be allowed home until it's passed. They're saying you might be a risk to the baby. Now, I know that's absurd. I know you'd never do anything to hurt Nell. But they don't know you like I do. And you want to come home, don't you, to be with me and the girls? Please, love, you have to listen. Nobody's taken our baby. She's right here, in my arms. And I just want the two of you to come home.'

He is trying to be kind – she can hear it in his voice, Bill is only ever trying to be kind – but today she does not want him to be kind, affable, easygoing. Today she needs him to be dogged, intransigent, determined. She needs him to tear through the place with his bare hands until they give him the address of the discharged woman from the bed opposite who has taken home Annie's baby by mistake.

'But, Bill—'

'Annie, please. Just try and get some rest now. I'll look after Nell. You get some sleep.' He leans back in the chair, strokes the baby's hair with his muscular fingers, every movement sending a shiver along Annie's spine.

She watches him treat this stranger's baby as their own and feels something sliding away from her. Cracks in reality become crevices and then chasms until she no longer knows what to believe, who to trust. The only thing she can hold on to is her certainty that the baby Bill is holding does not belong to them.

Lying on the bed, she feels herself falling down a bottomless well of despair. It is as though all the contents of her body have been scooped out and all that is left is an empty shell dotted with gaping holes for her rage and grief and fear to howl through. She knows, as fiercely as she has ever known anything in her life, that the baby the midwives have given them is not hers, just as she knows that she will not give up trying to convince them she is right. She does not care if they send an army of psychiatrists to see her, does not care how long she has to stay in hospital in order for them to believe her. All she has to do is hold on to what she knows and eventually somebody will have to believe she is telling the truth.

The thought of her child being out in the world with a stranger grips her with such force it is like being punched, winded, doubled over in pain.

Lying in a hospital bed that has become her temporary prison, she closes her eyes and remembers what her baby looked like when she held her in her arms yesterday morning. There is nobody who can tell her she does not know who her baby is. It is etched on every molecule of her being. Somehow, she just has to make them all see it.

NOW

'Who's Jane Whitworth? Is she my biological mother?' Nell's voice is thin, pinched, as though it is being squeezed through the eye of a needle.

Her mum does not turn to look at her. When she speaks, her voice is quiet, little more than a whisper. 'Please don't take my baby away . . . It wasn't my fault . . . The name tags, the poppers . . . I told them, in the hospital.' Her sentences collide so that it is difficult for Nell to separate one from the next.

'What do you mean? What about the name tags?'

Still her mum does not turn to look at her and Nell is not sure she has even heard. Out of the window the light is fading and Nell fears her mum's garbled memories may disappear with it.

'I knew she wasn't mine. But they didn't believe me.' Her mum's voice catches, as if snagging on a memory that will not let her go.

Thoughts scrabble towards meaning inside Nell's head. 'Who wasn't yours?'

Her mum begins to shake her head as a series of short plaintive syllables emerge from deep inside her throat: 'Please . . . No . . . Don't . . .'

Nell does not know how to coax more memories from her mum. She looks back down at the screen on her phone, at the face of the woman she is now convinced must be her birth mother. In the absence of any concrete facts, she does a general search for Dr Jane Whitworth, finds countless articles in scientific journals, links to conferences, memberships of various scientific organisations, but nothing that might elucidate whether her suspicion is true. Just more photographs bearing a startling resemblance to Nell.

And then, opening a fresh internet page, she types: *Jane Whitworth academic baby*. A voice in her head tells her to stop being foolish, that she is letting her imagination run away with her. Even if there is something to uncover she is not going to find it on the internet thirtyfive years later. But as her finger scrolls down the list of results, her eyes land on a collection of words that cause all the moisture to evaporate from her mouth.

Clicking on the link, she finds herself on a blog called *Light in the Dark: Stories of Life After Losing a Child*. At the top of the page is a short paragraph of text, explaining that the following article had been found in an old newspaper in the library. Nell clicks on the thumbnail image so that the photocopied cutting fills the screen, and all at once she feels she has tumbled down a rabbit hole so deep she will never reach the bottom.

THEN

Annie has just put Nell down for her daytime nap when she collects the local newspaper from the front doormat. It is not until a few minutes later, seated on the sofa with a cup of tea, that she sees the article that will tip her world upside down.

Countless times over the intervening years she will think about those few minutes, about that ellipsis in time between innocence and knowledge, and there will be no end to her selfrebuke that she had not thrown the newspaper straight into the bin without ever opening it, that she had not been able to live the rest of her life ignorant of the truth.

As soon as she sees the picture of the toddler beaming out at her, she knows. She does not need to retrieve the photograph albums from the sideboard, does not need to compare it to pictures of Clare and Laura at that age to see the startling resemblance. There is the same fine mousey hair that hangs without a single kink, refusing to be styled. The same oval eyes, the colour of a woodland forest. The same button nose, the same dimpled chin, the same telltale protrusion of the top lip over the bottom, producing a smile that is both impish and endearing.

She knows, without a doubt, that this is her child. That this is the little girl who was mistakenly swapped in the hospital two years and fourteen days ago, exchanged for the child who is now asleep upstairs. The accidental swap that everyone insisted could not possibly have happened. For a year and a half she has allowed herself to believe that she had made a terrible mistake, that the thick fog of postnatal depression had caused her to think those things. But now, staring at a photograph of a child that is undeniably hers, all the pain and panic and rage return.

There is a second photograph, of the child's mother, and Annie does not need to coax the memory from the corner of her mind. The recognition is immediate in the dark curls, pale skin, thoughtful blue eyes. It is the woman she had shared a ward with two years earlier, the woman from the bed opposite whom Annie had begged the hospital to locate, and with whom she had been denied any contact.

But it is only when her eyes drift to the headline, shouting at her in bold black font, that she senses all the air being sucked from her lungs.

TODDLER DIES IN ASTHMA ATTACK TRAGEDY

Shockwaves rippled through the Bromley community last week after the tragic death of two-yearold Amy Whitworth. The daughter of David and Jane Whitworth suffered a fatal asthma attack in the early hours of Wednesday morning. An ambulance was called after Amy's mother found the toddler distressed in her cot, wheezing and struggling to breathe. By the time the paramedics arrived, Amy had stopped breathing and was pronounced dead at the scene. She was later taken to University Hospital, where she had been born two years previously.

A neighbour said that Mr and Mrs Whitworth had no idea their daughter suffered from asthma, and speculated that the recent purchase of a puppy might have provoked the sudden attack. 'It just doesn't bear thinking about. If only they'd known, maybe they'd have been able to save her.'

David Whitworth is a highly respected member of the local community, where he is Chief Executive of the local council. His wife, Dr Jane Whitworth, is an academic specialising in Evolutionary Biology at Imperial College, London.

A friend of the couple commented: 'You've never seen two parents more smitten than David and Jane. They loved Amy with all their hearts. I can't imagine what this will do to them.'

Sandra Williams, head of Busy Fingers Nursery where Amy had been enrolled since Mrs Whitworth returned to work a year ago, said that Amy was 'a delightful child. She always had a smile for everyone.'

A postmortem is due to take place this week.

Amy Whitworth: 3 March 1986 – 10 March 1988.

Annie reads the article, the words darting in front of her eyes like fish that do not want to be caught. It is the name of the hospital and that final line – the date of birth, irrefutable proof – that cause her stomach to swirl, that send her rushing to the kitchen sink, where she regurgitates her lunch, wishing it could take every ounce of pain with it.

When her stomach is empty, she becomes aware of the hot tears streaming down her cheeks. She leans against the sink, grieving for the child she will now never meet, the daughter she held for less than five minutes before being taken from her arms and removed from her life forever. She closes her eyes, tries to recall the image she has spent the past eighteen months convincing herself was nothing more than a false memory: the image of Nell – the real Nell – lying in her arms just minutes after her birth, gazing up at her with those hazel eyes, that fine hair, that protruding top lip, as Annie's heart had swelled with love for her.

Her knees buckle beneath her and she does not know whether it is her body or the ground that is shaking so violently. She manages to stagger into the lounge, curl up on the sofa, bring her knees to her chest, but she does not know how she is supposed to get through the next few seconds, minutes, hours. It is preposterous and yet she knows it is true: her baby was taken from her and now her baby has died, and she will never get to hold her, comfort her, cradle her, smell her, touch her, kiss her, stroke her, caress her. Love her. Her baby is gone.

She thinks suddenly about the toddler upstairs asleep in her cot. She is not her child. Nell is not her biological child. She does not belong to her. And yet, at the same time, she is her daughter. Nell is her daughter, even while she is not. She is the child Annie now loves with a deep, intense, allconsuming love, as powerful as if she had given birth to her. It is a fierce love. A protective love. A mother's love. And she knows, without a shadow of a doubt, that they belong together now, whatever their DNA might say.

Nell is her daughter. She cannot lose her. She cannot lose them both.

Panic surges through her. She has to keep Nell. The child upstairs belongs to her now. Nell is her daughter, and she will not let anything or anyone take her away.

NOW

Time seems to warp, as though she is entering another dimension where she cannot be certain what she is seeing. Nell stares at the picture, blinks hard, stares again. But it is still there, just as it was before. A photograph of a woman in her midthirties. A woman with dark, curly hair and porcelain skin, at once both entirely familiar and completely unknown.

Nell's eyes dart to the top of the cutting where the date is printed in a font that newspapers have longsince abandoned. It is thirtythree years old. The cutting originates from two weeks after Nell's second birthday, thirtythree years ago.

She stares at the photograph, her thoughts a dark swirl. It does not make any sense, what she is seeing, and yet she knows it is the answer to a question she has only just begun to ask.

Because the woman in the photograph is Nell. Except it cannot possibly be Nell, she knows that. Because the date of the cutting is from when Nell was just two years old, and the woman in the photo is in her midthirties. And yet, looking at the picture now, Nell could be staring into the mirror.

Her eyes skim across the cutting to a second picture, of a toddler smiling into the camera, and the recognition hits Nell with such immediacy that it grips her lungs, squeezing tightly. Her eyes blur but she pulls them back into focus, fixes them on the headline at the top of the page, a sequence of words in thick, black letters.

And it is then that the world seems to tip on its axis.

TODDLER DIES IN ASTHMA ATTACK TRAGEDY

The walls of Nell's throat narrow as she reads the thirtythreeyearold article, her eyes scouring the text beneath the photographs, every word, every sentence unlocking a part of a puzzle she had never known needed solving.

A cold skein of dread stipples her skin. It is as though she is watching a car crash in slow motion, knows that the vehicles are about to collide moments before it happens, but can do nothing to stop it. It is the dates that make it possible. The dates and the hospital. The toddler in the article had been born on the same day, in the same hospital, as Nell.

Inside her head, Nell stumbles over her own thoughts as she looks at the two photographs. The photo of a toddler that could have been taken from one of the baby albums at home, such is the similarity to Clare and Laura. Next to it, the photo of a grown woman who so closely resembles Nell that to study it now is like watching a magician's illusion.

'It wasn't my fault . . . The name tags, the poppers . . . I told them, in the hospital . . . I knew she wasn't mine. But they didn't believe me.'

Pieces of her family history begin to slot into place, like a story written long ago from which chapters have been missing for years and have only now been found. Nell's centre of gravity shifts, her thoughts sliding into a twisted heap in the corner of her mind. Questions spiral inside her head and she looks at her mum's distant expression, her wrinkled face a map Nell does not know how to navigate.

Looking down at the newspaper cutting on her phone, grief winds its way around her throat, and she does not know for whom she is grieving the most: for herself or the other child. For the mother opposite her or the mother she has never met.

'Did you ever tell them the truth? Do my birth parents know what happened?' Her voice is strained, as though it is being wrung from a damp cloth, and she is unsure what she fears the most: that her real parents have been kept in the dark for thirtyfive years, or that they were once told the truth and decided against ever meeting her.

Her mum does not reply. Outside the window, the evening smudges into darkness and Nell panics that time is running out, that visiting hours will soon be over. Her mum's eyes narrow, and Nell does not know if it is something beyond the window or a memory inside her head that she is trying to pull into focus.

'Mum? Did you ever tell the Whitworths about me? Do they know . . . ?' She cannot finish the sentence, dare not follow where it may lead.

Still her mum does not look at her, fiddling with the plain gold wedding band that is now so deeply embedded in her flesh that it cannot be slid over her knuckle. 'He pretended he didn't think about her . . . I know he did . . .' Her mum's voice is quiet, childlike, as though unsure whether it wants to come out of hiding. 'That space he chose . . . He never told me . . . It must have been years ago . . .'

Nell repeats her mum's words in her head, trying to slot the fragments into place, like a jigsaw puzzle in which half the pieces are missing. 'What space?'

Her mum shakes her head. 'He said he wanted to be with his mum and dad . . . All those times I visited my Amy . . . It's my resting place too . . .' Annie's voice splinters and suddenly it dawns on Nell. She closes her eyes, remembers reading the plaques around her dad's plot in the graveyard just the day before.

Amy Imogen Whitworth
Two years on earth but forever in our hearts.
Sleep peacefully, angel.

Grief pulls taut inside Nell's chest. She thinks about her dad, never knowing his birth daughter and yet still wanting his ashes to be buried beside her. She tries to imagine the deep, primal urge that must have prompted him to buy that plot in the cemetery, does not know how to feel about this secret chamber of her father's heart that must have been reserved for the daughter whom he would never be able to parent, even while he loved the daughter who wasn't biologically his.

Her dad's final words to her in the hospital play inside her head, words which have haunted her for the past fortnight, and she does not know whether to feel grief or gratitude that he loved her in spite of the fact that she was never really his to love. He loved her unconditionally while all the time mourning the daughter he would never get to meet. And the thought of his love for this other little girl is like a needle in Nell's lungs, pricking her each time she breathes.

Nell opens her mouth to speak but finds there are no words ready to make their way into the world.

The two of them sit in silence, the blue sky slipping from corn-flower to sapphire. Nell thinks about her birth parents, about the loss they suffered, perhaps never knowing that their birth child was still alive and living just a few miles away. She thinks about Bill and Annie – the only parents she has ever known – and all the years they have been grieving, not one child but two. How they must have thought they had experienced the worst grief that death could inflict on them when Danny died, how raw and painful and irreparable that loss must have been. And then to have suffered again, so soon after, grieving a child they would never have the opportunity to love, a different loss and yet, perhaps, all the more debilitating. She thinks about the Hardys and the Whitworths, a quartet of lives shattered by a momentary mistake, by an unspeakable tragedy, and she does not know how any of them have managed to cope with the depth of their suffering.

'Why didn't you give me back?' Nell's voice is small, tentative, as though it knows the question is dangerous. She looks at her mum, sees that her lips are moving though no sound emerges. Nell reaches out, takes hold of her hand. But still her mum does not answer and Nell has only her own conjectures to fill the silence.

THEN

Annie pushes Nell back and forth on the swing in the playground.

'Higher! Higher!' Nell laughs, and Annie pushes, aware of the compression in her chest that is now a constant, ambient presence.

It is almost six months since she opened the newspaper and discovered a truth she wishes she had never learnt. It is knowledge that has seeped into the foundations of family life so that she can no longer trust the ground on which she walks, even within her own home. Neither she nor Bill choose to discuss it, not since she persuaded him that Nell is theirs to keep, that they must never divulge to anyone what has happened. But it is there in the silences, in the knowing glances, in the way he looks at her from across the room as she lifts Nell into her arms, showers her with kisses, tells her how much she loves her. It is there in the subtle ways Annie's behaviour towards Nell has changed, in the vigilant manner she now cares for her, as though Nell is a precious artefact in a museum with which she has been entrusted, and which she must ensure, at any cost, does not leave her sight. It is there in the invisible barrier that has been erected between those who know and those who do not: in the way she cannot fully relax around Clare and Laura for fear they will somehow deduce the truth. In the way she has avoided intimacy with even her closest friends as a means of patrolling the boundary protecting their secret. It is there all the nights she lies awake, unable to sleep, trying to picture the daughter she will never know, and in the endless, repetitive cycle of imagined scenes that spool through her mind: her birth daughter's first smile, first laugh, first words, first steps, first birthday, first paddle, first icecream. All those firsts Annie never got to witness with her biological child. And, beyond that, all those other firsts that Amy will now never get to experience because of the tragedy that prematurely ended her life.

It is there, perhaps most acutely, in the knowledge that had the babies never been swapped, Annie's birth child might still be alive. Because Annie and Bill would have been alert to the risk of their child having asthma. They would have known from the outset that Bill had already passed it on to Laura, would have been vigilant about the possibility that their fourth child may have been afflicted too. They would never have bought a puppy, knowing how dog hair aggravated Bill's condition. They would have known, as soon as their child started coughing and wheezing, why she was struggling to breathe, would have been able to fetch Laura's inhaler and spacer from the bathroom, would have been able to administer the salbutamol before the attack got out of hand.

There is every possibility that they would have been able to save her life.

Annie feels the muscles in her throat tighten and she swallows against the grief lodging in her throat.

'Higher, Mama, higher!'

Annie pushes the swing higher still and Nell squeals with delight.

'Mum, can we go and do something else now? It's boring here.' Clare scratches at a patch of eczema on her arm, Laura next to her, wideeyed and hopeful.

'I want to go on da slide!'

Annie glances between her daughters: Nell on one side, Clare and Laura on the other, her loyalties divided. 'Nell's having such a lovely time. Just another ten minutes, okay?'

'You said that ten minutes ago.'

Annie hesitates. She knows that the tiny playground is no fun for a fifteenyearold and an elevenyearold, but there are no activities that suit all three of them.

'Da slide, Mama, da slide!'

Annie lifts Nell out of the swing, kisses her forehead. 'Just let her have a bit more time. And then we'll go home and you two can watch TV while Nell and I make cakes.'

Clare and Laura slouch off, sit on the big swings on the far side of the playground, their heads bent close together, exchanging complaints, Annie suspects.

Following Nell to the toddler slide, Annie watches her climb the eight metal stairs to the top, holds out her arms ready to catch Nell if she falls. She watches her slide down before Nell runs back to the steps to do it all over again. Annie loses count of how many times Nell goes up and then down, over and over again, and as she watches her, a door opens up in her mind on a series of alternative lives she might be leading. A life in which Danny had not died, in which she is now standing in the playground supervising a four-yearold on the brink of school. A life in which her fourth child had never been born because her third baby had survived. A life in which the name tags had never been mistakenly swapped in the hospital, in which the child she is now supervising is genetically hers. A life in which they had told the Whitworths about the cata-strophic mixup, had suffered the consequences, whatever they may have been. They are doors onto other lives she has got used to enter-ing over the past six months, corridors she has become accustomed to roaming. But at the thought of Nell living somewhere else, with her birth parents, the door slams shut and she turns her back on it.

Grief, she is learning, is love's echo: it is not possible to have one without the other.

At the top of the slide Nell gazes up, following the contrail of an aeroplane across the clear blue September sky. Annie knows she will never stop blaming herself for what happened. She will always feel that it is her fault for not shouting loud enough, not fighting hard enough to make someone believe her during those early days in the hospital. She will never stop criticising herself for not having pursued more doggedly her certainty that the baby she had been handed was not hers. For a month she had tried to convince the doctors and midwives that she was right, and for a month they had kept her imprisoned there, subjected to daily visits from a psychiatrist similarly determined not to believe her. They had refused to let her go home, had said she was a risk to the baby, that they needed to keep them both under supervision. She had not been able to convince them that she would never have harmed the baby. Not just because it wasn't in her character to do something like that, but because she had to keep this baby safe. She had to believe that whoever was looking after her biological child was keeping her safe too. She had to trust that when she finally found her real child, the two mothers would be able to swap them back knowing that each child had been cared for with utmost diligence. And yet, after four weeks in the hospital, with Bill imploring her to get better and come home, she had pretended to relinquish her conviction, had pretended to accept this baby as her own, just so that she could escape. And, in the subsequent months, she had come to believe that Nell was hers. It is a belief she may have held on to for the rest of her life had it not been for the newspaper article that had spun her world out of control.

Nell reaches the bottom of the slide for the umpteenth time and runs back round to the metal steps, clambering up them with joyful abandon. Annie watches, her heart swelling with love. She loves Nell as if she were her own child, more perhaps for knowing that she is not, and for the fear that if she and Bill are careless, Nell may be taken away from them. The Whitworths have moved away, their house sold, left for destinations unknown, but that does not end the constant fluttering in her chest that somehow they will find out and come back to claim the daughter who is rightfully theirs.

Annie watches Nell run to the pirate ship, clamber to the top and look out of the crow's nest, hand flat above her eyes as if gazing out to sea. There are times when she does not know how she will manage to hold on to this secret. It is so powerful, so allconsuming that she cannot imagine living with it for the rest of her life. She cannot comprehend how the years will roll by without her knowing every detail about her birth daughter's short life, details she knows she can never discover without disclosing the truth. Sometimes she fears the secret will burst from her chest without any means of containment, that it will erupt into the world, destroying everything in its wake. Other times it burns so fiercely inside her that she imagines it scorching her from the inside out. There are moments when she tries to envisage the future – Nell starting primary school, secondary school, beginning work, getting married, having children of her own – but she cannot imagine ever allowing Nell to run free without the constant, gnawing anxiety that if she travels too far from home she may never come back.

'Mama! Watch me climb!'

Annie turns to where Nell is scrambling up a latticed climbing net, hurries to her side to catch her should she fall. 'Well done, angel. That's amazing, you clever girl!' She waits until Nell has reached the top before scooping her into her arms, kissing her cheek, holding her tight.

Nell is her daughter. Irrespective of DNA, she is hers. And Annie will never let anyone take her away.

NOW

They sit in silence, Nell's mind spiralling, her feelings refusing to be packaged into neat, tidy boxes. She is angry and yet she is full of love. She is confused and yet somehow it all makes sense. The woman sitting next to her is both her mum and yet she is not, and Nell doesn't know how both these things can be true at the same time. She feels as though her world has been turned upside down and yet here she is, sitting with the only woman she has ever known to be her mother, the woman she loves more than any other, and it is as though everything and nothing has changed.

Memories throb inside Nell's head, too many thoughts and feelings to decipher. So many things she has not been able to explain over the years, so many moments she has not understood, but now it is as if the frosted glass through which she has viewed her family all these years is beginning to clear.

All those class trips for which her mum volunteered as a parent helper so that she was always there, by Nell's side. All those sleepover invitations her mum had persuaded her not to accept. All those bewildering conversations when she passed the elevenplus. All those residential trips during secondary school that her mum would find excuses for her not to attend. All those exasperating questions when she got her offer from Oxford about why she had not chosen a university closer to home. Her mum's palpable disappointment when she decided to move north of the river rather than within walking distance of her parents' house.

She thinks about all the occasions she has thought her mum cloying and overprotective, not understanding her mum's fear of the possible consequences if Nell strayed too far. All those times she wished her mum would take a little more pride in her achievements, not realising that every notable difference between her and her parents must have been a painful reminder of her true origins, heightening the fear that one day, surely, somebody was going to notice the disparity and start asking questions.

The wall of Nell's throat narrows. There is so much she wants to say – so much she needs to say – but she does not know where to begin. There is the anger that she has never been told the truth, that she has uncovered the story only by accident. There is the shock that her parents have kept it secret all this time, have maintained the deception all these years. There is the frustration that she is making the discovery too late, when the only two people who could fill in the blanks are no longer able to do so.

Neither of them speaks, her mum staring out of the window, Nell studying her face as she tries to imagine what it must have been like for her parents, knowing she was not their child and yet raising her as if she were. How their hearts must have cleaved in two, one half keeping secret their love and grief for a child they would never have the chance to know, the other half raising Nell as if she were their flesh and blood.

She thinks about how they must have lived with the constant fear of exposure, how a small part of them must have jumped every time the phone rang, every time there was a knock at the door, every time she brought a new friend home from school, wondering if this was the moment their secret would be discovered, this was the moment Nell would be taken away.

She thinks about her birth parents, about Jane and David Whitworth, about the grief they must have suffered. A part of her tries to imagine what they might be like – what her life might have been like had she spent it with them – but here her imagination fails her, a sluice falling across the stream of her thoughts.

The last gasp of evening light filters through the window. She takes hold of her mum's hand, runs her fingers along the back where a mosaic of liver spots are dotted across the skin, like points on a map she is only now beginning to read. Her mum turns to look at her, and Nell searches in her expression for a glimmer of recollection. For a second she thinks it is there, her lungs inflating with hope, but then it is gone, as quickly as it arrived, like a flame extinguished under the cap of a metal snuffer. Instead her mum reaches across to the bedside table, pulls a tissue from a box and hands it to her.

Nell takes it, wipes the tears from her cheeks, feels her voice begin to fracture as she starts to speak. 'I love you, Mum. I need you to know that. I will always love you, even if you were never really mine to love.'

NOW

There is a young woman sitting opposite her, leaning forward and holding her hand, tears slipping down her cheeks. She is pretty, slender, and there is something familiar in her face, though Annie cannot place what it is. She has a sense that she knew, only moments ago, why this woman is here, what she had come for. But now it has gone, like day sliding into night.

There is a residue of something though, a thought or a feeling, she is not sure which. A sense that she is expecting the woman to be angry with her though she does not know why. It is a notion that hovers on the periphery of her thoughts, but whenever she tries to focus on it, it floats further away, out of sight.

This woman does not look angry. She looks sad. Tears spill over the lids of her eyes. Perhaps, Annie thinks, whatever it was she had done to make the woman angry has been forgiven. Perhaps it is all in the past.

Reaching across to the box of tissues by the bed, she pulls one out and hands it to the woman, hopes she stops crying soon.

The woman takes the tissue, wipes her cheeks. 'I love you, Mum. I need you to know that. I will always love you, even if you were never really mine to love.'

The young woman's voice cracks and more tears spring from her eyes. Annie pats the young woman's knee, feels a warmth from the woman's words even though she does not know what they mean or why they are being said to her.

She remembers another little girl who sometimes had a sad face too. How this little girl would stand on the sofa, looking out of the window through net curtains, as if waiting for something, or someone, to arrive. Annie remembers how she would study the little girl's watchful expression and how panic would grip her heart that somehow the child knew more than Annie had ever told her. She can feel it now, that anxiety pressing down on her chest, making her fear she might never be able to fill her lungs again. She remembers an overpowering urge to protect the little girl – to do everything possible to ensure that no harm comes to her – recalls lifting the little girl off the sofa and into her arms, shrouding her in a blanket of love and kisses until the little girl is laughing.

Annie tugs at the thread of memory that might tell her who the little girl is and what she was trying to protect her from. But the thread is tangled and knotted and she cannot unwind it, cannot find her way back to the start.

She thinks of a fairy tale, the name of which she cannot recall, but there is a tower and a girl, and the girl is locked in the tower, and Annie knows she is supposed to think it is wrong, but instead she thinks it is the safest place for the girl to be, even if the girl does not understand why. It is safe because there no one can reach her, no one can find her and take her away.

The young woman sitting on the edge of the bed blows her nose and crumples the tissue into a ball, slips it into the handbag at her feet. Annie can see that the young woman is trying to smile, but the fractional upending of her lips cannot disguise the sadness in her eyes.

Another image tugs at the vine of Annie's memory. It is a photograph of a child, about two years of age, no more. The child is smiling, she is happy, there is no doubt about it. And yet the photograph makes Annie unbearably sad. She can feel it now, that sadness, pulsing through her blood as though it is a virus that cannot be cured. But it is not only sadness she feels. There is love too – a great swell of love – and she feels her heart unlatch and let the little girl in. It is such a strong, visceral memory of such overwhelming grief and love that she does not know where one ends and the other begins.

The young woman next to her takes another tissue, wipes more tears from her cheeks, and the sight of it stirs another memory in Annie though she does not know where it has come from or where it belongs. It is a birthday party, a little girl's birthday party, perhaps her fifth or sixth, Annie cannot be sure. There is a space rocket cake on the table and the little girl blows out the candles and then flings her arms around Annie's waist with such vigour that Annie has to reach out to steady herself against the doorframe. She bends down and hugs the little girl, who whispers into her ear. '*I know I'm not supposed to tell anyone, but I wished I could stay living with you and Daddy forever and ever and never have to get grownup and leave.*' The little girl pulls her head away from Annie's face, grins at her, and before Annie knows it, before she can do anything to stop it, tears are gliding down her cheeks. '*What's wrong, Mummy? Why are you crying?*' The little girl's smile has flattened, her voice full of concern.

'*Nothing, sweetheart. I'm just being silly. I'm just happy you're having such a lovely birthday, that's all.*' She kisses the top of the little girl's head, helps her cut the cake, hands the child a slice on a paper plate. She knows that her answer is not truthful, knows it is not the first lie she has told the little girl, and that it won't be the last, but she also knows that she has spoken not out of deceit but out of love. She is doing her best. It is all she can do. She is full of love for this little girl and she is just doing the best she can.

The memory slips away and Annie's head aches. Her chest is tight with feelings she does not know how to keep still. She closes her eyes. She does not want to remember any more. There are too many things she would rather forget.

The door opens and Annie looks up, sees another young woman standing in the doorway. This woman is wearing a blue, baggy tunic with matching cotton trousers, and she smiles at them both, even though Annie does not recall ever having seen her before.

'I'm really sorry but visiting hours are over. We're about to settle everyone down for the night.' The woman standing in the doorway has a strange accent and Annie wonders where she has come from, what she is doing in her bedroom.

And then the young woman who has been sitting on the bed crouches down in front of Annie, takes hold of both her hands, looks at her again with those sad eyes.

'I'll come and see you again soon, okay? Next weekend, I promise.' The sad young woman leans forward and kisses her cheek and the warmth of it travels through Annie's skin and down into her chest and there is a brief moment of panic that she doesn't want this young woman to leave, she doesn't want to be all by herself in this strange place. But then the young woman kisses her again and squeezes her hand and the panic subsides.

Annie watches the tearful young woman leave, waves a hand as the woman looks back over her shoulder, and hopes she comes to visit her again soon.

FOUR MONTHS LATER

The summer has been and gone, and Nell has considered long and hard what she is about to do.

For the past four months, she feels as though she has lived a double life. There is the lie she had not known she was living, the pretence she continues to uphold: with her sisters, with her friends, with her colleagues. The lie that she is her parents' child. And then there is the truth, a story still so new it has not yet found a permanent space inside her. She does not know how she would have survived these recent weeks – emotionally, psychologically – had there not been Elsa and Josh to talk to, had they not been her confidantes, generous with their time, open with their hearts, devoid of any judgement.

It had taken only a matter of days after she had discovered the truth for her to entrust it to Josh. Despite her having pushed him away the weekend of the house clearance, he had continued to text and call, had demonstrated a level of patience and love of which she did not feel worthy, but for which she was profoundly grateful nonetheless. It was not until she told him the truth that she'd realised how fearful she had been of his reaction, afraid that in confiding in him she would be leaving herself raw, vulnerable, exposed. But she had summoned the courage, told him the whole story, and in his response she had found exactly what she needed:

to be held, to be allowed silence, to be afforded space to gather her scattered thoughts. Over the subsequent days and weeks, as they had talked it over, Josh had so often seemed to know what she was thinking and feeling without her needing to articulate it. He had understood, instinctively, how the news had distorted her sense of identity, how it had made her feel untethered from the world, like a dinghy let loose at sea with no compass, no map, no sun in the sky, no stars in the darkness. He had recognised that her feelings could not be neatly categorised: that her love and her anger, her confusion and anxiety, her regrets and tentative hopes overlapped in one complex, evershifting Venn diagram.

She has not told her sisters what she uncovered that evening in the nursing home. She has told neither of them that she is not, in fact, their sister, has kept hidden the secret their parents held on to for so long. Whether or not to tell Clare and Laura is a dilemma about which she has agonised during the past four months. In the early days after the discovery, she had felt an instinctive sense that they had a right to know, that she had a responsibility to tell them. She did not think she could continue to live the lie that she was their sister when she knew she was no more related to them than to strangers she passed in the street. But as the weeks passed, the complexities of her new reality took shape in her mind, and she began to realise the full ramifications of telling them the truth. As she watched Laura at work, washing and bathing their mum with such tenderness, as she listened to Clare chat to her with such love and patience, she had known that to reveal her parents' secret could be devastating. She does not want to be the one to shatter the perception her sisters have of their parents, cannot predict what their reactions might be: whether they will be angry at having been lied to all these years; whether they will be horrified by the decision to keep Nell from her biological family; whether it will reframe indelibly the prism through which they view their mum and dad. The knowledge could, Nell knows, change their relationship with them forever, long after their mother is no longer with them. To tell them might be an act not of kindness but of destruction. She has spent hours thinking about it, talking it over with Elsa and Josh, and she is almost certain now that to hold on to what she knows is the most compassionate thing she can do for her sisters.

But that is not the only reason for not telling them. She has thought so much about Bill and Annie over the past four months, about the decision they took to keep her. She will never know what it was like for them, sharing such a dangerous, explosive secret: a secret that must have sealed them off from the rest of the world, a twoperson cocoon of trust, isolating themselves against the possibility of discovery. But she does know that her father died with the knowledge locked inside his heart, that her mother still fears the arrival of Jane Whitworth, still dreads the possibility of Nell being taken away. It is not, she has come to realise, her secret to tell. If her parents have kept it to themselves all this time, there is a reason they did not want their daughters – all three of them – to know, and it is not, Nell feels, her place to betray that.

Sometimes she wonders whether these are the only reasons or whether, perhaps, there is something more: whether she does not have the courage to unhook the ties that have bound her and her sisters together for the past thirtyfive years, whether she is not yet brave enough – whether she will ever be brave enough – to find out if, once those hooks are undone, they will be reattached in a different formation.

Every time she is at the nursing home with Clare or Laura, she feels it, needling beneath her ribs: the knowledge of what she is keeping from them, the lie at the heart of their family. But she understands now that lies and the truth are not always easily divisible, that they do not always fit into neat, separate compartments.

Sometimes they blur, like white paint with black until all that is left is a murky, inconclusive grey. She knows that her life as her parents' child – as Bill and Annie's child – is not simply a lie. It cannot be a lie because they loved her, cared for her, encouraged and supported her. They taught her to crawl, to walk, to talk, to read, to write, to laugh, to love and be loved. They allowed her to become the person she wanted to be, the person, she thinks in more fanciful moments, she was destined to be. If they had done none of these things then perhaps she could claim that her place in their family had been a lie. But these are all acts of love, of care, of parental devotion. They are selfless acts her parents performed even while knowing she was not biologically their child.

And yet, for all the truth of their love, she knows that her place as their daughter is also a lie. Because she was never theirs to raise. They knew she belonged to another set of parents who would love and support and encourage her in different ways, but they never gave her birth parents the chance. Bill and Annie's love for her was at once both the greatest truth and the most profound lie. An act both of infinite kindness and acute selfishness. And the coexistence of those things in the same people, in the same relationship, is a paradox Nell is not sure she will ever be able to fully comprehend. The knowledge leaves her feeling as though she is a halfformed thing, a featherless bird emerged too soon from its egg. As though she materialised in the wrong place, at the wrong time, and has been unfinished ever since.

The double doors swing open and Nell's eyes dart towards them. Two women enter, clutching books to their chests and talking in low voices. Nell stays seated on the wooden hardback chair in the senior combination room, adrenaline racing through her veins.

It was Josh who had unearthed all the stories online about babies being swapped at birth. A few days after she told him, he had woken her long before the alarm was due to chime, shown her the string of links he had saved, all of them telling different versions of the same story. Stories of the wrong tags being put on the wrong babies, of no tags being put on at all, of tags being mistakenly switched. Stories about babyswaps being discovered the moment parents arrived home, the mistake immediately rectified. Other stories where it had been six months, a year, two years until the error had been uncovered, when parents had been forced to make the heartwrenching decision whether to continue raising a child who was not genetically theirs and yet whom they loved as their own, or to switch the children back to their biological families. He had found one story from overseas in which a baby boy and girl had been mistakenly swapped in the hospital, their mothers labelled delusional when they had insisted that the baby they had given birth to had been the opposite sex.

Reading all these stories, Nell has thought of her mum, in hospital for a month after giving birth, insisting that the baby in the crib beside her was not hers while everyone around her maintained Annie was wrong. Mad. Unhinged. That she was not to be listened to. She has imagined how unbearable, how isolating, how disempowering it must have been. She has felt, often, an impotent rage on her mum's behalf.

In recent weeks, Nell has begun to accept that she will probably never find out the definitive truth about what happened in the hospital on the day of her birth. Whether, amidst the panic of her mum's haemorrhage and the baby's breathing difficulties, an overworked, stressed midwife forgot to attach a nametag to her mother's real child and accidentally swapped her for another baby. She will never know whether both babies had originally been fitted with correct name tags that had somehow come loose and were wrongly exchanged. She will never know whether there is another explanation, one that has yet to cross her mind. There is, she accepts, no way for her to find out. All she has is a wealth of other people's stories, enough evidence to know that it is possible. And together with those stories, there are the dozens of photographs she has poured over online of the woman she has no doubt is her birth mother. The proof is there in the bright blue eyes, the dark curly hair, the pronounced Cupid's bow of her top lip.

It had been more difficult to locate her father. It was the internet from which she'd deduced that her biological parents were no longer together: her mother a professor at Cambridge, her father now living in the Scottish Highlands having retired from an illustrious career in local government. She has wondered whether they have been separated for long, whether it was grief that wormed its way into their marriage and wedged itself between them. It is just one of the many questions she has, one of the many unknowns that remain to be uncovered.

She looks down at her hands, at nails freshly bitten to the quick. This morning, before she left, Josh had placed his hands on her shoulders, asked her if she was sure she wanted to do this, reminded her that it was not too late to change her mind. She had reassured him that she was ready, that she needed to do it, whatever the outcome. But now, as she peels her tongue from the roof of her mouth, she is not so sure.

She thinks about when she last saw Annie, the day before yesterday, and guilt weighs heavily in her chest. There is very little of her mum's memory left now. It is like a picture drawn in the sand, being washed away by the tide, leaving barely any trace. Nell visits her every weekend but they do not converse. Instead, she holds her mum's hand, listens to her halfformed sentences like loose threads in the bottom of a sewing basket, longsince abandoned and tangled into balls, which Nell has stopped trying to weave into meaningful narratives.

Sometimes she tells her mum stories of their shared past: day trips to Brighton, summer afternoons at the local lido, birthday parties and Christmas mornings. All those hours spent together in the garden. Nell speaks of all the things her mum has helped fix over the years, from grazed knees to fractured friendships. Sometimes she thinks that perhaps these reminiscences are less an act of remembrance, more an act of love. Perhaps it is not about igniting memories in her mum. Perhaps it is simply the hope that somehow, somewhere, in listening to these stories, her mum will hear Nell's love and gratitude for the childhood her parents gave her.

Pulling a bottle of water from her bag, Nell takes a sip, replaces the lid. A week ago, when she and Josh had been returning from a weekend in Wiltshire staying with Josh's parents, he had asked her if she was clear in her own mind why she was doing this, whether she knew what she wanted from it. Whether she was prepared for the meeting not to go the way she hoped. She had paused before replying, wanting to be sure she was being honest before committing herself aloud. And now she is certain that her answer is the truth. She is here not because she wants to replace her mum. Bill and Annie will always be her parents. Familial love, she now understands, bears little relation to biology. Love transcends genetics, that much she has learnt. Her mum and dad were everything good parents should be – kind, loving, caring, supportive – whatever the DNA report says. And yet, in spite of all that, she cannot unknow what she has learnt. She cannot pretend that she has never seen that newspaper article, cannot disregard the fact that she has another, parallel story, one that has never been written. Knowing that her biological parents are out there is a fact it is impossible to ignore.

Her palms are damp and she wipes them on a tissue. She has not told Jane Whitworth the real reason for the meeting that is scheduled to begin in five minutes' time. She has contacted her under false pretences, fabricating a story about a conference she is putting together. This was never a conversation that could have taken place over email or on the phone. She needs to be able to look into Jane's eyes when she tells her what she has learnt. She needs to see her reaction to know where the news may lead them both.

All summer long she has deliberated whether this is the right thing to do, whether it is an act of kindness or cruelty. She has tried to imagine whether her birth parents will want to know the truth: whether it will make the loss they suffered over three decades ago even more acute knowing that it was, in one sense, never their grief to bear. Whether it will reignite their mourning, knowing that there is a second tragedy that can never be repaired: all those lost years they have been denied access to Nell. She knows there is a chance they may reject her, has tried to convince herself that she is prepared for it even as her mind shuts down whenever she tries to imagine it.

For the first few weeks after she found out the truth, she had been locked in a state of perpetual speculation, imagining hypothetical, parallel lives. She had been obsessed with thoughts of where she might be, how her life might be different, had the two babies never been switched. There had been a stubborn, uncompromising belief that her life had been split onto twin tracks when she was less than twentyfour hours old, frustration that she could never know where that other journey might have taken her. There have been times when she has felt as though she will never be able to move forward because she cannot reconcile herself to the past.

Now, four months later, those thoughts are still there, especially in the middle of the night when she cannot sleep. But they are quieter now, a whisper rather than a roar, and she has accepted they are thoughts that might never be silenced. She will never know how her life might have turned out had she not been swapped, had the nurses believed her mum, had her parents given her back when they realised the truth. There is no way to turn back the clock and live her life again, with different parents, in a different house, a different upbringing. Her life to date is the only one she has, the only one she will ever know. There is no option to live a life twice. The only decision for her now is how she will respond to the facts she has learnt, to the choices other people made.

The heavy wooden doors swing open again and a woman steps into the room. Nell's heart begins to race, her head spinning as though she would fall over if she weren't already sitting down. Every word in her vocabulary seems to seep out of her mind and she does not know how she will conjure up a greeting when the time comes.

Jane Whitworth stops at a small wooden table by the entrance, at which are seated two academics about the same age as Nell, and the three of them exchange words too quiet for her to hear. Her mother's hair is different from the photograph on the university website – shorter, greyer – but Nell would know her anywhere. Jane laughs at something the man says, and the sound is so familiar – so like Nell's own laughter – that she has to grab the arms of the chair to steady herself.

She watches Jane walk away from her colleagues, cast her eyes around the room. They settle on Nell and there is a flash of something across her face, a look that causes goosebumps to rise on Nell's arms. They hold one another's gaze for a second, perhaps more, Nell's heart thumping in her chest, all the stories, revelations, truths suspended between her ribs, waiting to see what will happen next.

And then the moment passes and Jane is heading towards her, smiling, her face brimming with kindness. The knot in Nell's stomach loosens and into its place slips a tentative ribbon of hope.

Her birth mother stands in front of her, holding out her hand, and Nell has to remind herself to lift her arm from her body, return the greeting. As their two hands meet in the space between them, Nell feels something travel through her fingers, across the skin of her arm, around her shoulders, down into her chest. There is not, she thinks, a name for this feeling. It is an uncanny sense of connection, of affinity, of belonging. It is yearning and kinship and hope and trust wrapping themselves around her heart.

'Nell Hardy? Jane Whitworth. It's nice to meet you. Are you okay to sit in here and talk?'

Nell feels herself falter, takes in a deep breath. 'Thank you for seeing me. I wondered if we might . . . perhaps we could go and get a coffee? There's something I need to tell you.'

ACKNOWLEDGMENTS

This book might never have found its way into your hands (or onto your Kindle) without the dynamic team at Lake Union, Amazon Publishing. Huge thanks to Sammia Hamer for bringing me into the Amazon fold, and for her passion and commitment to this book and my writing: you are the champion every writer dreams of. Thanks to Sophie Wilson for such an incisive structural edit and sensitive read of the novel. Thanks to Bekah Graham in marketing and the uber-efficient Nicole Wagner for always answering my questions, however random. In editorial, thanks to Victoria Pepe and Victoria Oundjian for helping to steer the book towards publication. Book jackets are notoriously difficult beasts, so I'm enormously grateful to Emma Rogers for such a striking cover (and for the many iterations we went through to get it right). Also at Amazon, thanks to Melissa Hyder for the copyedit and Jon Pennock for overseeing the audiobook production.

Agents are, in many ways, the silent partners in any writer's success. Heartfelt thanks to Sheila Crowley for keeping the faith and never being afraid to have difficult conversations. Thanks to the whole team at Curtis Brown, especially Sabhbh Curran for the patient fielding of queries, Ligeia Marsh in screen rights, and Katie McGowan and Callum Mollison in translation.

The PR team at FMcM have been a dream to work with: special thanks to Kealey Rigden and Emma Mitchell for spearheading the campaign with such calm and supportive professionalism.

Trusted early readers are crucial to any writer's progress, so special thanks to Ruth Jones for meticulous readings throughout the process, not least for the invaluable guidance in how (not) to write dialogue. Any residual clunkiness is entirely my own. Thanks, too, for *The Archers* gossiping and WhatsApp chats: lockdown would have been significantly more tedious without them.

Thanks to Alex Michaelides and Lucy Atkins for their thoughtful early reads of this novel: it's an act of huge generosity to read and comment on a fellow author's work, and I'm enormously grateful to you both.

I had seemingly endless medical queries for this novel, so many thanks to Adam Kay for answering them all with such patience and comprehensiveness. Any medical errors are, of course, mine.

Plenty of people outside the publishing world help keep a writer fuelled with love and laughter. Thanks to Katie Leah and Georg Ell for friendship I hope never to be without: let's still be putting the world to rights in our eighties (and beyond). Thanks to my brother and sister-in-law, Matthew and Sally Bush, for their boundless generosity and kindness. Thanks to my stepdad, Jerry Bowler, for always being so proud and supportive, and to my mum, Tania Bowler, for everything: the love, the encouragement, the fact that nothing is ever too much trouble, the phone chats on the school run, and the brilliantly eagle-eyed proofread.

My biggest thanks, as always, to my husband, Adam, and my daughter, Aurelia. Thank you, Aurelia, for your infinite and infectious enthusiasm for life, for teaching me so much (when you're older, and you read this, you will see the extent of your influence) and for your ability to come up with so many excellent similes and metaphors, many of which I have shamelessly purloined for this book. Thank you, Adam, for affording me the freedom to write even when we've not been certain where it would lead, and for being the best possible partner I could wish for. There is a reason this book is dedicated to you both: because if this is a novel about love and family and about how our identity is inextricably linked to both, then you two are the cornerstone of everything – the writing, the motivation, the happiness and the adventures. Covid has made this not the most exciting couple of years, but I have no doubt the three of us will make up for it in the not-too-distant future.

And finally, to D and her mother, who probably don't even remember me. Thirty years ago, over dinner, you told me a story: a curious anecdote, narrated in jest and yet seemingly so much more. It has haunted me ever since, and this novel is the result of three decades of imagining what might have been.

Resources and Further Reading

I'm indebted to many organisations (and their extensively informative websites) in the research for this book. Below is a list of some of the resources used, and where further information and advice can be found.

- Dementia UK : https://www.dementiauk.org/
- Alzheimer's Society: https://www.alzheimers.org.uk/
- Lullaby Trust: https://www.lullabytrust.org.uk/
- Tommy's: https://www.tommys.org/
- Mind: https://www.mind.org.uk/

ABOUT THE AUTHOR

Author photo © 2018 Adam Jackson

Hannah Beckerman is an author, journalist and broadcaster. She is a book critic and features writer for a range of publications including the *Observer*, the *Guardian* and the *FT Weekend Magazine*. A regular chair at festivals and events across the UK, she has interviewed a host of authors and celebrities, as well as appearing as a book pundit on BBC Radio 2 and Times Radio. Prior to becoming a full-time writer, Hannah worked in television as a producer and commissioning editor. *The Impossible Truths of Love* is her third novel.